TO JAMES AND MICHAEL —
REMEMBER THAT BROTHERS STICK
TOGETHER, NO MATTER WHAT.

AND TO ERIN —
YOU ARE THE LOVE OF MY LIFE.

JOEY ELLIS

WOLFIE MONSTER AND THE BIG BAD PIZZA BATTLE

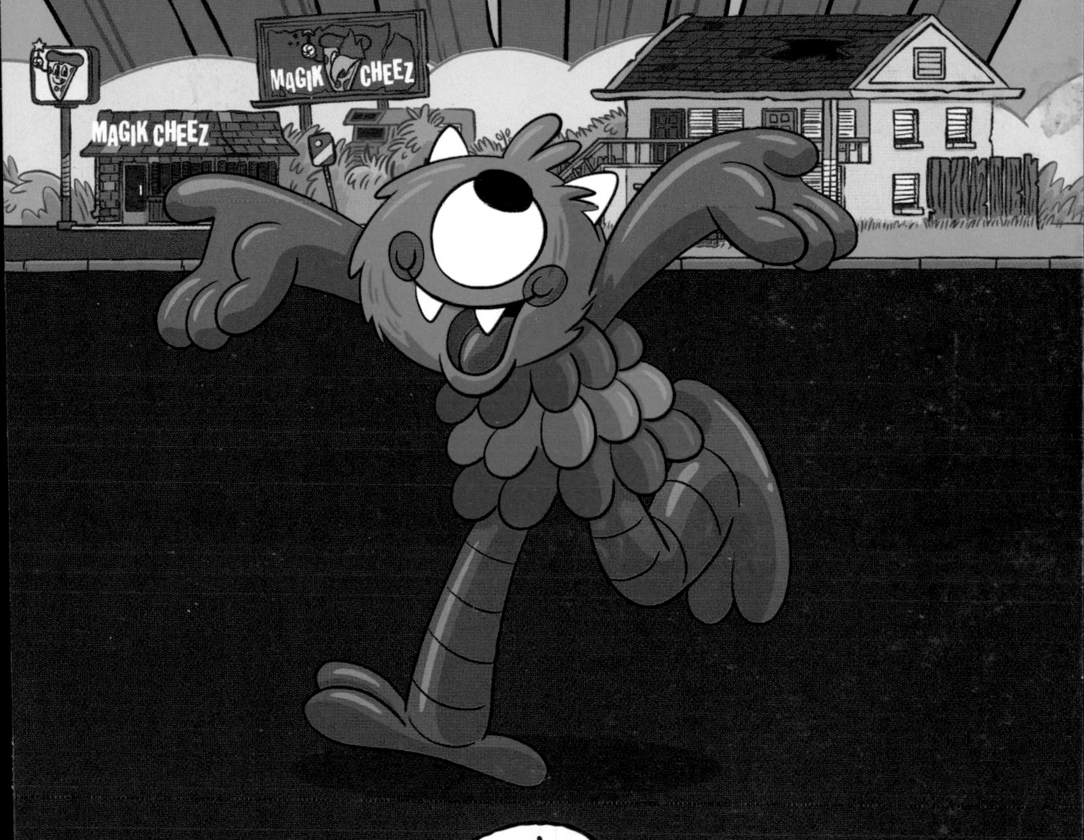
MAGIK CHEEZ
MAGIK CHEEZ

graphix

An Imprint of

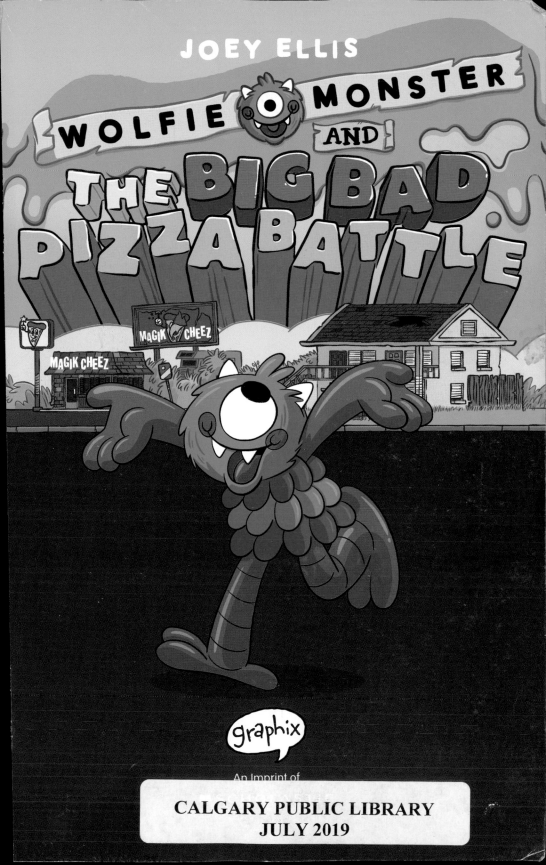

Library of Congress Control Number: 2018949525

ISBN 978-1-338-18604-8 (hardcover)
ISBN 978-1-338-18603-1 (paperback)

10 9 8 7 6 5 4 3 2 1   19 20 21 22 23

Printed in China   62
First edition, July 2019
Edited by Adam Rau
Book design by Phil Falco
Publisher: David Saylor

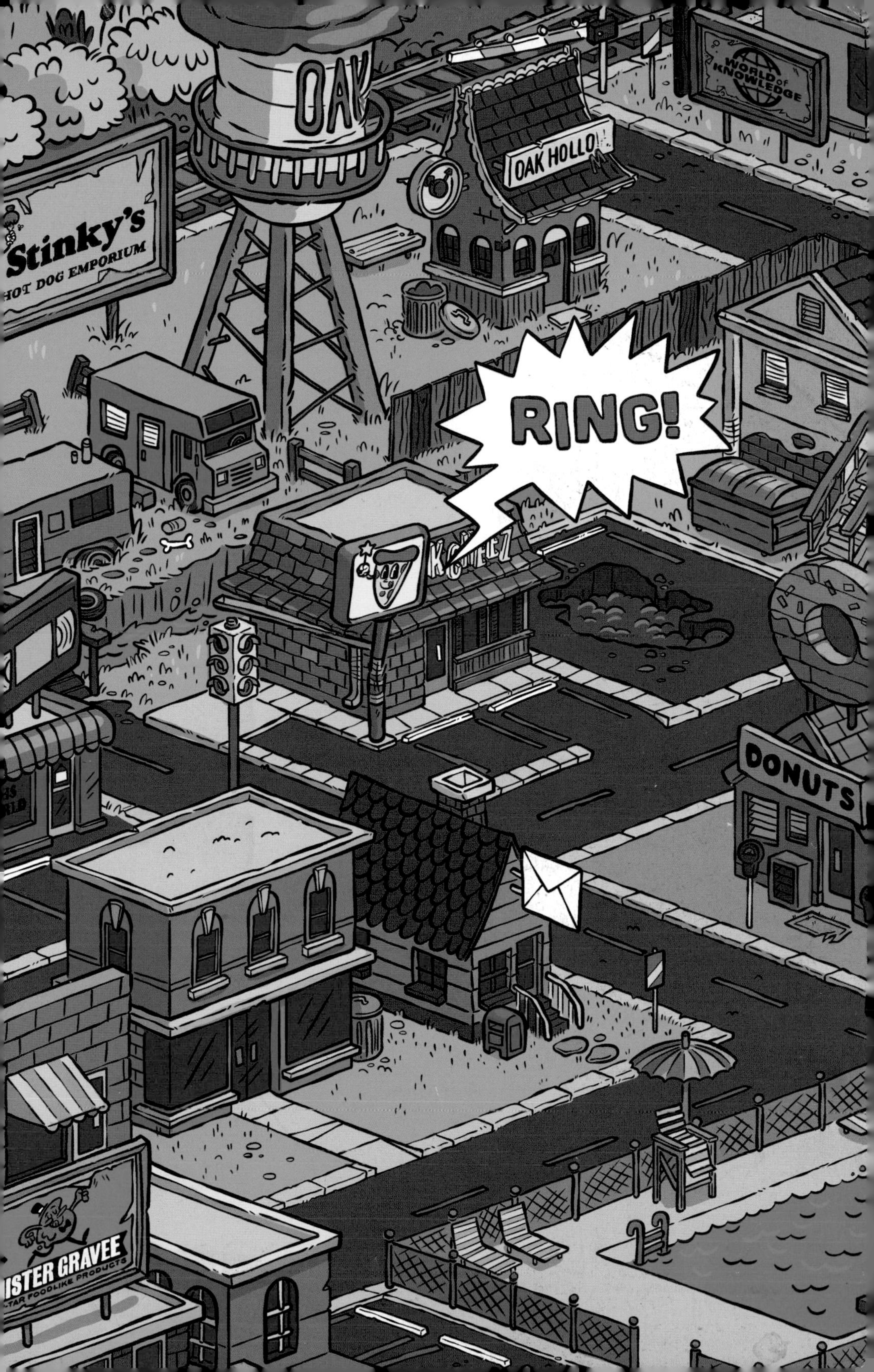

OAK
Stinky's
HOT DOG EMPORIUM
OAK HOLLO
WORLD OF KNOWLEDGE
RING!
DONUTS
MISTER GRAVEE

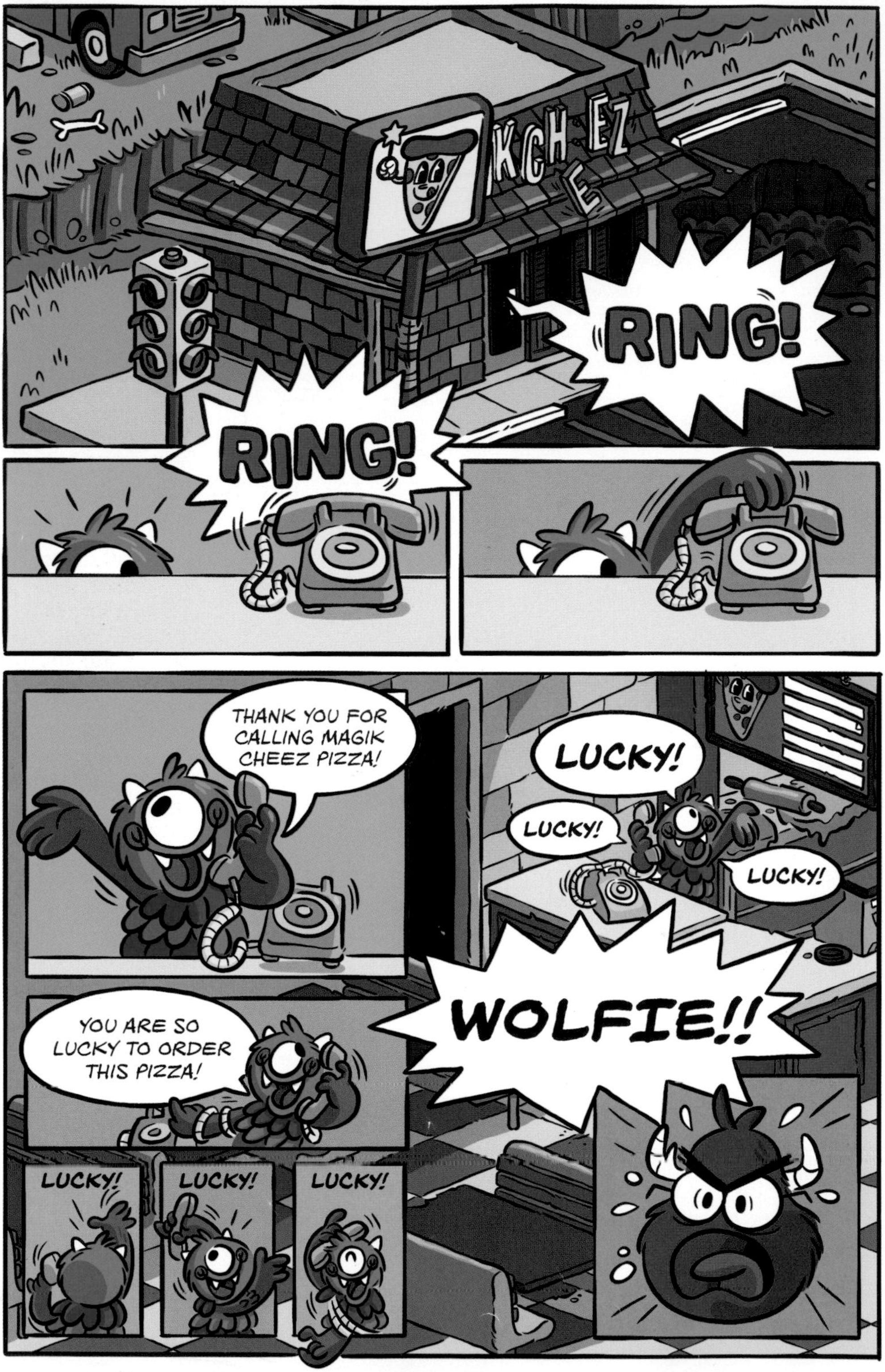
KCH EZ
E
RING!
RING!
THANK YOU FOR CALLING MAGIK CHEEZ PIZZA!
LUCKY!
LUCKY!
LUCKY!
YOU ARE SO LUCKY TO ORDER THIS PIZZA!
LUCKY!
LUCKY!
LUCKY!
WOLFIE!!

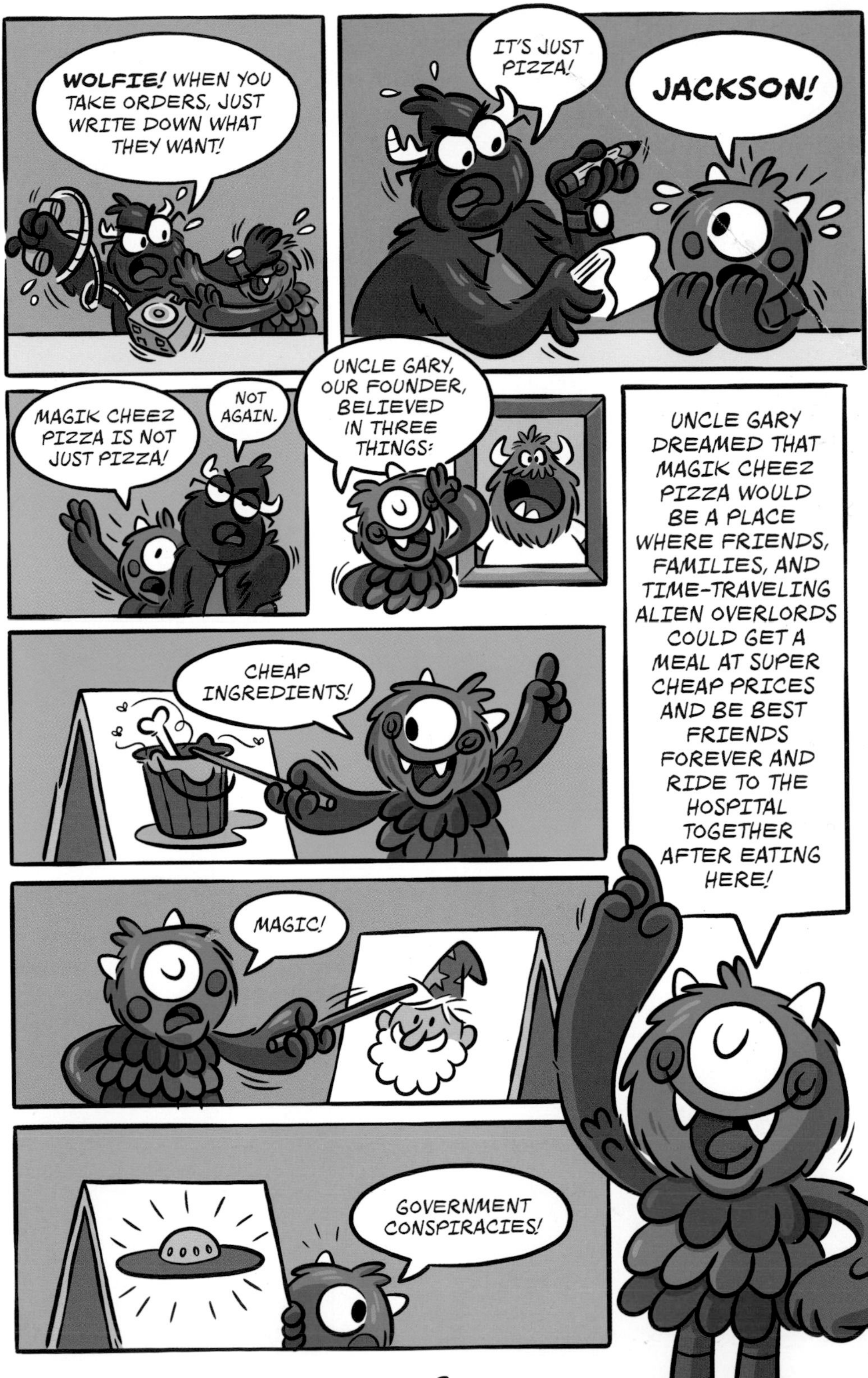
WOLFIE! WHEN YOU TAKE ORDERS, JUST WRITE DOWN WHAT THEY WANT!
IT'S JUST PIZZA!
JACKSON!
MAGIK CHEEZ PIZZA IS NOT JUST PIZZA!
NOT AGAIN.
UNCLE GARY, OUR FOUNDER, BELIEVED IN THREE THINGS:
UNCLE GARY DREAMED THAT MAGIK CHEEZ PIZZA WOULD BE A PLACE WHERE FRIENDS, FAMILIES, AND TIME-TRAVELING ALIEN OVERLORDS COULD GET A MEAL AT SUPER CHEAP PRICES AND BE BEST FRIENDS FOREVER AND RIDE TO THE HOSPITAL TOGETHER AFTER EATING HERE!
CHEAP INGREDIENTS!
MAGIC!
GOVERNMENT CONSPIRACIES!

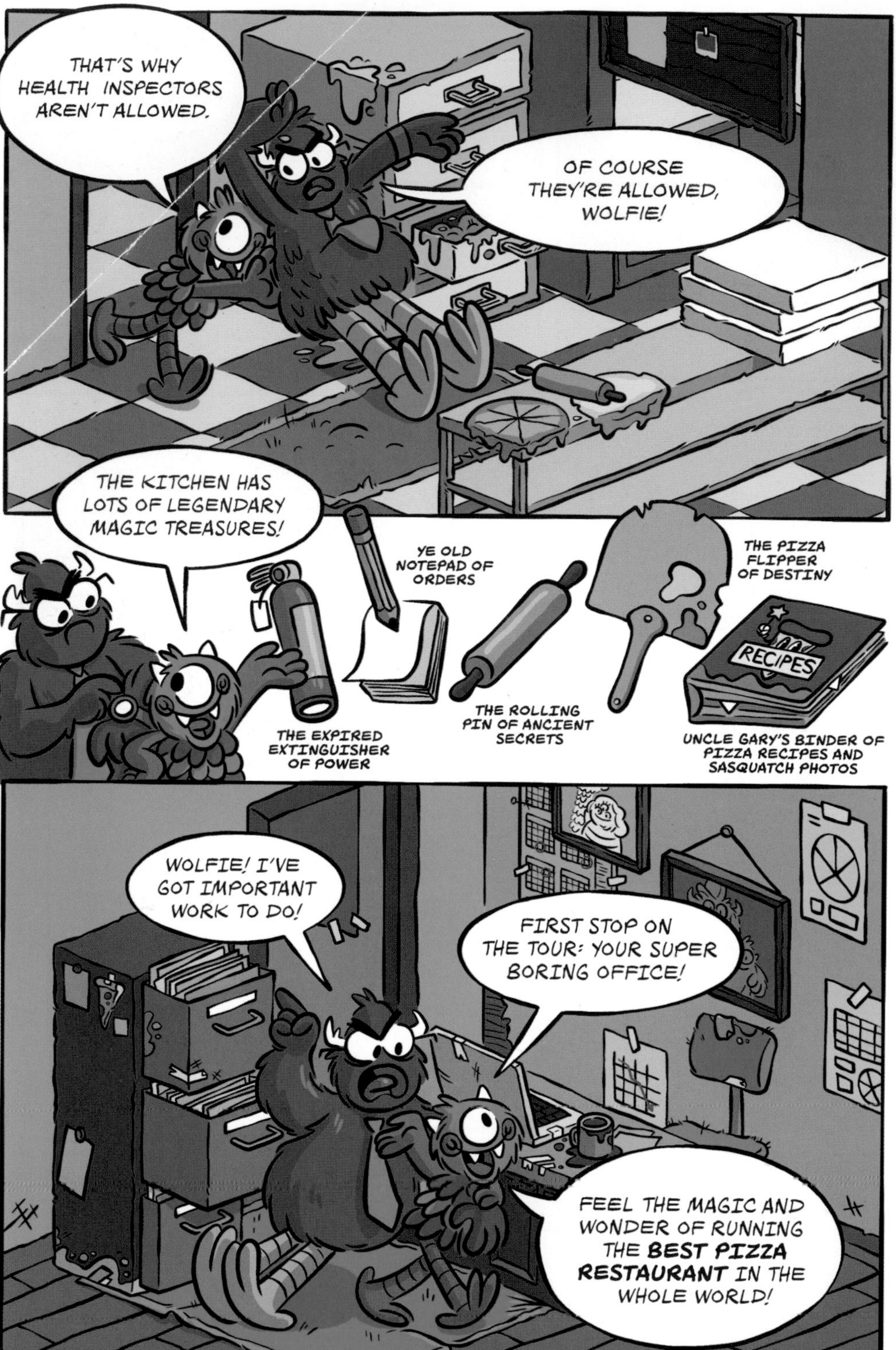
THAT'S WHY HEALTH INSPECTORS AREN'T ALLOWED.
OF COURSE THEY'RE ALLOWED, WOLFIE!
THE KITCHEN HAS LOTS OF LEGENDARY MAGIC TREASURES!
THE EXPIRED EXTINGUISHER OF POWER
YE OLD NOTEPAD OF ORDERS
THE ROLLING PIN OF ANCIENT SECRETS
THE PIZZA FLIPPER OF DESTINY
RECIPES
UNCLE GARY'S BINDER OF PIZZA RECIPES AND SASQUATCH PHOTOS
FIRST STOP ON THE TOUR: YOUR SUPER BORING OFFICE!
WOLFIE! I'VE GOT IMPORTANT WORK TO DO!
FEEL THE MAGIC AND WONDER OF RUNNING THE **BEST PIZZA RESTAURANT** IN THE WHOLE WORLD!

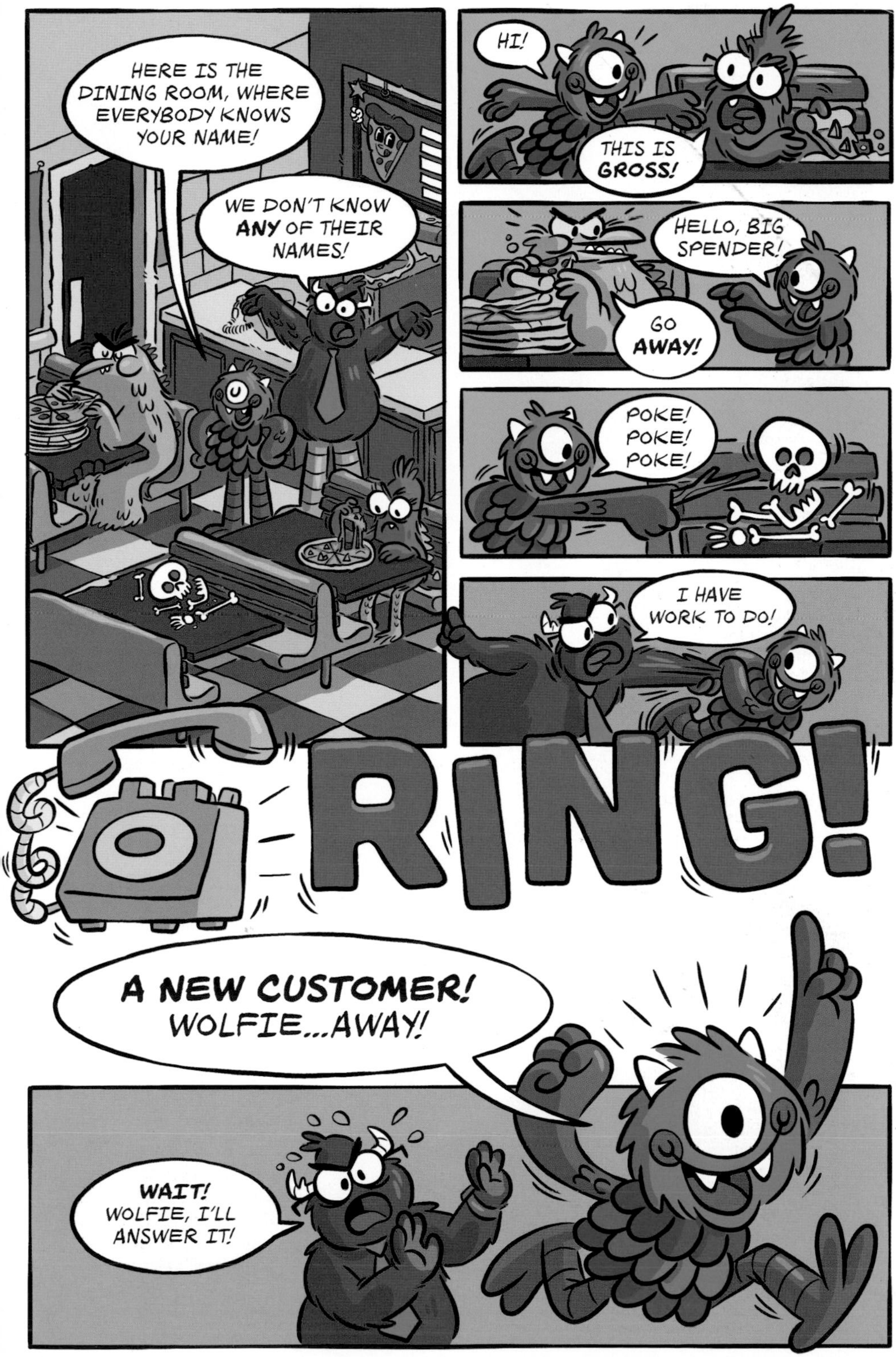
HERE IS THE DINING ROOM, WHERE EVERYBODY KNOWS YOUR NAME!
WE DON'T KNOW **ANY** OF THEIR NAMES!
HI!
THIS IS **GROSS!**
HELLO, BIG SPENDER!
GO **AWAY!**
POKE! POKE! POKE!
I HAVE WORK TO DO!
RING!
A NEW CUSTOMER! WOLFIE...AWAY!
WAIT! WOLFIE, I'LL ANSWER IT!

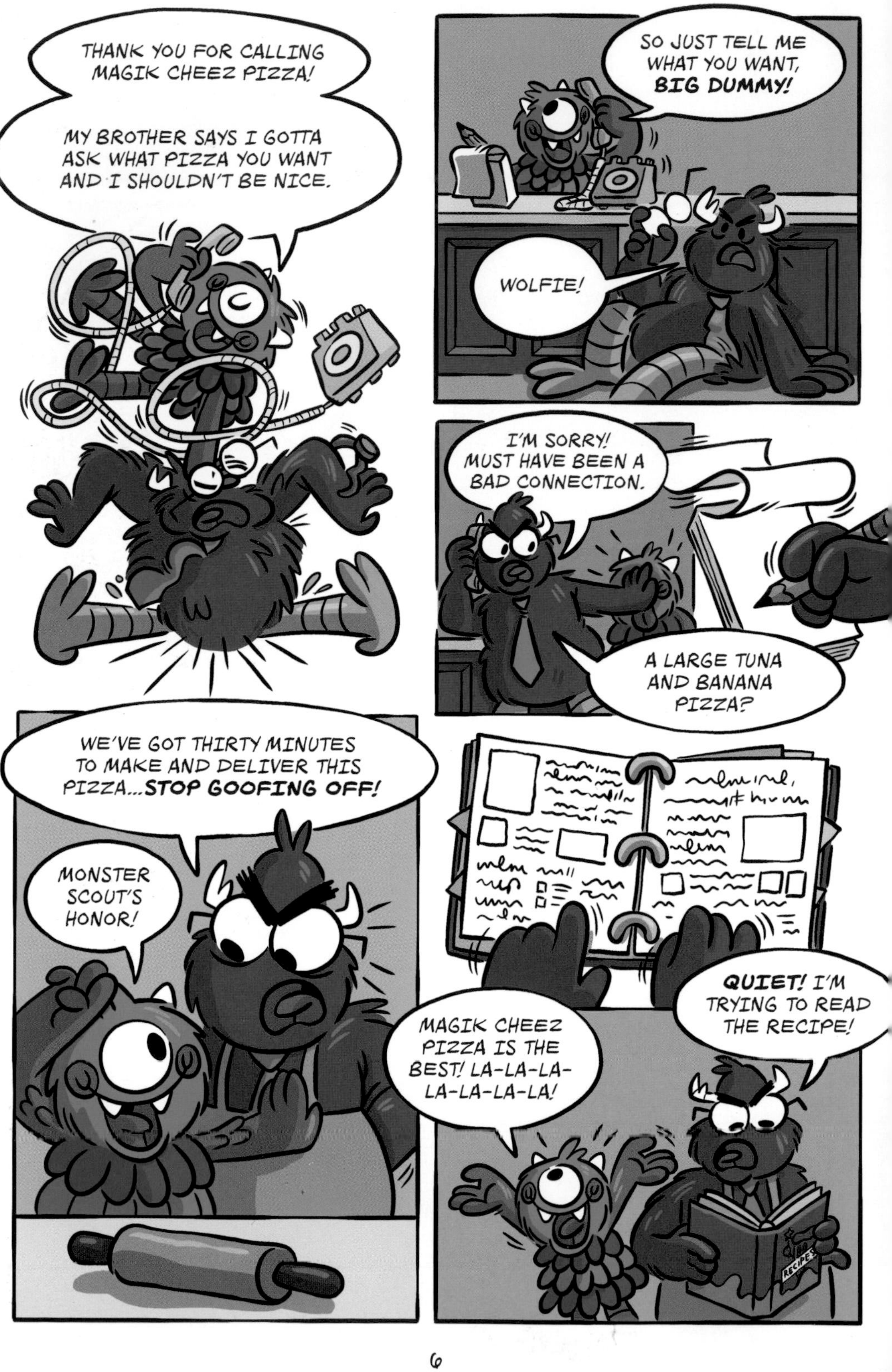
THANK YOU FOR CALLING MAGIK CHEEZ PIZZA!
MY BROTHER SAYS I GOTTA ASK WHAT PIZZA YOU WANT AND I SHOULDN'T BE NICE.
SO JUST TELL ME WHAT YOU WANT, **BIG DUMMY!**
WOLFIE!
I'M SORRY! MUST HAVE BEEN A BAD CONNECTION.
A LARGE TUNA AND BANANA PIZZA?
WE'VE GOT THIRTY MINUTES TO MAKE AND DELIVER THIS PIZZA...**STOP GOOFING OFF!**
MONSTER SCOUT'S HONOR!
QUIET! I'M TRYING TO READ THE RECIPE!
MAGIK CHEEZ PIZZA IS THE BEST! LA-LA-LA-LA-LA-LA!
RECIPES

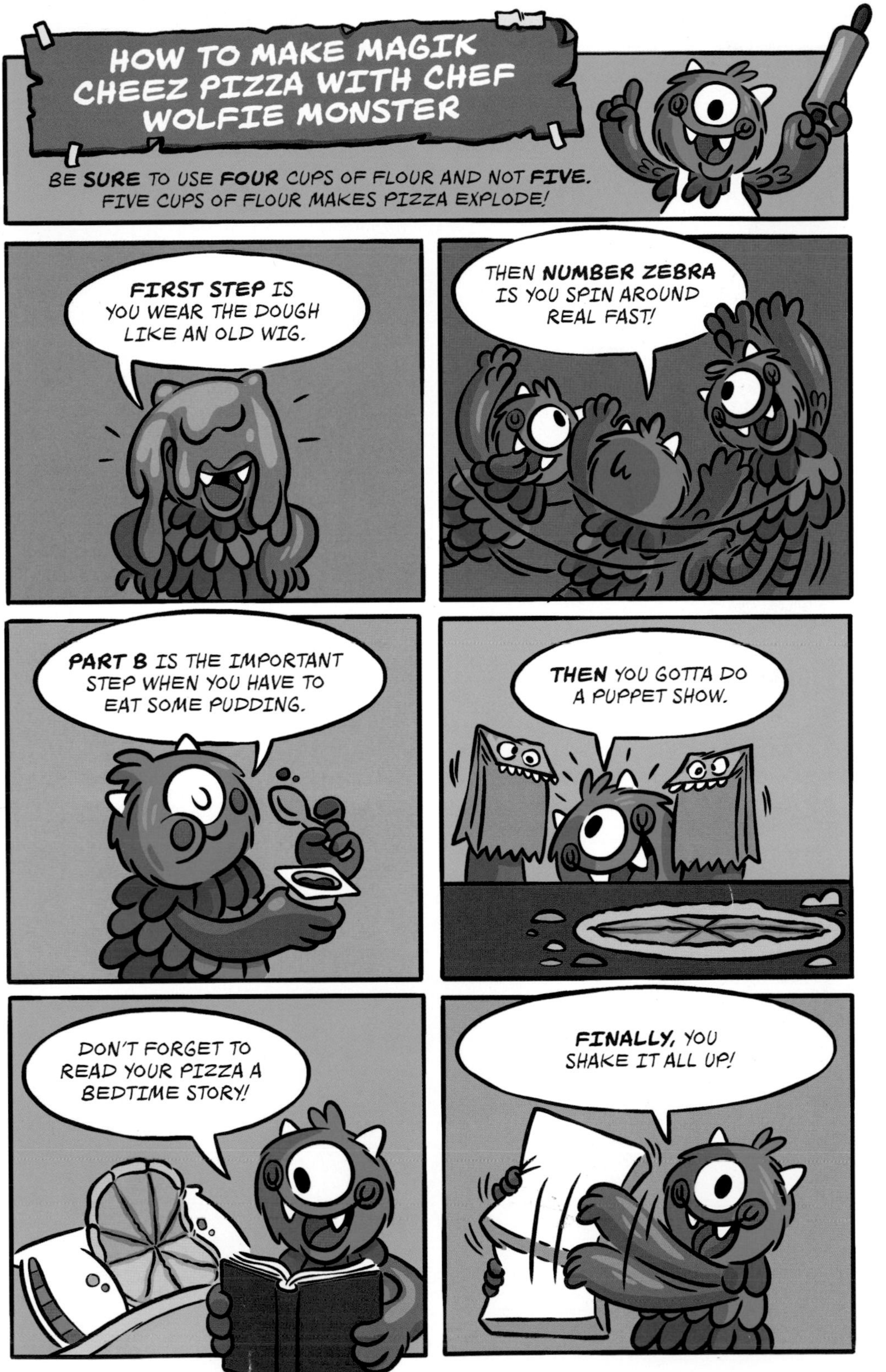
HOW TO MAKE MAGIK CHEEZ PIZZA WITH CHEF WOLFIE MONSTER
BE SURE TO USE FOUR CUPS OF FLOUR AND NOT FIVE. FIVE CUPS OF FLOUR MAKES PIZZA EXPLODE!
FIRST STEP IS YOU WEAR THE DOUGH LIKE AN OLD WIG.
THEN NUMBER ZEBRA IS YOU SPIN AROUND REAL FAST!
PART B IS THE IMPORTANT STEP WHEN YOU HAVE TO EAT SOME PUDDING.
THEN YOU GOTTA DO A PUPPET SHOW.
DON'T FORGET TO READ YOUR PIZZA A BEDTIME STORY!
FINALLY, YOU SHAKE IT ALL UP!

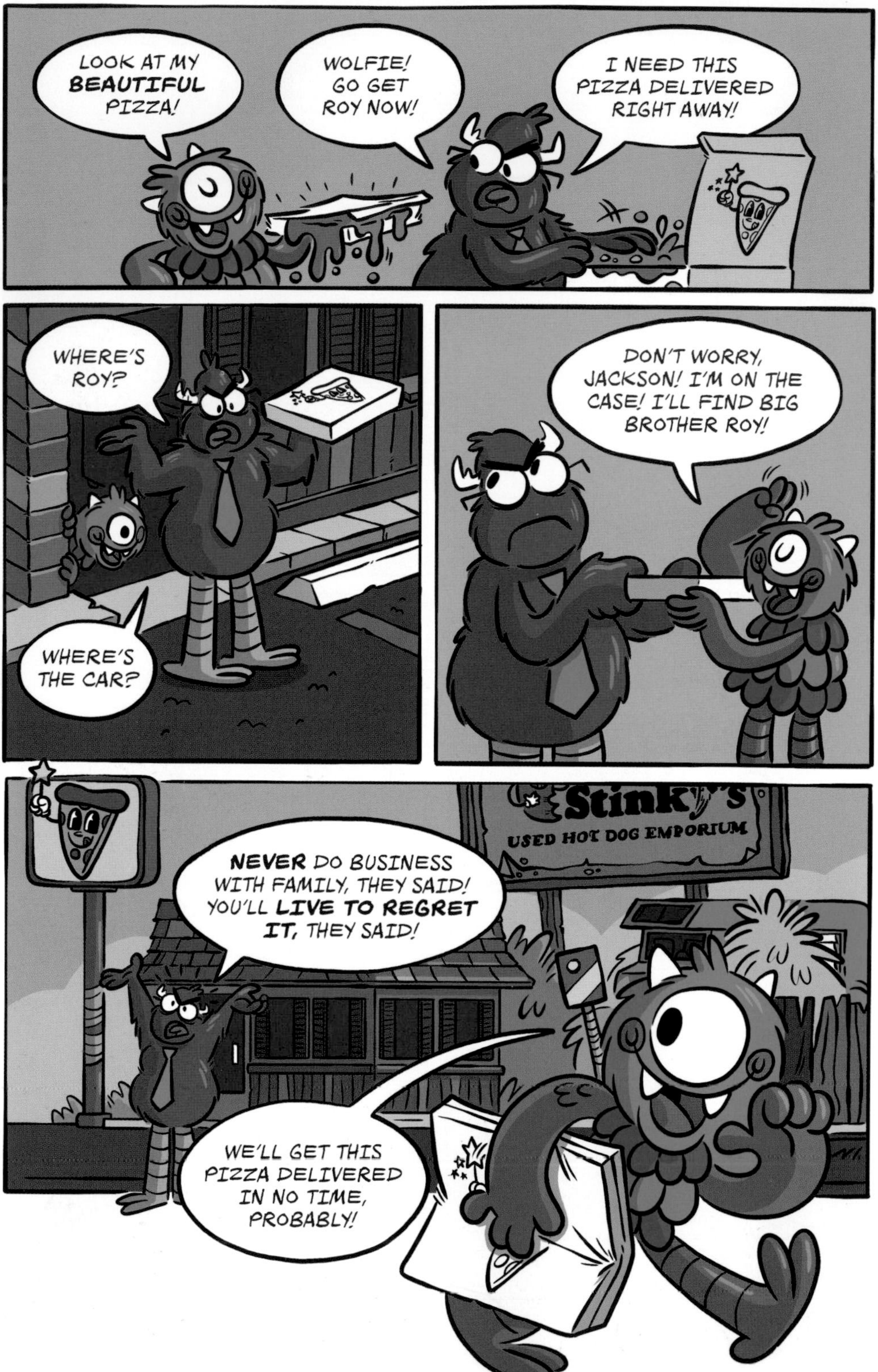
LOOK AT MY **BEAUTIFUL** PIZZA!
WOLFIE! GO GET ROY NOW!
I NEED THIS PIZZA DELIVERED RIGHT AWAY!
WHERE'S ROY?
WHERE'S THE CAR?
DON'T WORRY, JACKSON! I'M ON THE CASE! I'LL FIND BIG BROTHER ROY!
USED HOT DOG EMPORIUM
NEVER DO BUSINESS WITH FAMILY, THEY SAID! YOU'LL **LIVE TO REGRET IT,** THEY SAID!
WE'LL GET THIS PIZZA DELIVERED IN NO TIME, PROBABLY!

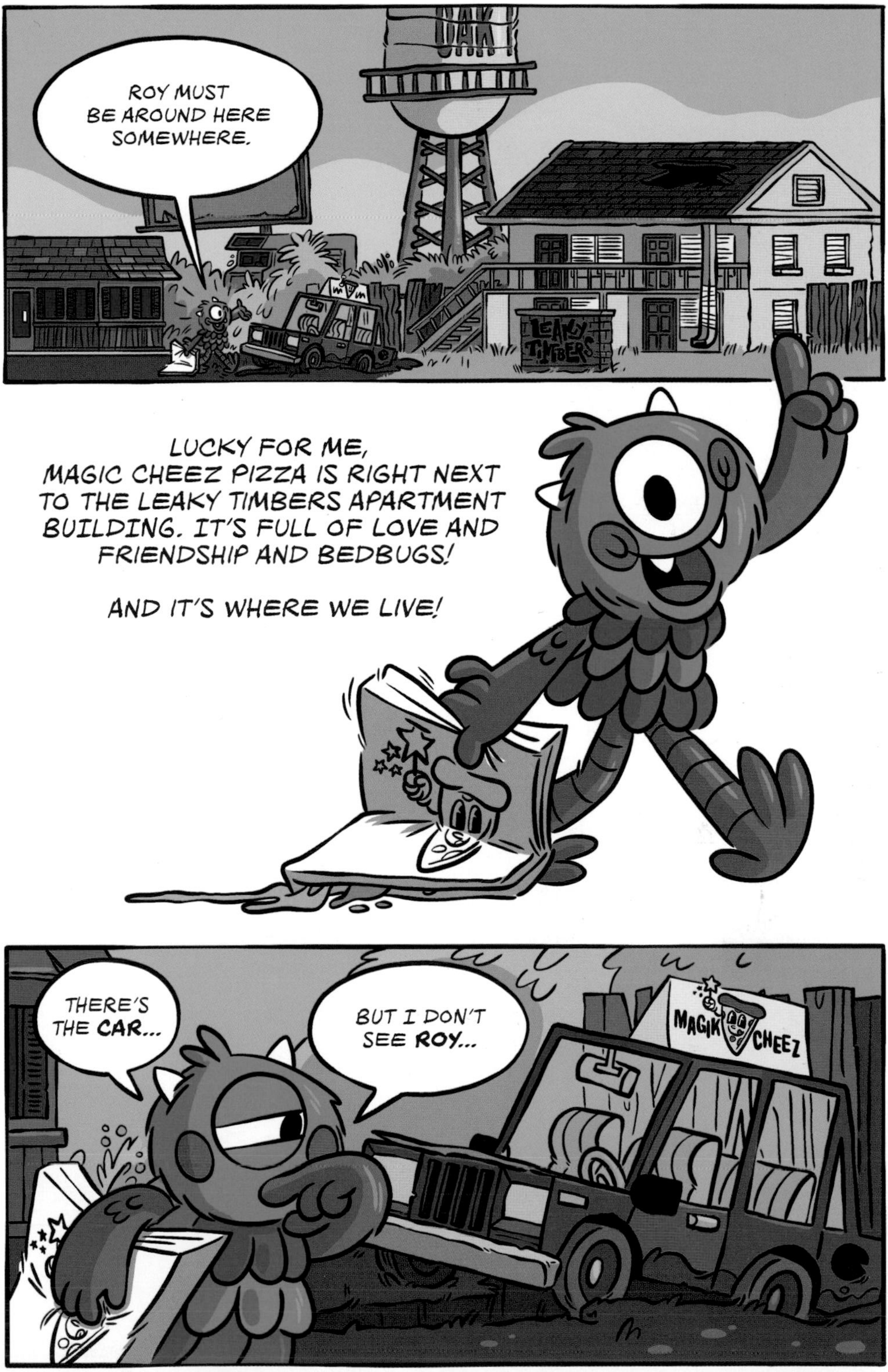
ROY MUST BE AROUND HERE SOMEWHERE.
LEAKY TIMBERS
LUCKY FOR ME, MAGIC CHEEZ PIZZA IS RIGHT NEXT TO THE LEAKY TIMBERS APARTMENT BUILDING. IT'S FULL OF LOVE AND FRIENDSHIP AND BEDBUGS!
AND IT'S WHERE WE LIVE!
THERE'S THE **CAR**...
BUT I DON'T SEE **ROY**...
MAGIK CHEEZ

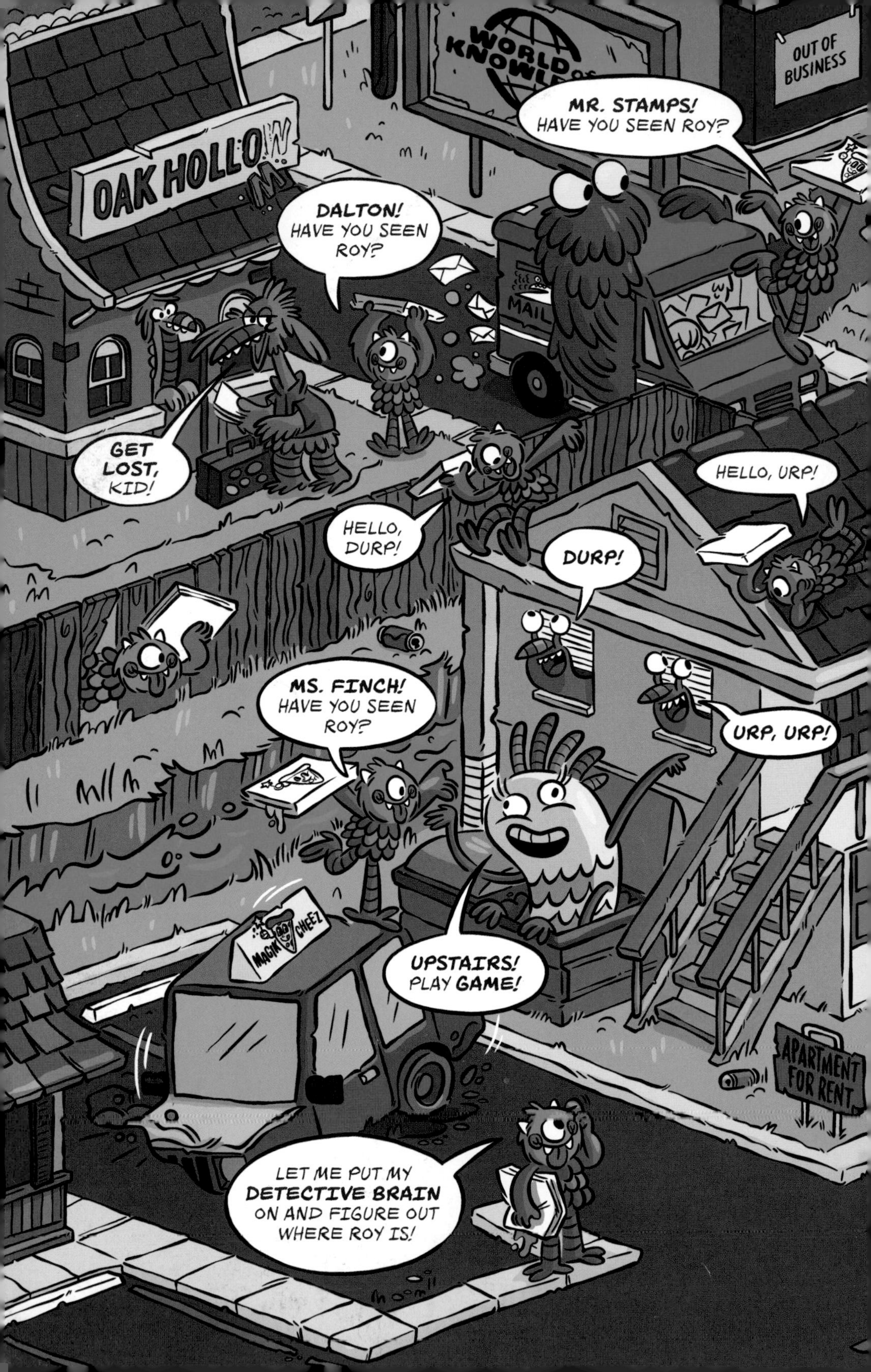
OAK HOLLOW
WORLD OF KNOWL...
OUT OF BUSINESS
MR. STAMPS! HAVE YOU SEEN ROY?
DALTON! HAVE YOU SEEN ROY?
GET LOST, KID!
HELLO, DURP!
HELLO, URP!
DURP!
URP, URP!
MS. FINCH! HAVE YOU SEEN ROY?
MAIL
MAGIK CHEEZ
UPSTAIRS! PLAY GAME!
APARTMENT FOR RENT
LET ME PUT MY DETECTIVE BRAIN ON AND FIGURE OUT WHERE ROY IS!

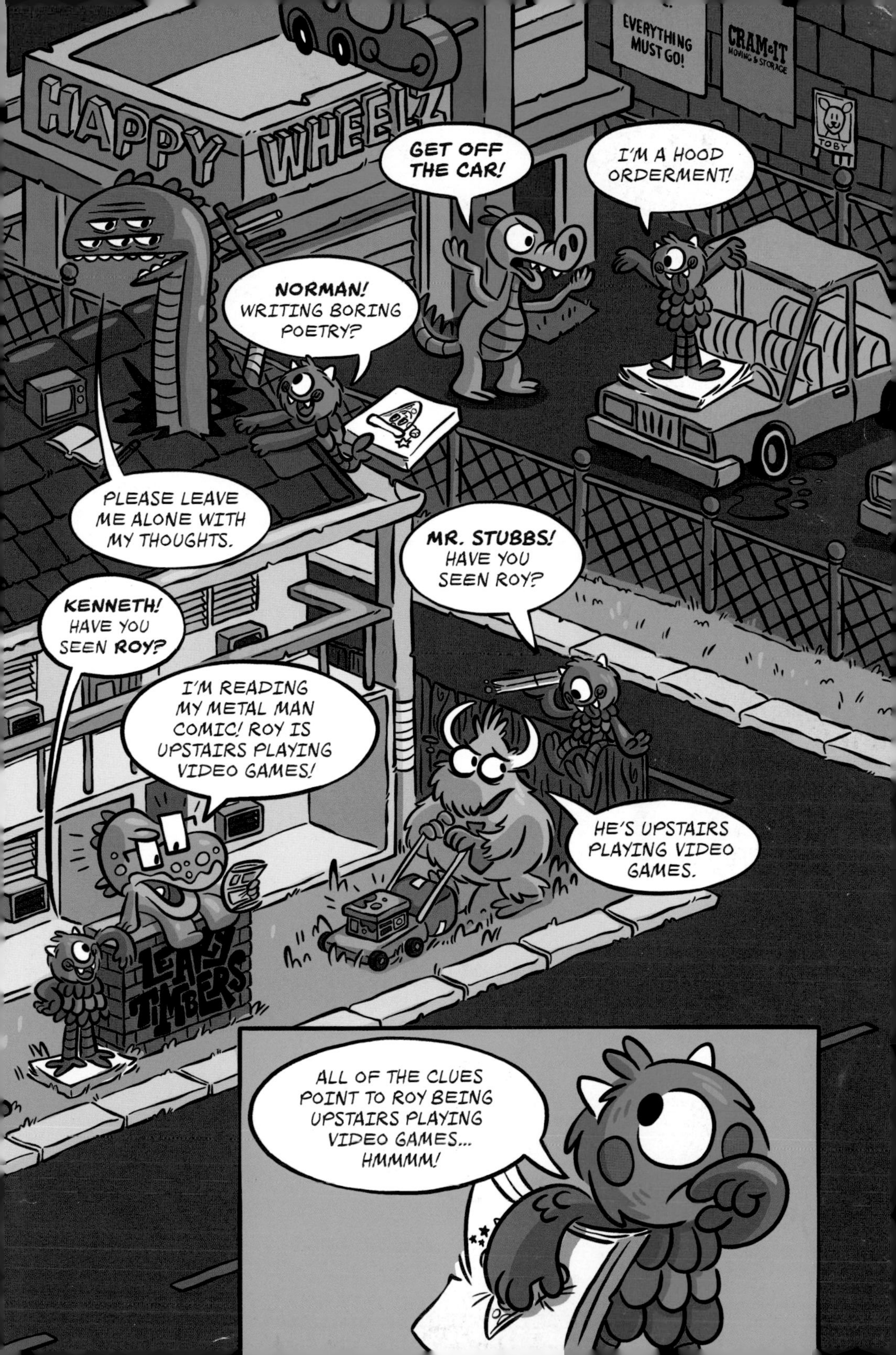
HAPPY WHEELZ
EVERYTHING MUST GO!
CRAM-IT MOVING & STORAGE
TOBY
NORMAN! WRITING BORING POETRY?
PLEASE LEAVE ME ALONE WITH MY THOUGHTS.
GET OFF THE CAR!
I'M A HOOD ORDERMENT!
MR. STUBBS! HAVE YOU SEEN ROY?
HE'S UPSTAIRS PLAYING VIDEO GAMES.
KENNETH! HAVE YOU SEEN ROY?
I'M READING MY METAL MAN COMIC! ROY IS UPSTAIRS PLAYING VIDEO GAMES!
LEAKY TIMBERS
ALL OF THE CLUES POINT TO ROY BEING UPSTAIRS PLAYING VIDEO GAMES... HMMMM!

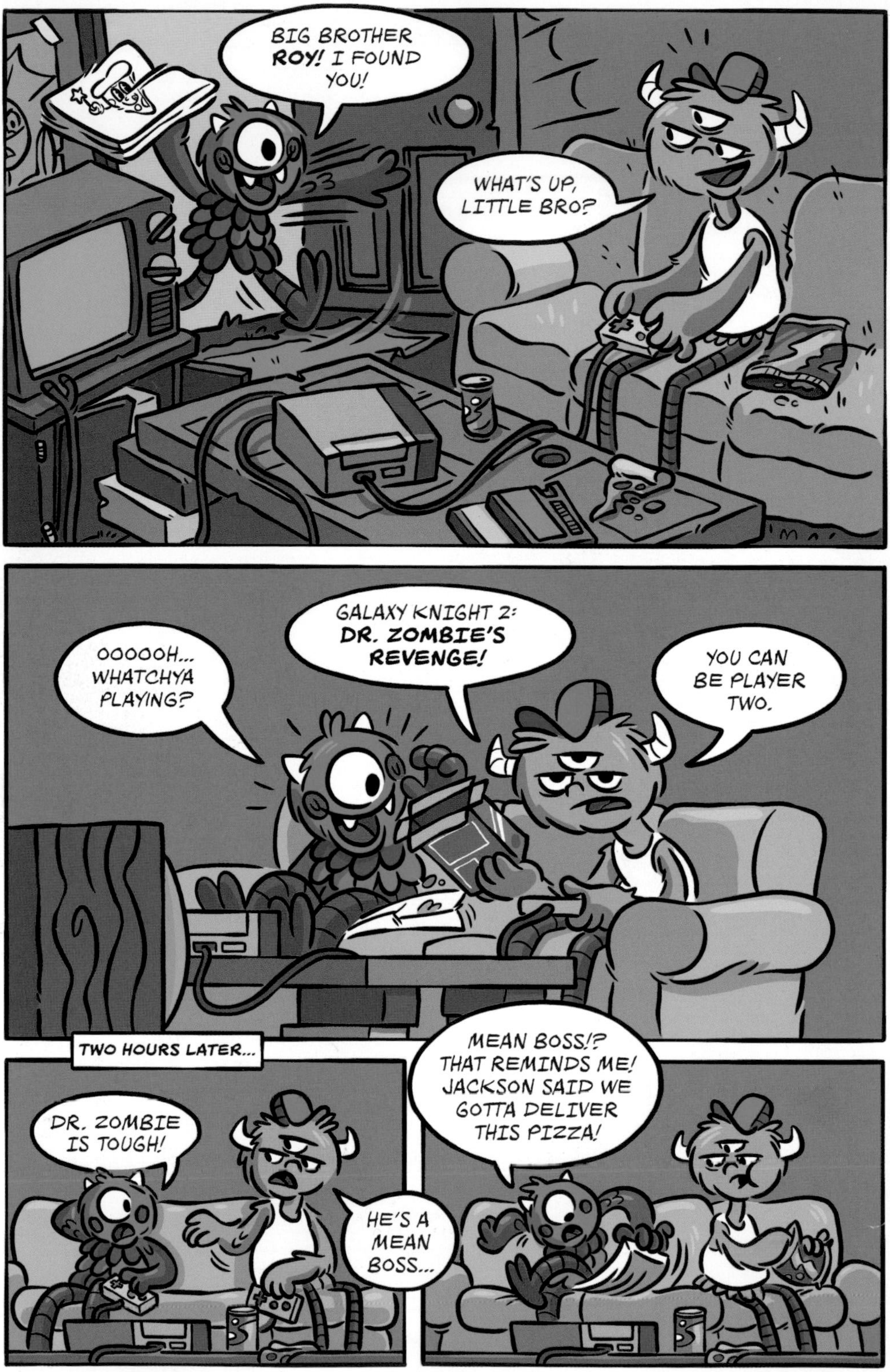
BIG BROTHER **ROY!** I FOUND YOU!
WHAT'S UP, LITTLE BRO?
OOOOOH... WHATCHYA PLAYING?
GALAXY KNIGHT 2: **DR. ZOMBIE'S REVENGE!**
YOU CAN BE PLAYER TWO.
TWO HOURS LATER...
DR. ZOMBIE IS TOUGH!
HE'S A MEAN BOSS...
MEAN BOSS!? THAT REMINDS ME! JACKSON SAID WE GOTTA DELIVER THIS PIZZA!

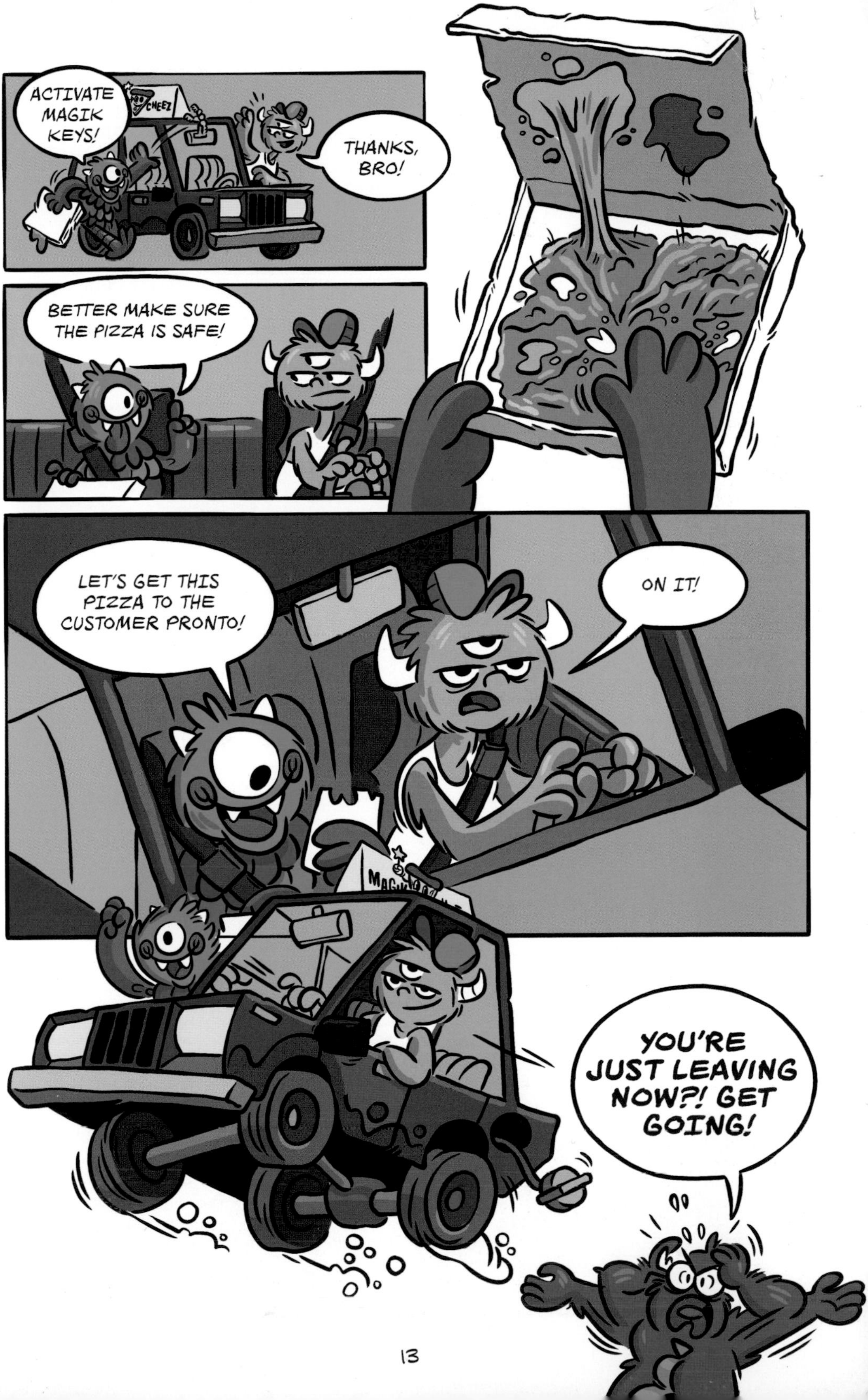
ACTIVATE MAGIK KEYS!
CHEEZ
THANKS, BRO!
BETTER MAKE SURE THE PIZZA IS SAFE!
LET'S GET THIS PIZZA TO THE CUSTOMER PRONTO!
ON IT!
YOU'RE JUST LEAVING NOW?! GET GOING!

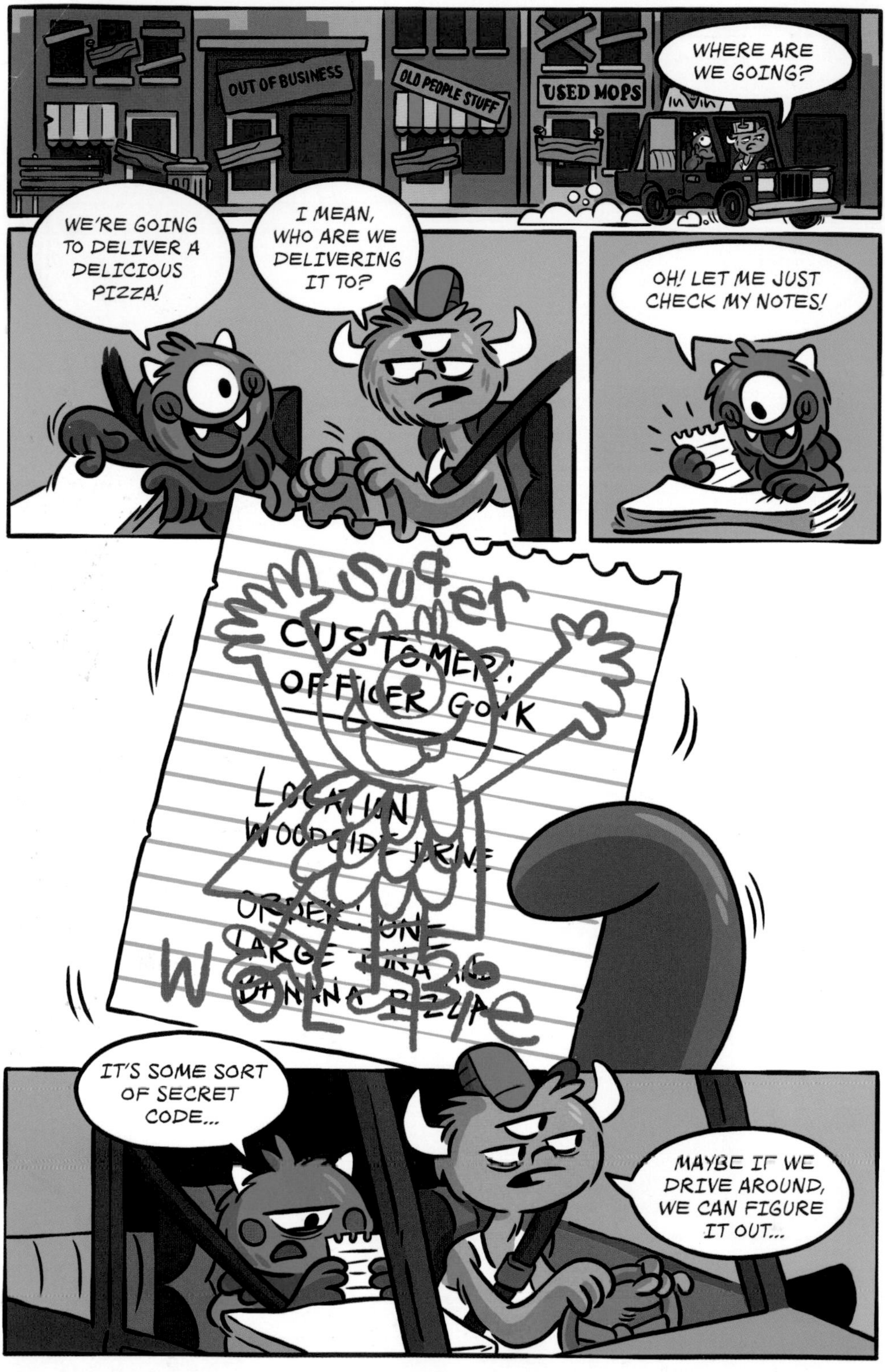
OUT OF BUSINESS
OLD PEOPLE STUFF
USED MOPS
WHERE ARE WE GOING?
WE'RE GOING TO DELIVER A DELICIOUS PIZZA!
I MEAN, WHO ARE WE DELIVERING IT TO?
OH! LET ME JUST CHECK MY NOTES!
super
CUSTOMER:
OFFICER GONK
IT'S SOME SORT OF SECRET CODE...
MAYBE IF WE DRIVE AROUND, WE CAN FIGURE IT OUT...

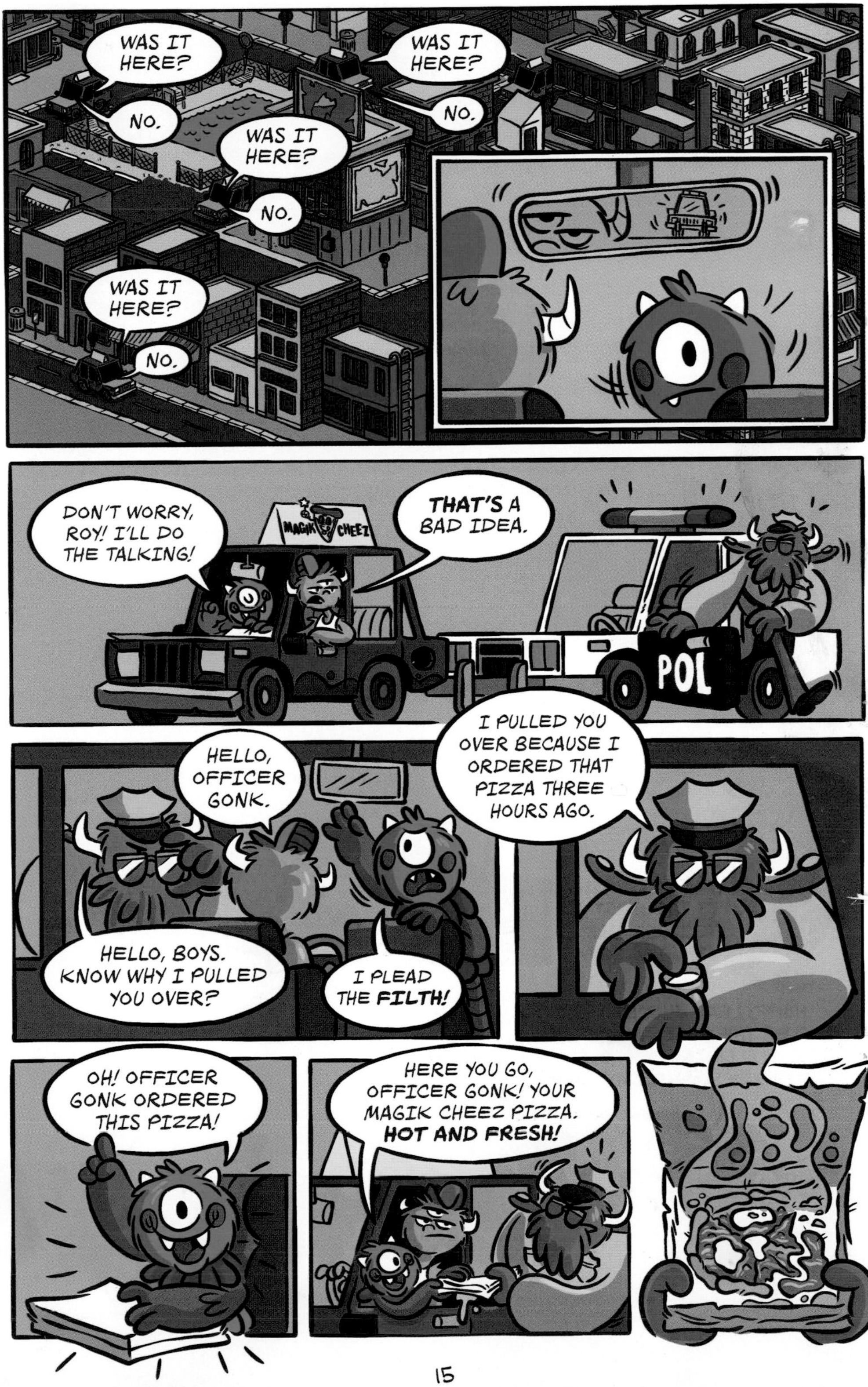
WAS IT HERE?
NO.
WAS IT HERE?
NO.
WAS IT HERE?
NO.
WAS IT HERE?
NO.
DON'T WORRY, ROY! I'LL DO THE TALKING!
MAGIK CHEEZ
THAT'S A BAD IDEA.
POL
HELLO, OFFICER GONK.
HELLO, BOYS. KNOW WHY I PULLED YOU OVER?
I PLEAD THE FILTH!
I PULLED YOU OVER BECAUSE I ORDERED THAT PIZZA THREE HOURS AGO.
OH! OFFICER GONK ORDERED THIS PIZZA!
HERE YOU GO, OFFICER GONK! YOUR MAGIK CHEEZ PIZZA. HOT AND FRESH!

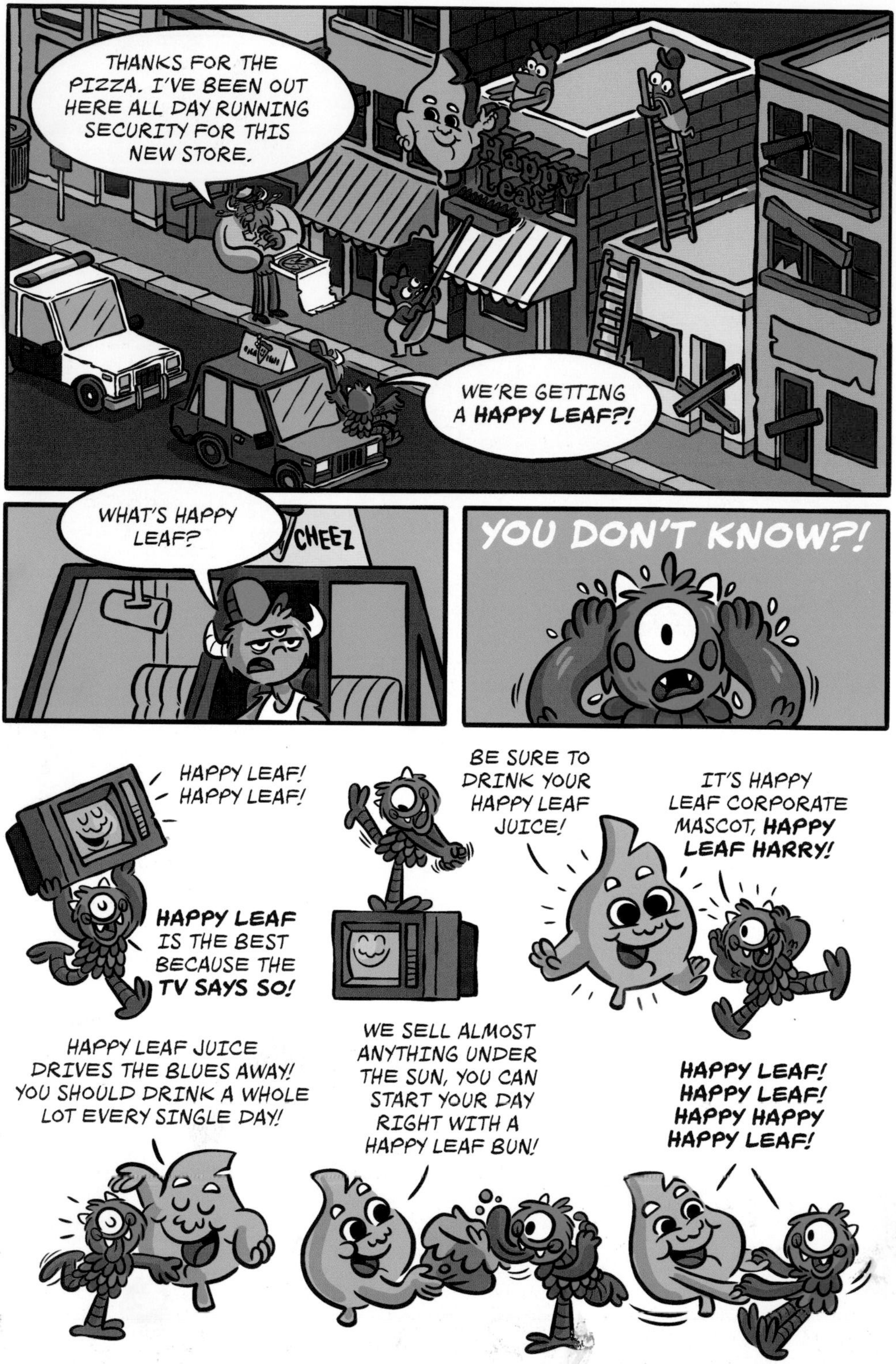

THANKS FOR THE PIZZA. I'VE BEEN OUT HERE ALL DAY RUNNING SECURITY FOR THIS NEW STORE.
Happy Leaf
WE'RE GETTING A **HAPPY LEAF?!**
WHAT'S HAPPY LEAF?
CHEEZ
YOU DON'T KNOW?!
HAPPY LEAF! HAPPY LEAF!
HAPPY LEAF IS THE BEST BECAUSE THE **TV SAYS SO!**
BE SURE TO DRINK YOUR HAPPY LEAF JUICE!
IT'S HAPPY LEAF CORPORATE MASCOT, **HAPPY LEAF HARRY!**
HAPPY LEAF JUICE DRIVES THE BLUES AWAY! YOU SHOULD DRINK A WHOLE LOT EVERY SINGLE DAY!
WE SELL ALMOST ANYTHING UNDER THE SUN, YOU CAN START YOUR DAY RIGHT WITH A HAPPY LEAF BUN!
HAPPY LEAF! HAPPY LEAF! HAPPY HAPPY HAPPY LEAF!

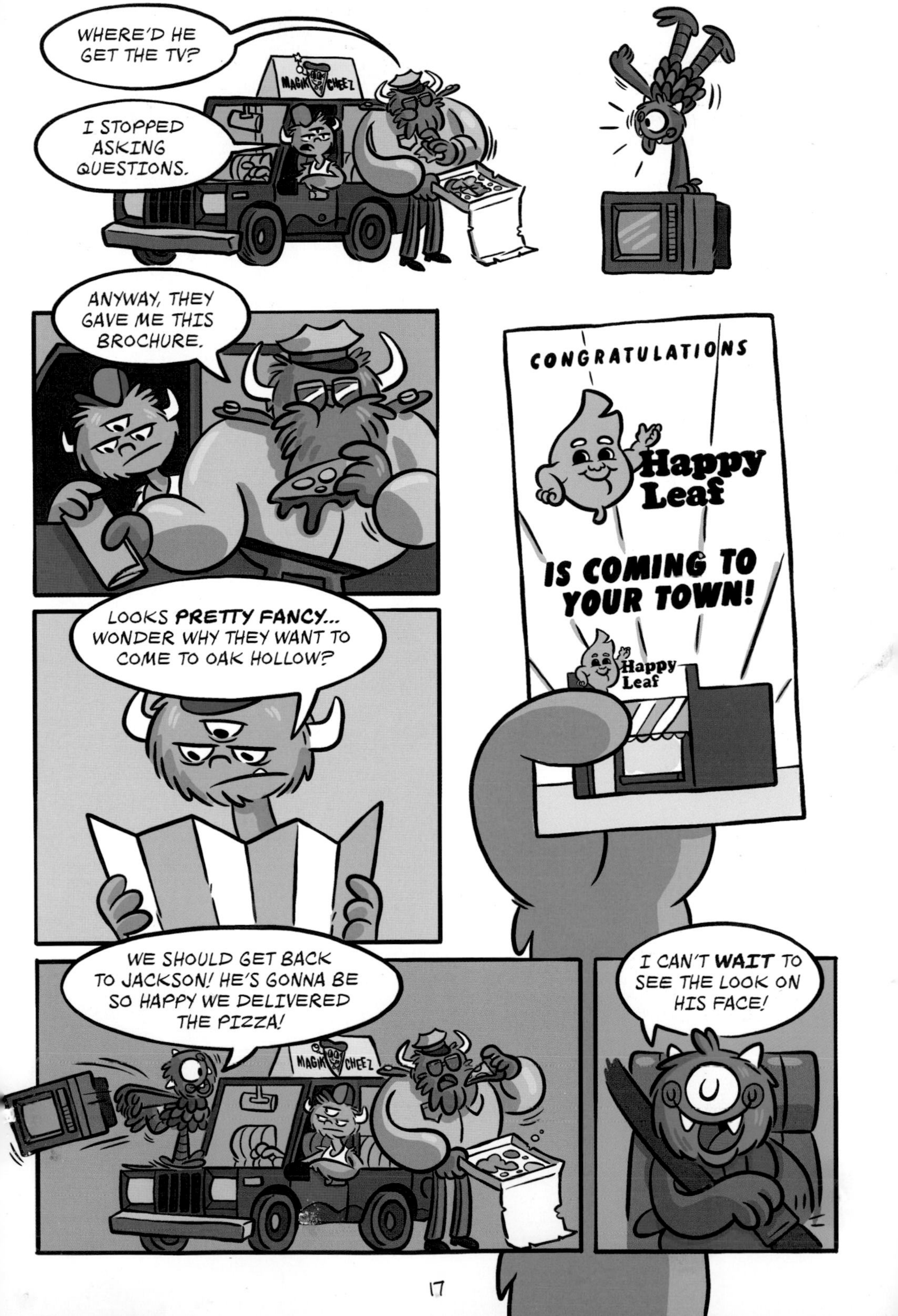
WHERE'D HE GET THE TV?
I STOPPED ASKING QUESTIONS.
MAGIK CHEEZ
ANYWAY, THEY GAVE ME THIS BROCHURE.
CONGRATULATIONS
Happy Leaf
IS COMING TO YOUR TOWN!
Happy Leaf
LOOKS **PRETTY FANCY...** WONDER WHY THEY WANT TO COME TO OAK HOLLOW?
WE SHOULD GET BACK TO JACKSON! HE'S GONNA BE SO HAPPY WE DELIVERED THE PIZZA!
MAGIK CHEEZ
I CAN'T **WAIT** TO SEE THE LOOK ON HIS FACE!

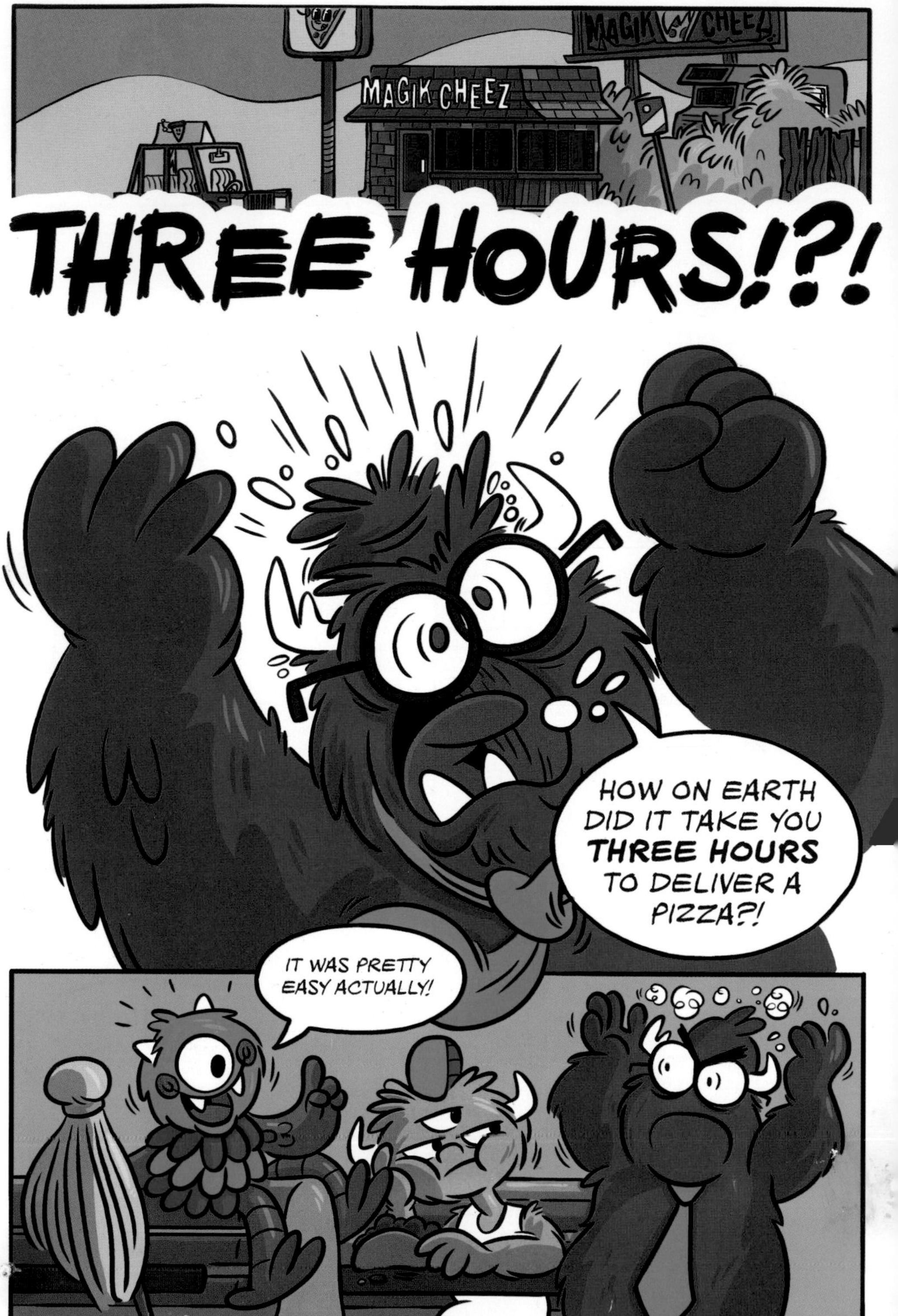
MAGIK CHEEZ
MAGIK CHEEZ
THREE HOURS!?!
HOW ON EARTH DID IT TAKE YOU **THREE HOURS** TO DELIVER A PIZZA?!
IT WAS PRETTY EASY ACTUALLY!

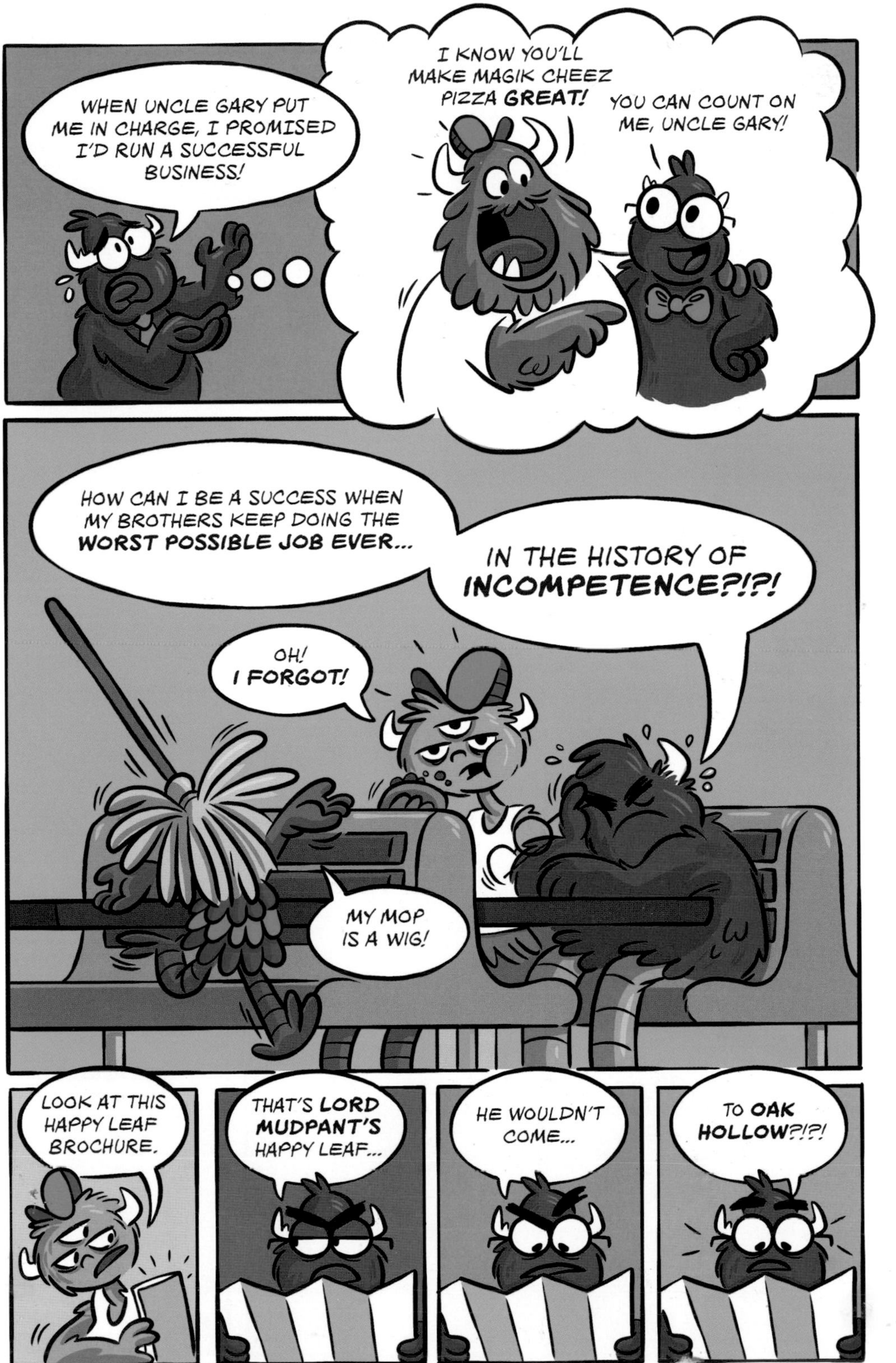
WHEN UNCLE GARY PUT ME IN CHARGE, I PROMISED I'D RUN A SUCCESSFUL BUSINESS!
I KNOW YOU'LL MAKE MAGIK CHEEZ PIZZA **GREAT!**
YOU CAN COUNT ON ME, UNCLE GARY!
HOW CAN I BE A SUCCESS WHEN MY BROTHERS KEEP DOING THE **WORST POSSIBLE JOB EVER...**
IN THE HISTORY OF **INCOMPETENCE?!?!**
OH! **I FORGOT!**
MY MOP IS A WIG!
LOOK AT THIS HAPPY LEAF BROCHURE.
THAT'S **LORD MUDPANT'S** HAPPY LEAF...
HE WOULDN'T COME...
TO **OAK HOLLOW?!?!**

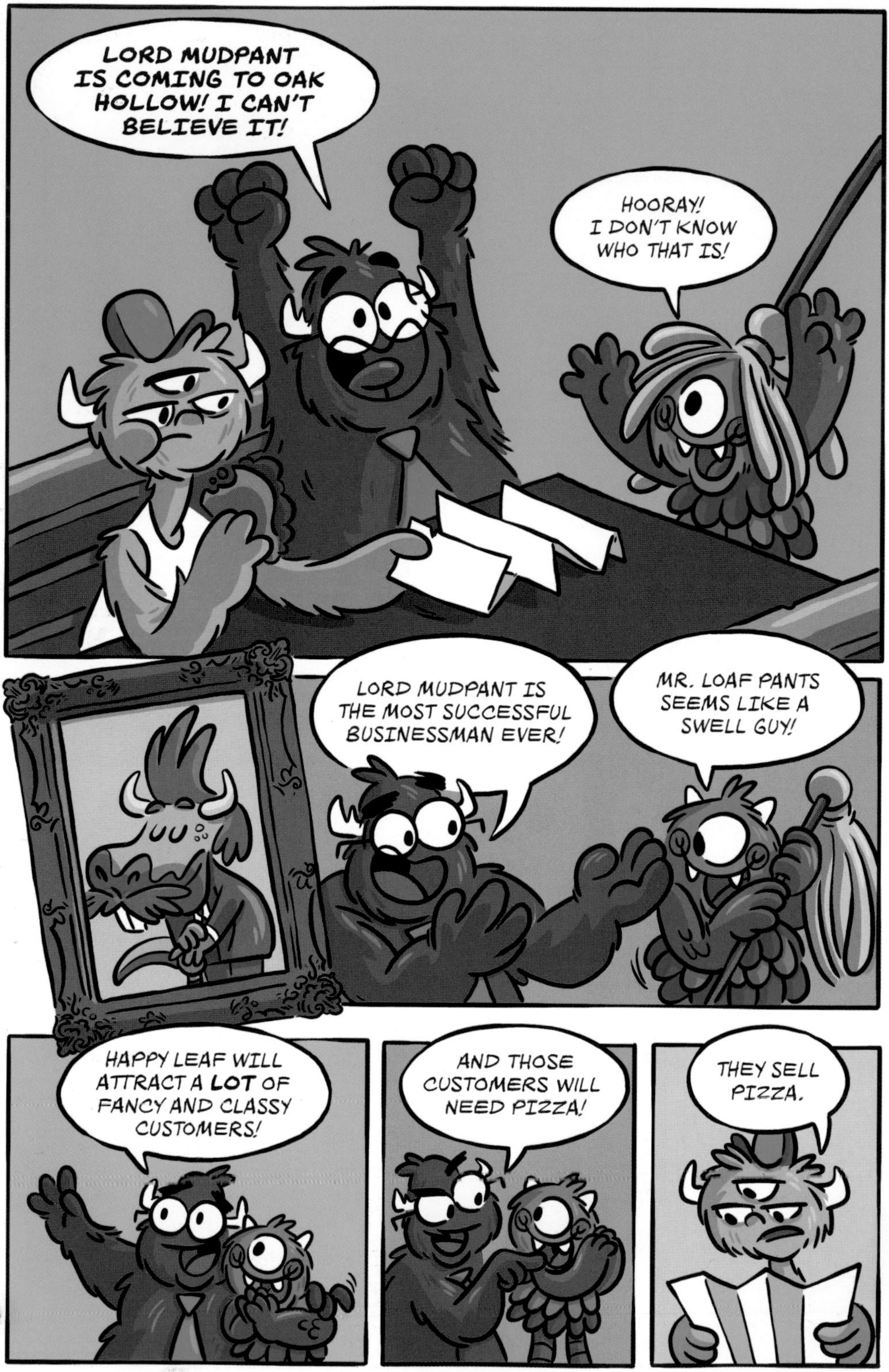
LORD MUDPANT IS COMING TO OAK HOLLOW! I CAN'T BELIEVE IT!
HOORAY! I DON'T KNOW WHO THAT IS!
LORD MUDPANT IS THE MOST SUCCESSFUL BUSINESSMAN EVER!
MR. LOAF PANTS SEEMS LIKE A SWELL GUY!
HAPPY LEAF WILL ATTRACT A **LOT** OF FANCY AND CLASSY CUSTOMERS!
AND THOSE CUSTOMERS WILL NEED PIZZA!
THEY SELL PIZZA.

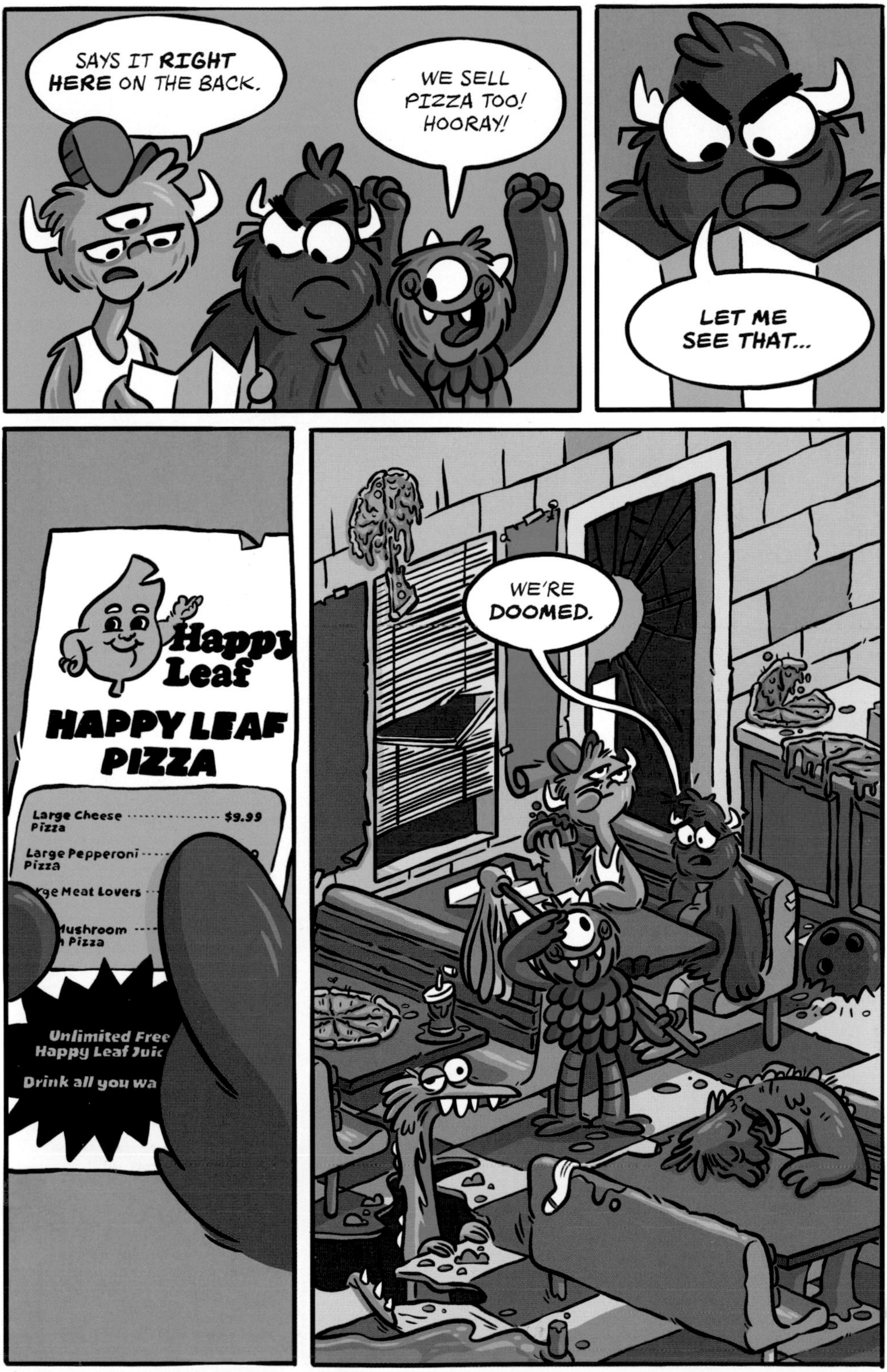
SAYS IT **RIGHT HERE** ON THE BACK.
WE SELL PIZZA TOO! HOORAY!
LET ME SEE THAT...
Happy Leaf
HAPPY LEAF PIZZA
Large Cheese Pizza $9.99
Large Pepperoni Pizza
Meat Lovers
Mushroom
Pizza
Unlimited Free
Happy Leaf
Drink all you
WE'RE **DOOMED.**

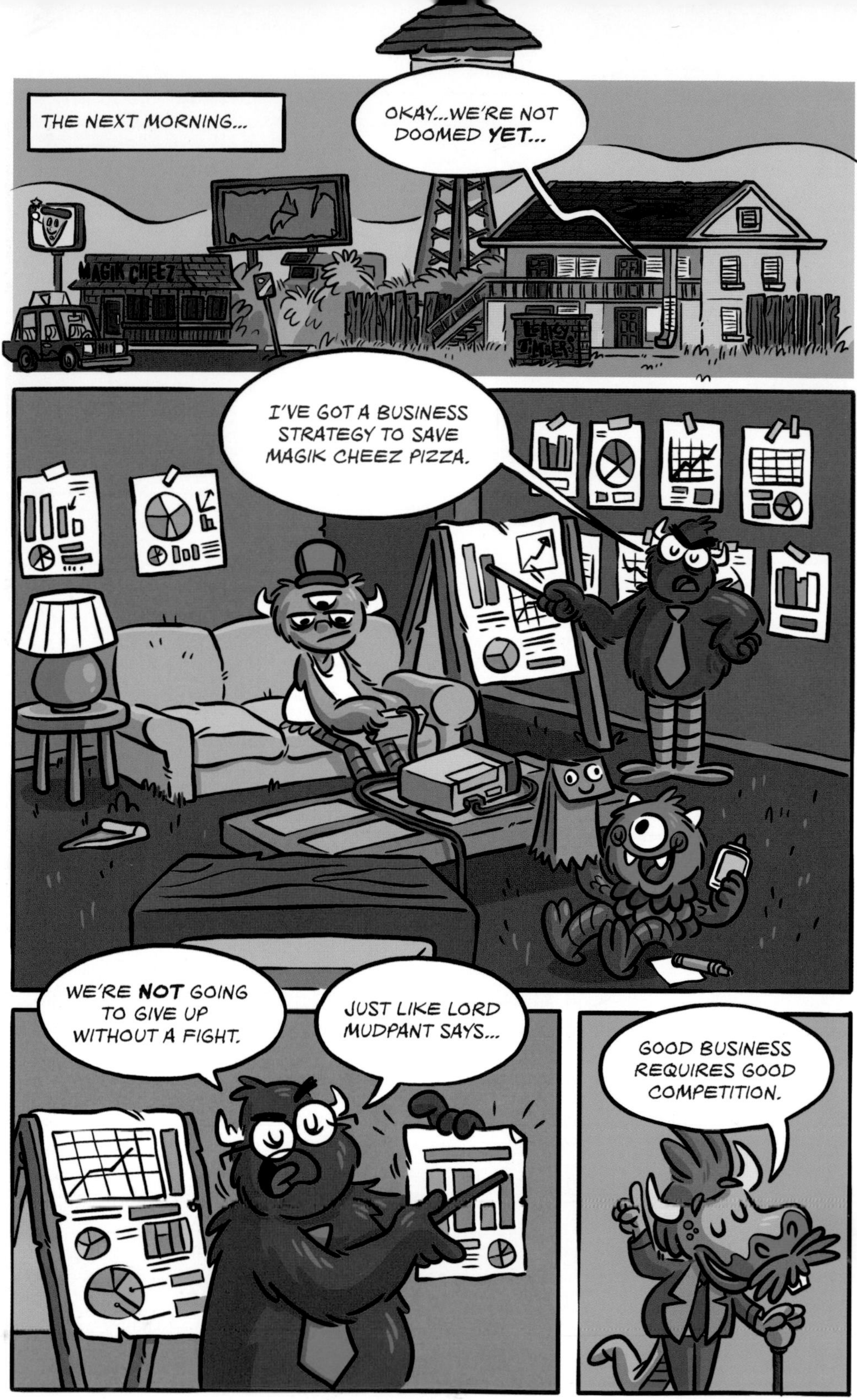
THE NEXT MORNING...
OKAY...WE'RE NOT DOOMED YET...
MAGIK CHEEZ
I'VE GOT A BUSINESS STRATEGY TO SAVE MAGIK CHEEZ PIZZA.
WE'RE NOT GOING TO GIVE UP WITHOUT A FIGHT.
JUST LIKE LORD MUDPANT SAYS...
GOOD BUSINESS REQUIRES GOOD COMPETITION.

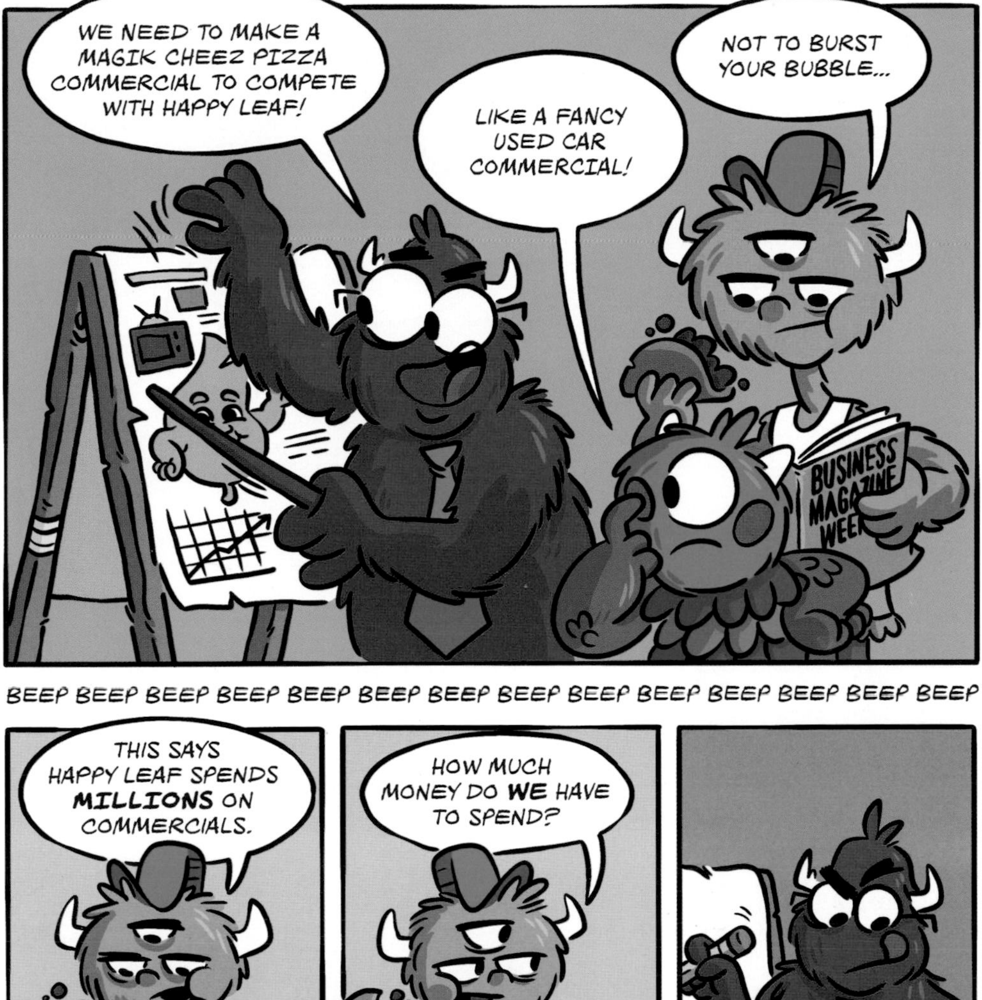
WE NEED TO MAKE A MAGIK CHEEZ PIZZA COMMERCIAL TO COMPETE WITH HAPPY LEAF!
LIKE A FANCY USED CAR COMMERCIAL!
NOT TO BURST YOUR BUBBLE...
BUSINESS MAGAZINE WEEK
BEEP BEEP BEEP BEEP BEEP BEEP BEEP BEEP BEEP BEEP BEEP BEEP BEEP BEEP
THIS SAYS HAPPY LEAF SPENDS **MILLIONS** ON COMMERCIALS.
HOW MUCH MONEY DO **WE** HAVE TO SPEND?
BEEP BEEP BEEP BEEP BEEP BEEP BEEP BEEP BEEP BEEP BEEP BEEP BEEP BEEP
$73.12
WE HAVE **TENS** OF DOLLARS!

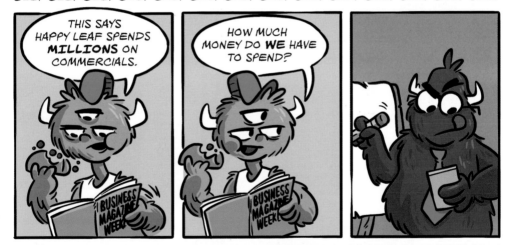

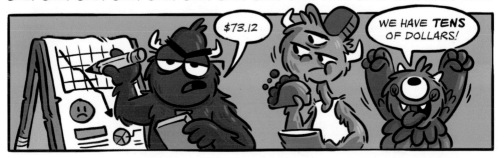

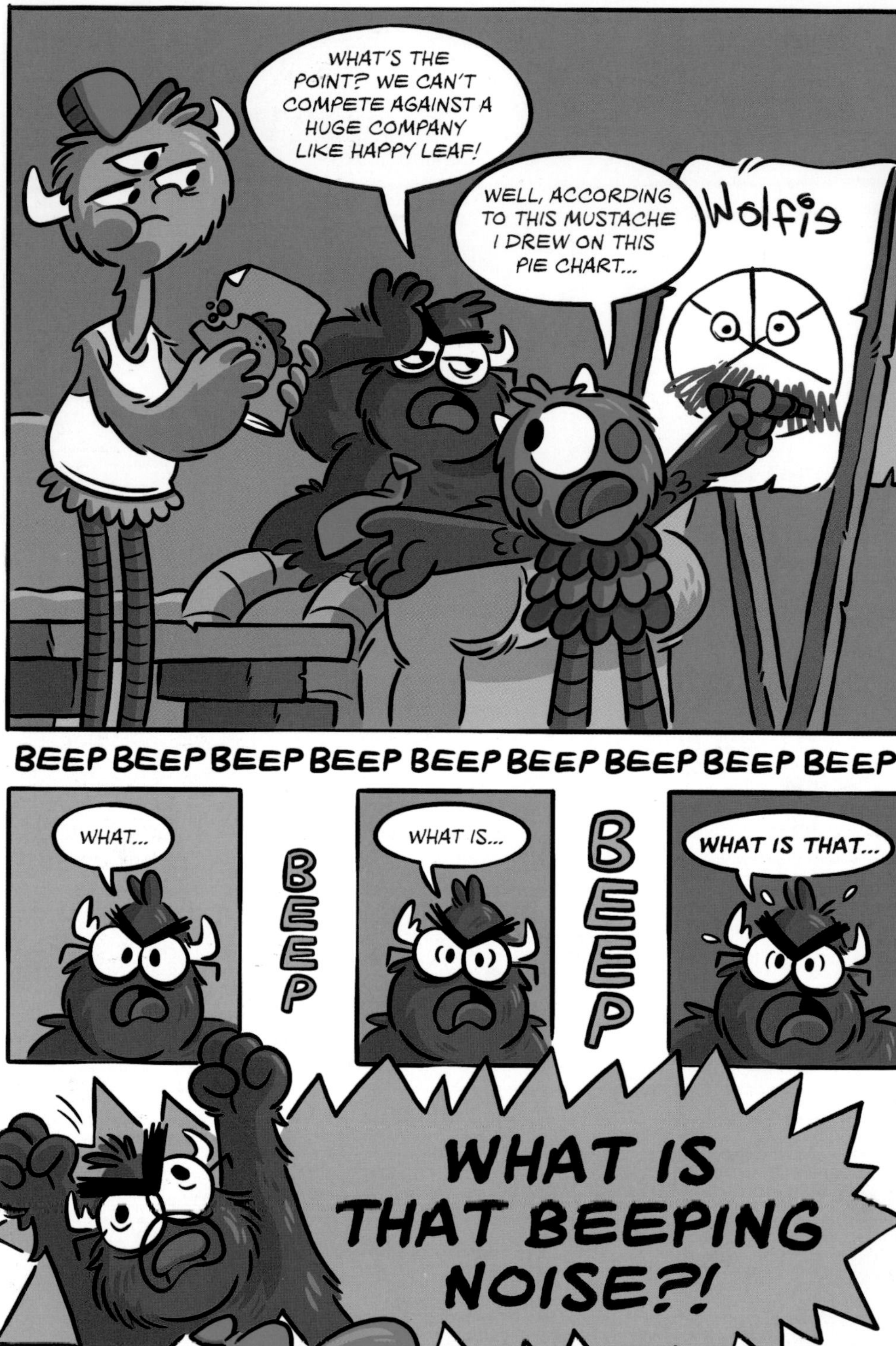

WHAT'S THE POINT? WE CAN'T COMPETE AGAINST A HUGE COMPANY LIKE HAPPY LEAF!
WELL, ACCORDING TO THIS MUSTACHE I DREW ON THIS PIE CHART...
Wolfie
BEEP BEEP BEEP BEEP BEEP BEEP BEEP BEEP BEEP
WHAT...
BEEP
WHAT IS...
BEEP
WHAT IS THAT...
WHAT IS THAT BEEPING NOISE?!

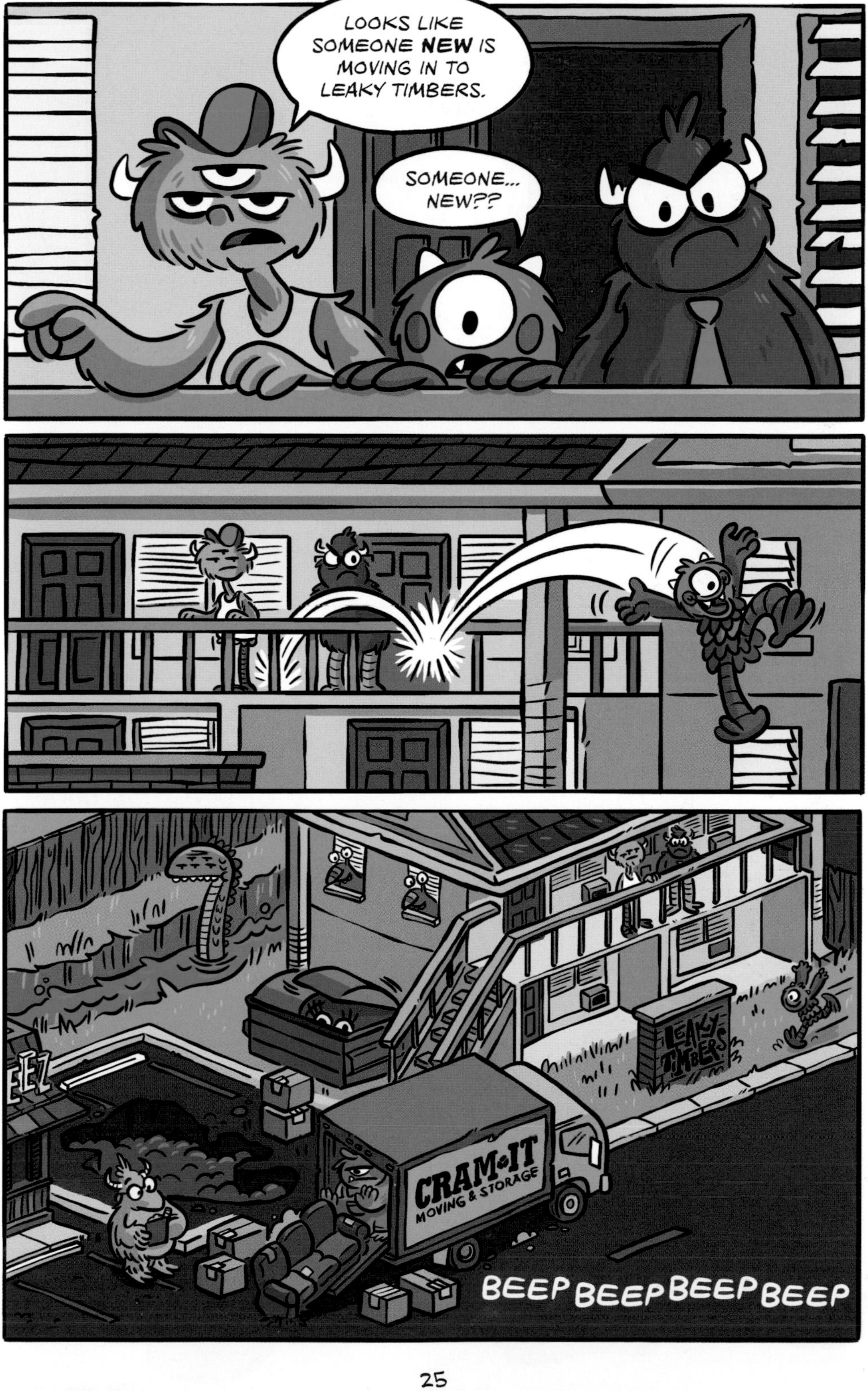
LOOKS LIKE SOMEONE NEW IS MOVING IN TO LEAKY TIMBERS.
SOMEONE... NEW??
LEAKY TIMBERS
CRAM-IT MOVING & STORAGE
BEEP BEEP BEEP BEEP

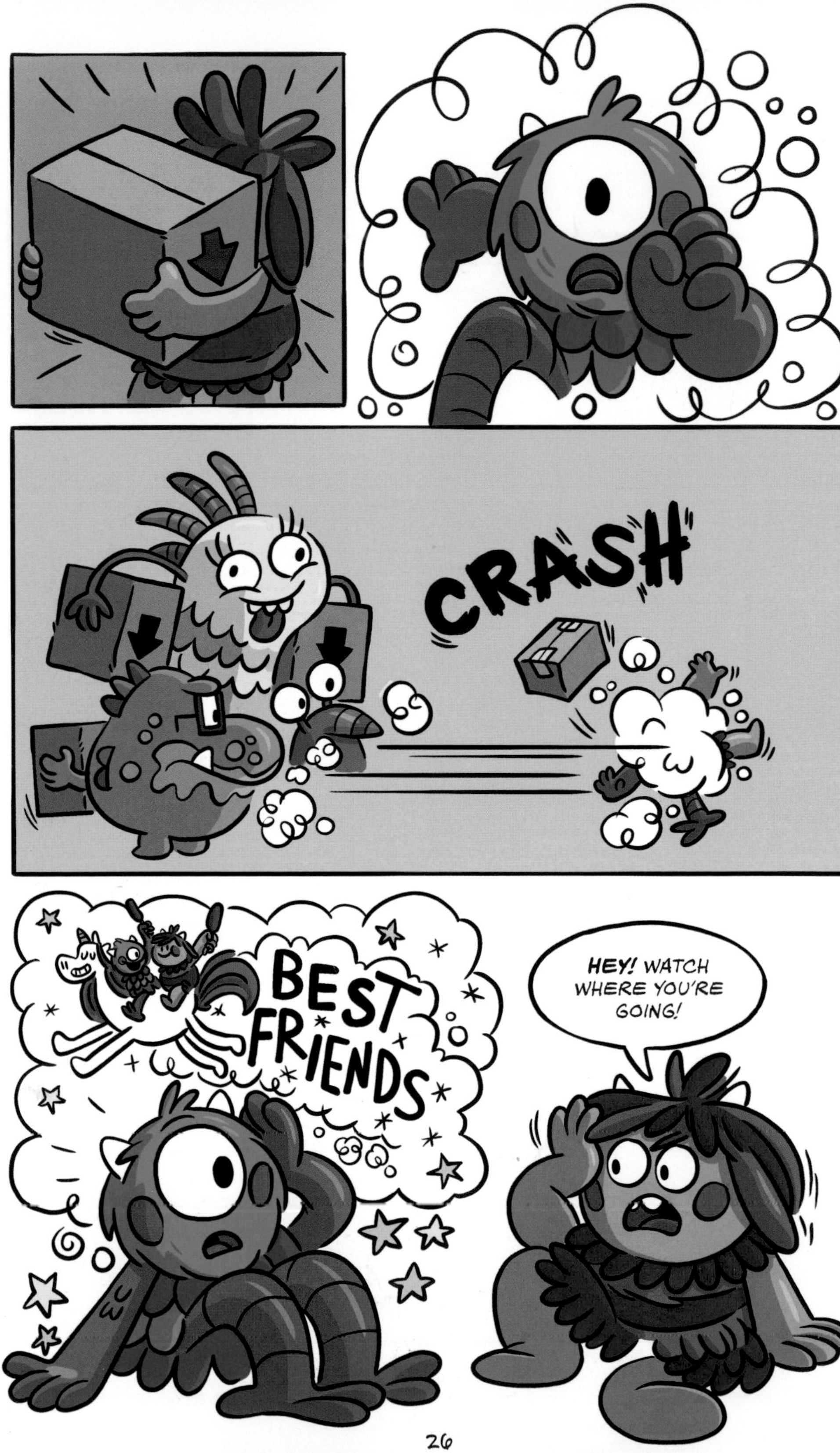
CRASH
BEST FRIENDS
HEY! WATCH WHERE YOU'RE GOING!

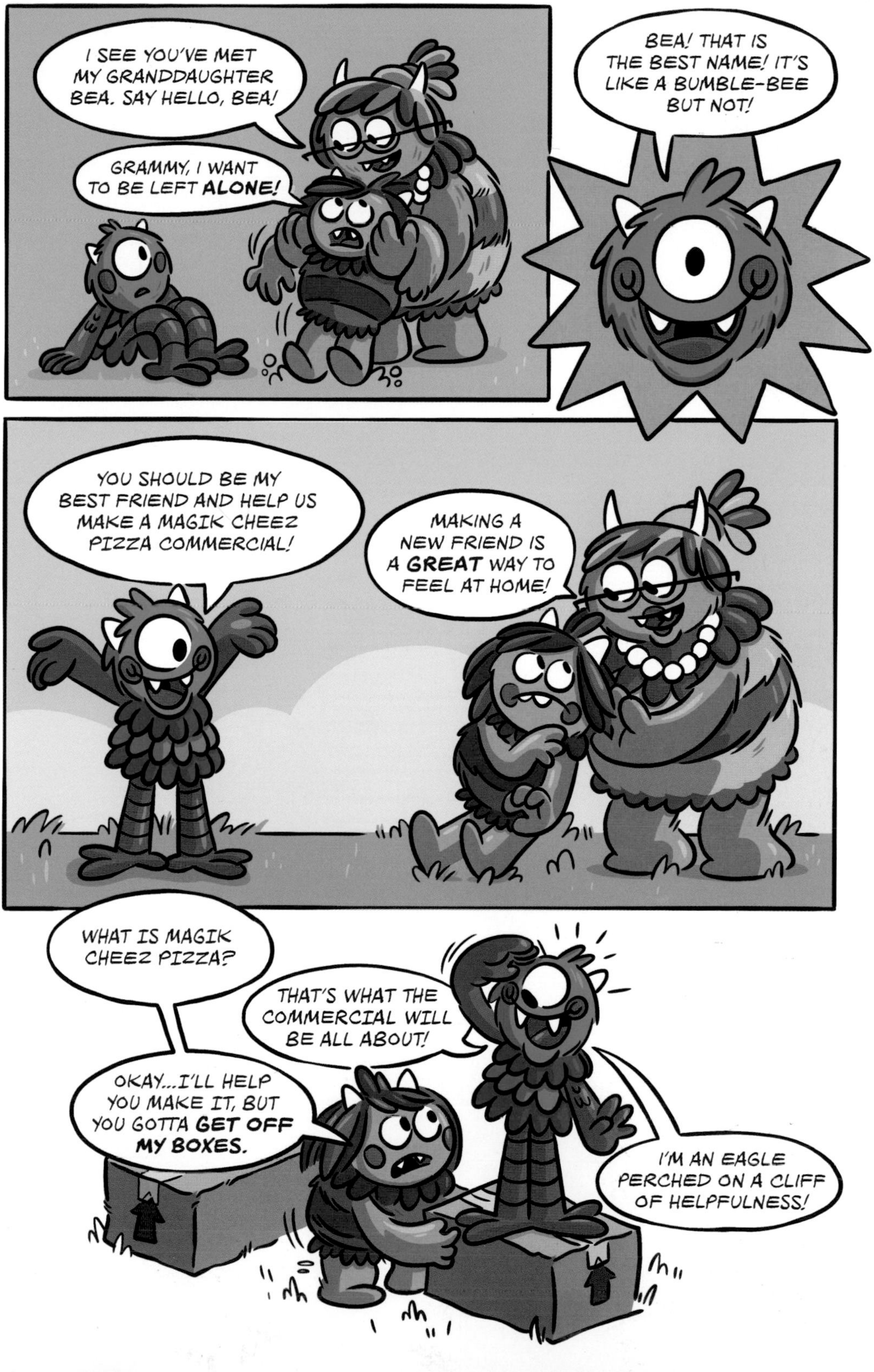
I SEE YOU'VE MET MY GRANDDAUGHTER BEA. SAY HELLO, BEA!
GRAMMY, I WANT TO BE LEFT **ALONE**!
BEA! THAT IS THE BEST NAME! IT'S LIKE A BUMBLE-BEE BUT NOT!
YOU SHOULD BE MY BEST FRIEND AND HELP US MAKE A MAGIK CHEEZ PIZZA COMMERCIAL!
MAKING A NEW FRIEND IS A **GREAT** WAY TO FEEL AT HOME!
WHAT IS MAGIK CHEEZ PIZZA?
THAT'S WHAT THE COMMERCIAL WILL BE ALL ABOUT!
OKAY...I'LL HELP YOU MAKE IT, BUT YOU GOTTA **GET OFF MY BOXES.**
I'M AN EAGLE PERCHED ON A CLIFF OF HELPFULNESS!

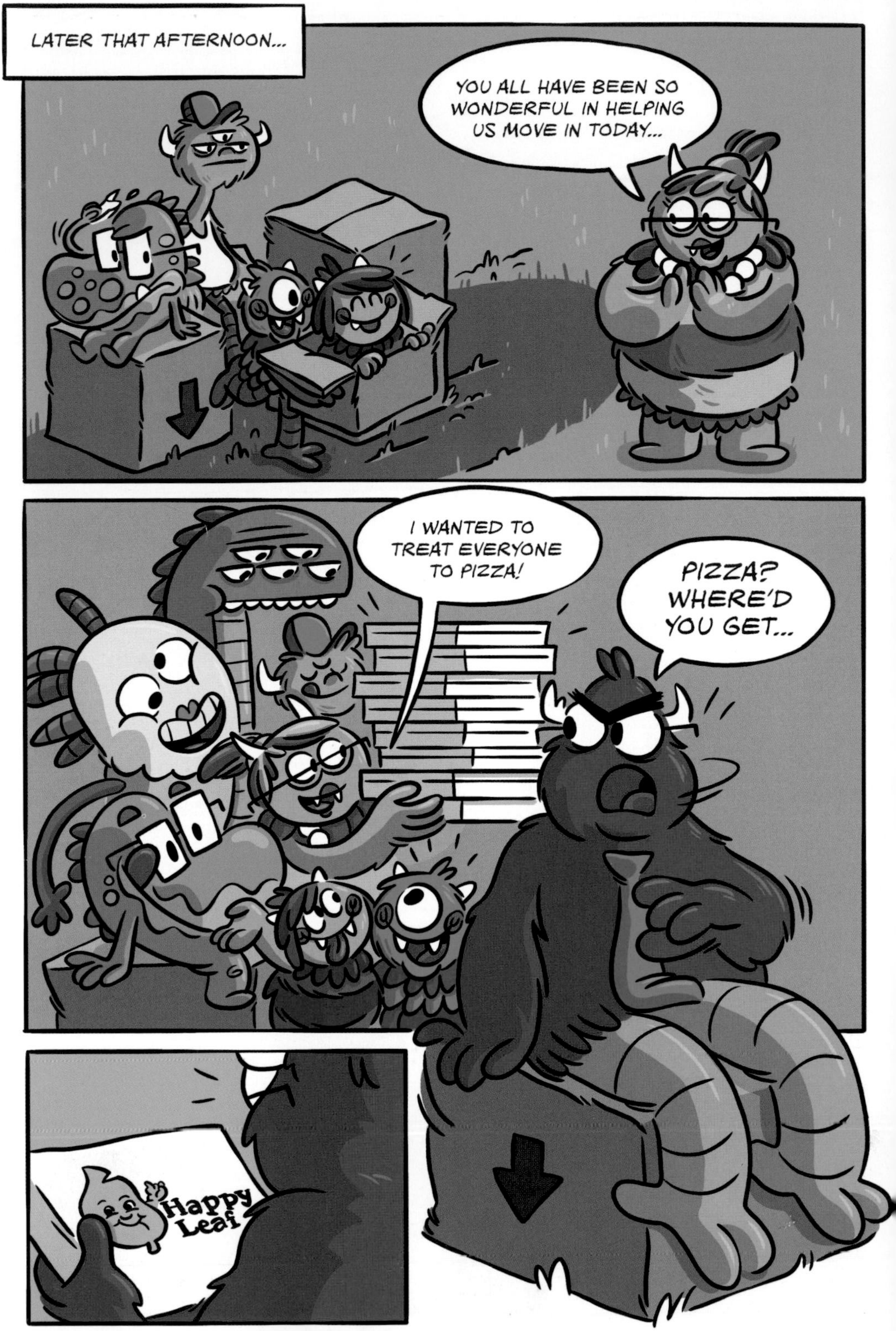
LATER THAT AFTERNOON...
YOU ALL HAVE BEEN SO WONDERFUL IN HELPING US MOVE IN TODAY...
I WANTED TO TREAT EVERYONE TO PIZZA!
PIZZA? WHERE'D YOU GET...
Happy Leaf

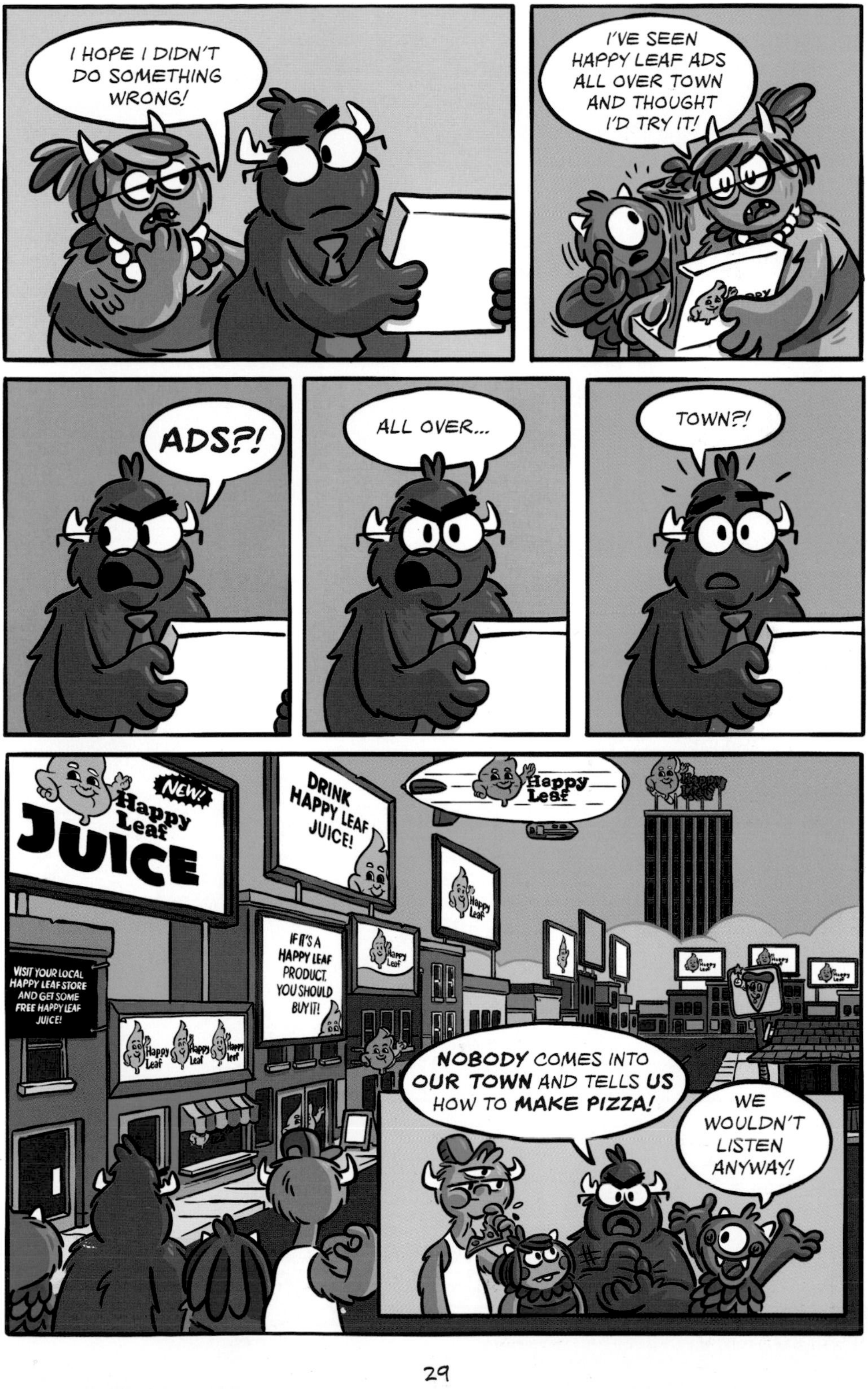
I HOPE I DIDN'T DO SOMETHING WRONG!
I'VE SEEN HAPPY LEAF ADS ALL OVER TOWN AND THOUGHT I'D TRY IT!
ADS?!
ALL OVER...
TOWN?!
NEW! Happy Leaf JUICE
DRINK HAPPY LEAF JUICE!
Happy Leaf
Happy Leaf
VISIT YOUR LOCAL HAPPY LEAF STORE AND GET SOME FREE HAPPY LEAF JUICE!
IF IT'S A HAPPY LEAF PRODUCT, YOU SHOULD BUY IT!
Happy Leaf
Happy Leaf Happy Leaf Happy Leaf
NOBODY COMES INTO OUR TOWN AND TELLS US HOW TO MAKE PIZZA!
WE WOULDN'T LISTEN ANYWAY!

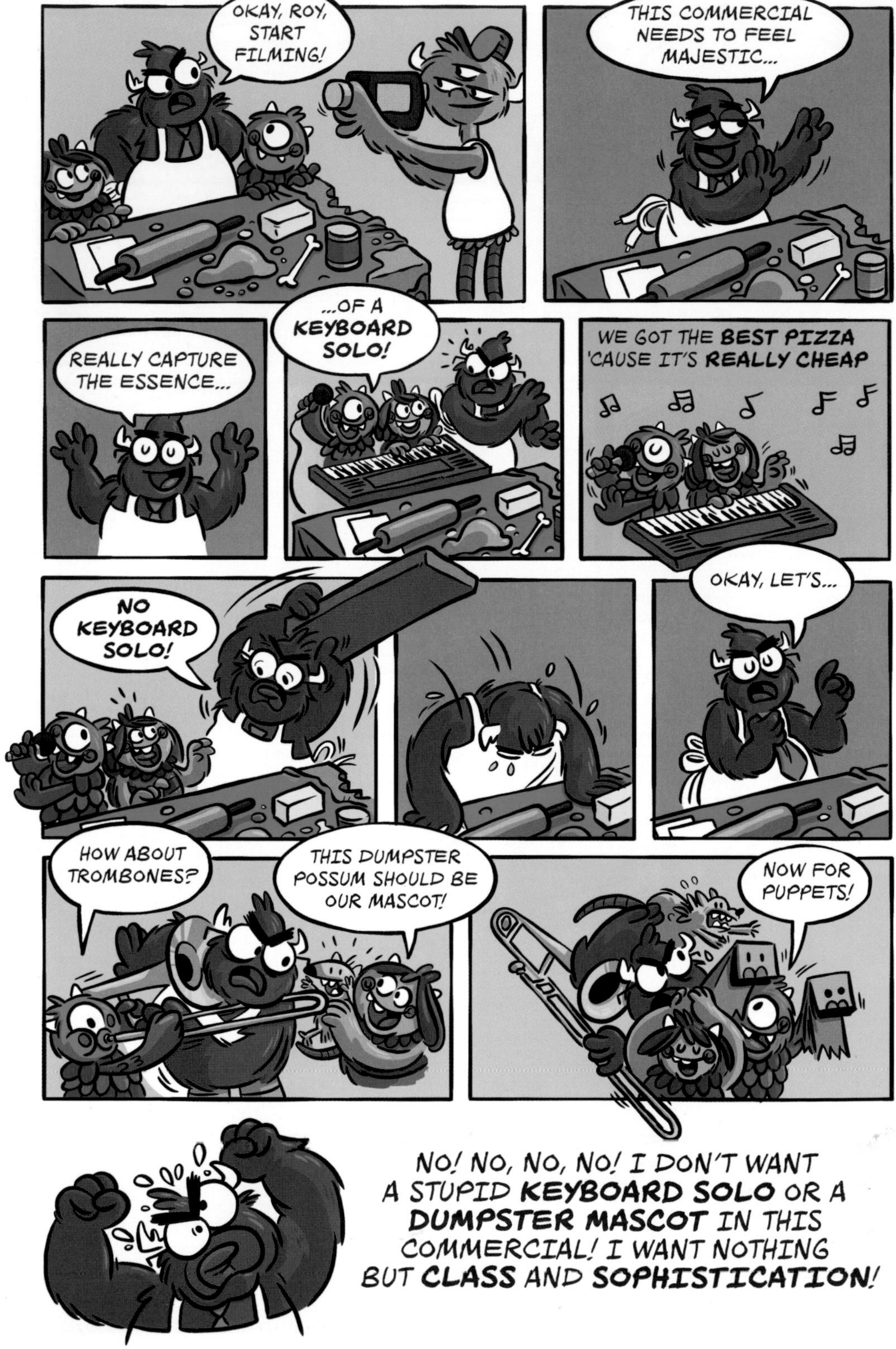
OKAY, ROY, START FILMING!
THIS COMMERCIAL NEEDS TO FEEL MAJESTIC...
REALLY CAPTURE THE ESSENCE...
...OF A KEYBOARD SOLO!
WE GOT THE BEST PIZZA 'CAUSE IT'S REALLY CHEAP
NO KEYBOARD SOLO!
OKAY, LET'S...
HOW ABOUT TROMBONES?
THIS DUMPSTER POSSUM SHOULD BE OUR MASCOT!
NOW FOR PUPPETS!
NO! NO, NO, NO! I DON'T WANT A STUPID KEYBOARD SOLO OR A DUMPSTER MASCOT IN THIS COMMERCIAL! I WANT NOTHING BUT CLASS AND SOPHISTICATION!

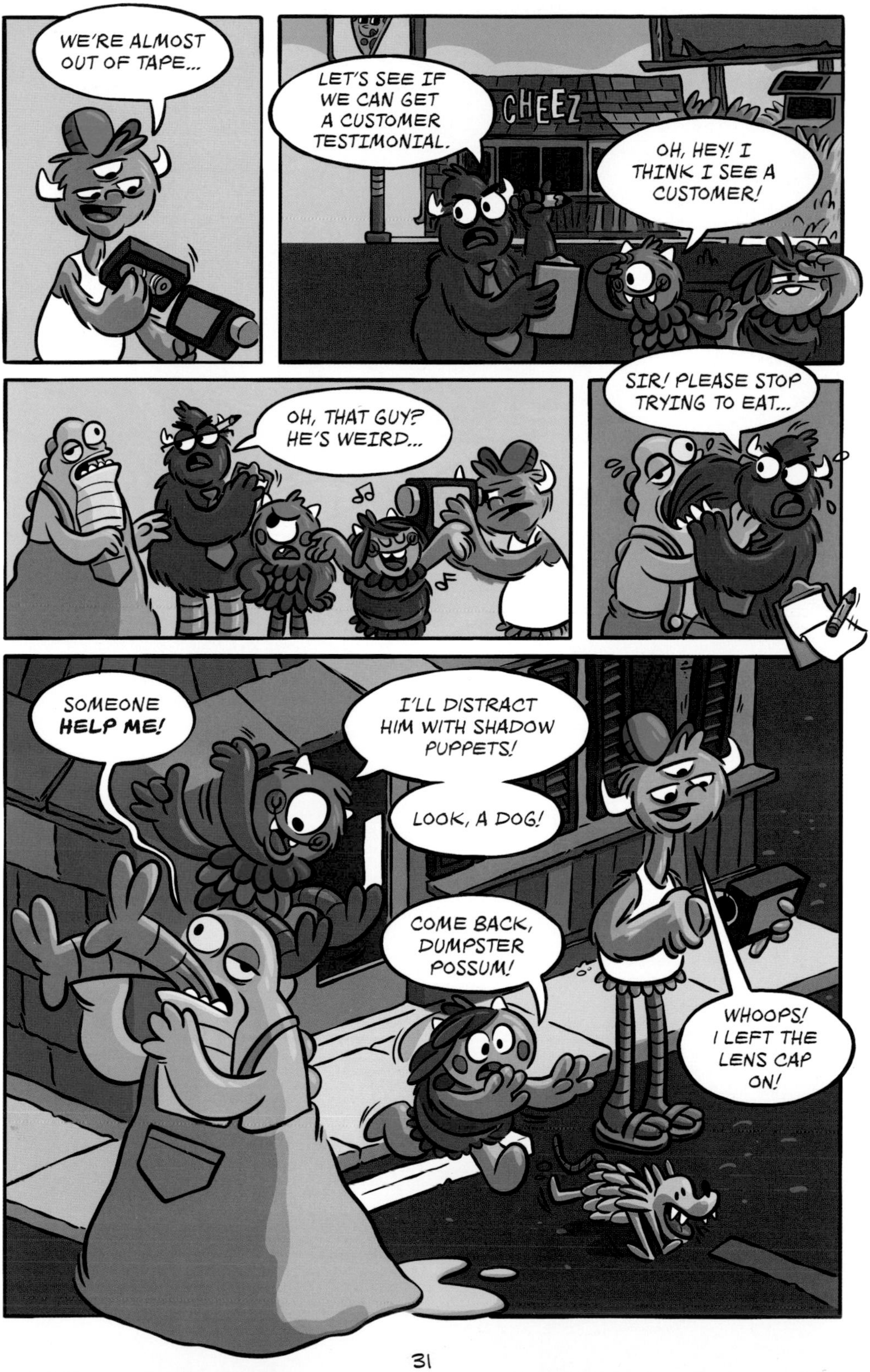
WE'RE ALMOST OUT OF TAPE...
LET'S SEE IF WE CAN GET A CUSTOMER TESTIMONIAL.
CHEEZ
OH, HEY! I THINK I SEE A CUSTOMER!
OH, THAT GUY? HE'S WEIRD...
SIR! PLEASE STOP TRYING TO EAT...
SOMEONE HELP ME!
I'LL DISTRACT HIM WITH SHADOW PUPPETS!
LOOK, A DOG!
COME BACK, DUMPSTER POSSUM!
WHOOPS! I LEFT THE LENS CAP ON!

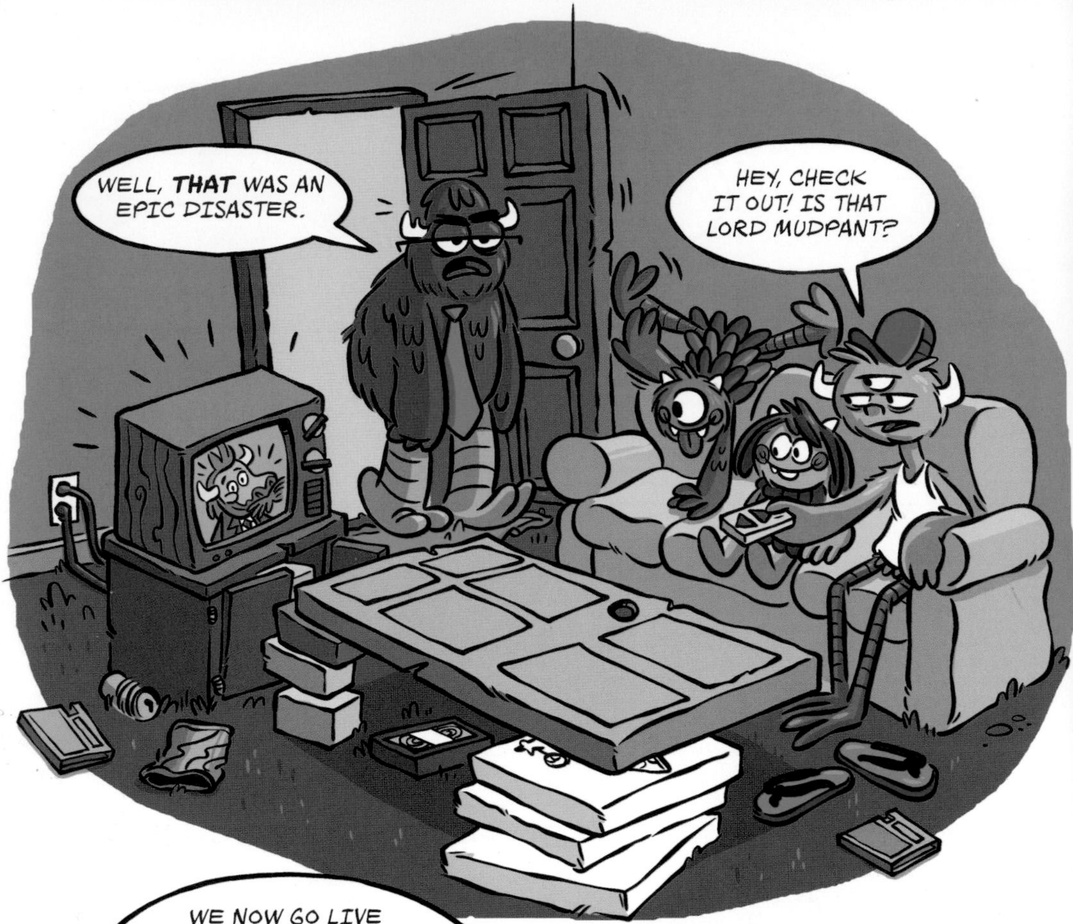
WELL, **THAT** WAS AN EPIC DISASTER.
HEY, CHECK IT OUT! IS THAT LORD MUDPANT?

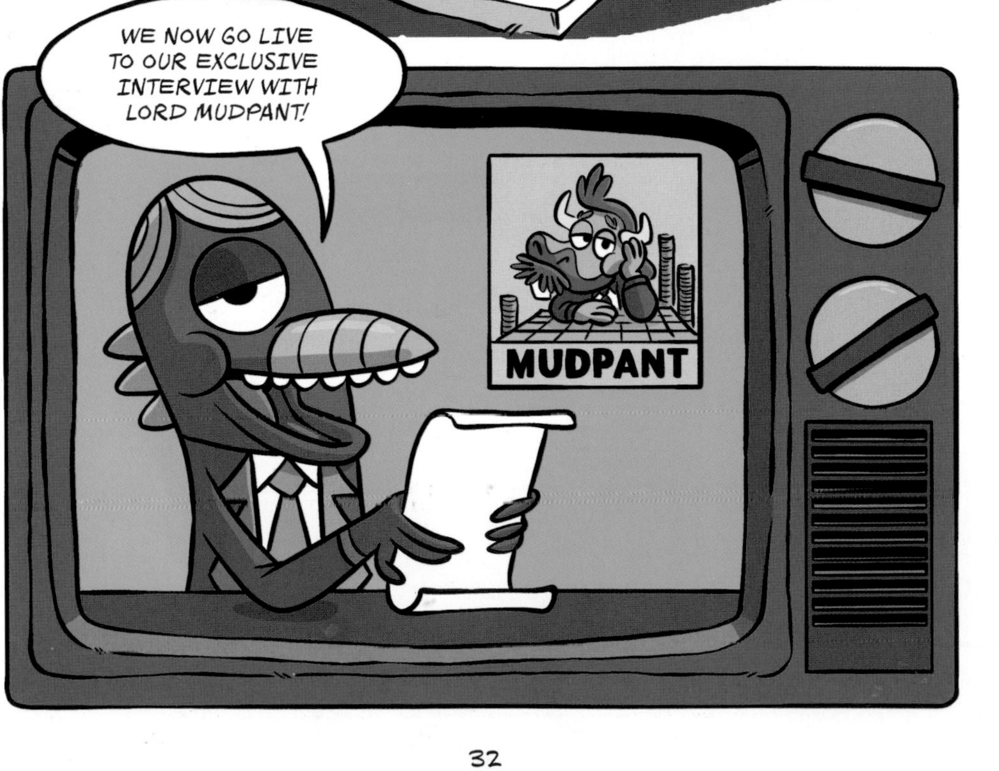
WE NOW GO LIVE TO OUR EXCLUSIVE INTERVIEW WITH LORD MUDPANT!
MUDPANT

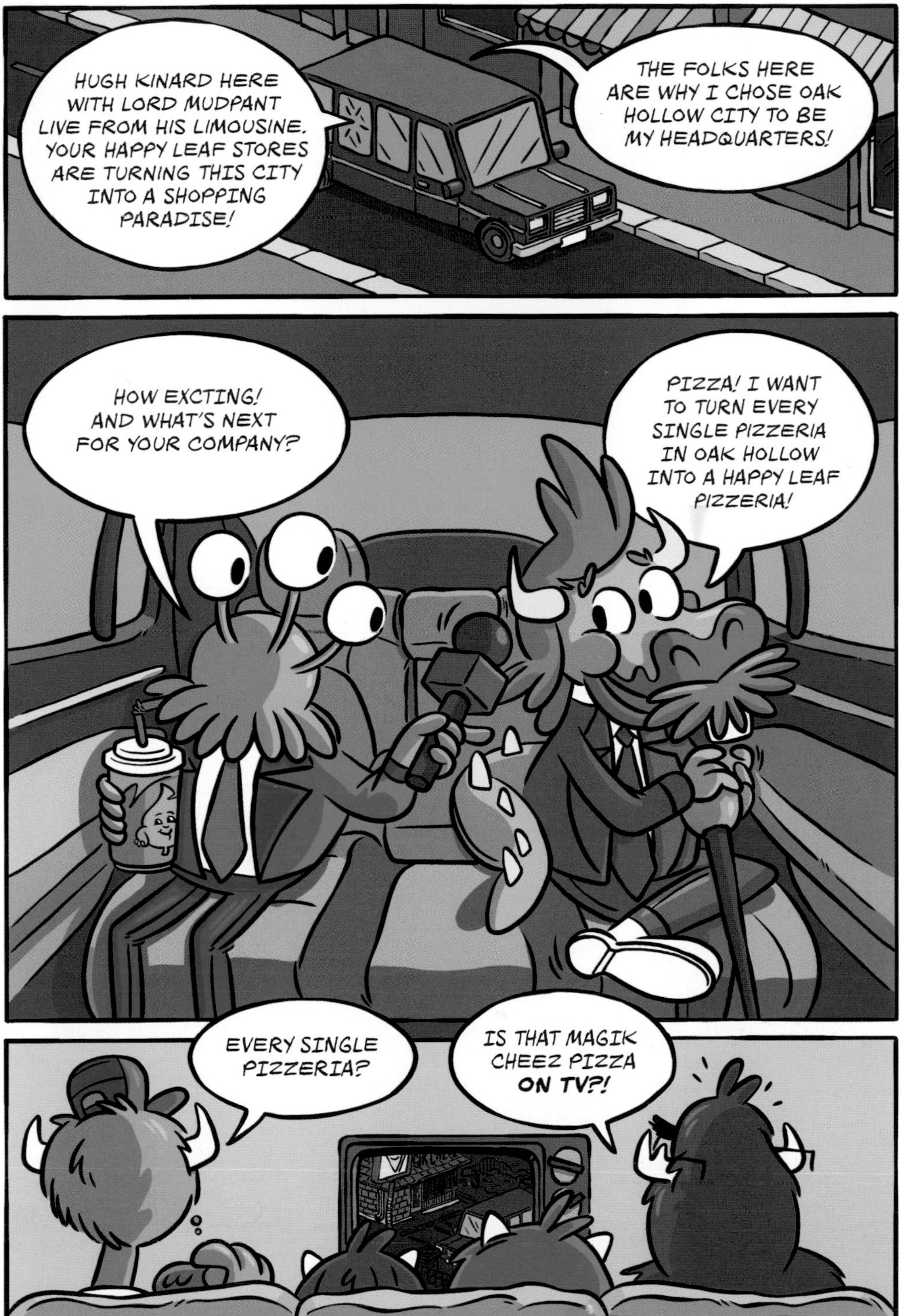
HUGH KINARD HERE WITH LORD MUDPANT LIVE FROM HIS LIMOUSINE. YOUR HAPPY LEAF STORES ARE TURNING THIS CITY INTO A SHOPPING PARADISE!
THE FOLKS HERE ARE WHY I CHOSE OAK HOLLOW CITY TO BE MY HEADQUARTERS!
HOW EXCTING! AND WHAT'S NEXT FOR YOUR COMPANY?
PIZZA! I WANT TO TURN EVERY SINGLE PIZZERIA IN OAK HOLLOW INTO A HAPPY LEAF PIZZERIA!
EVERY SINGLE PIZZERIA?
IS THAT MAGIK CHEEZ PIZZA **ON TV?!**

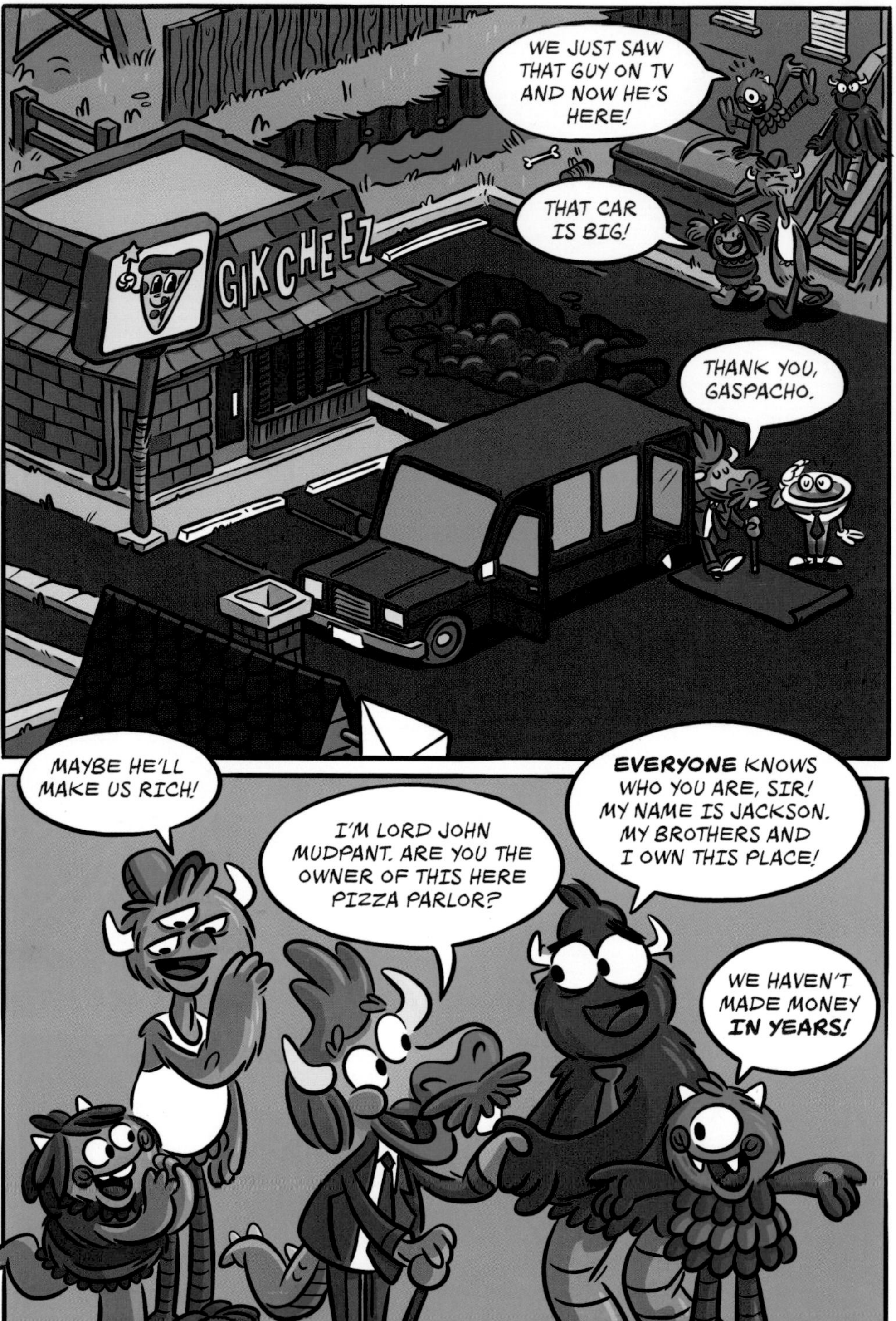
WE JUST SAW THAT GUY ON TV AND NOW HE'S HERE!
THAT CAR IS BIG!
GIKCHEEZ
THANK YOU, GASPACHO.
MAYBE HE'LL MAKE US RICH!
I'M LORD JOHN MUDPANT. ARE YOU THE OWNER OF THIS HERE PIZZA PARLOR?
EVERYONE KNOWS WHO YOU ARE, SIR! MY NAME IS JACKSON. MY BROTHERS AND I OWN THIS PLACE!
WE HAVEN'T MADE MONEY **IN YEARS!**

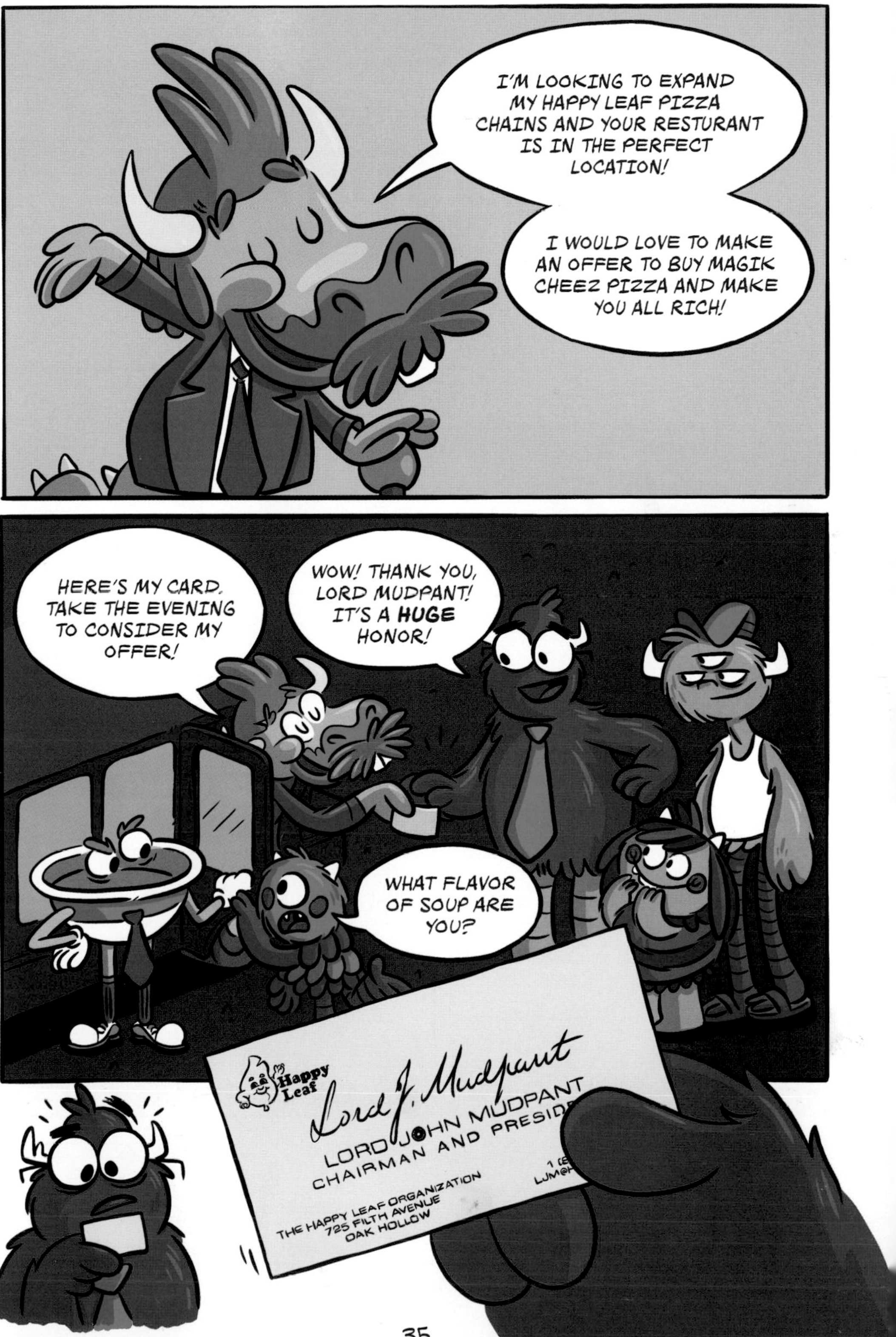
I'M LOOKING TO EXPAND MY HAPPY LEAF PIZZA CHAINS AND YOUR RESTURANT IS IN THE PERFECT LOCATION!
I WOULD LOVE TO MAKE AN OFFER TO BUY MAGIK CHEEZ PIZZA AND MAKE YOU ALL RICH!
HERE'S MY CARD. TAKE THE EVENING TO CONSIDER MY OFFER!
WOW! THANK YOU, LORD MUDPANT! IT'S A **HUGE** HONOR!
WHAT FLAVOR OF SOUP ARE YOU?
Happy Leaf
Lord J. Mudpant
LORD JOHN MUDPANT
CHAIRMAN AND
THE HAPPY LEAF ORGANIZATION
725 FILTH AVENUE
OAK HOLLOW

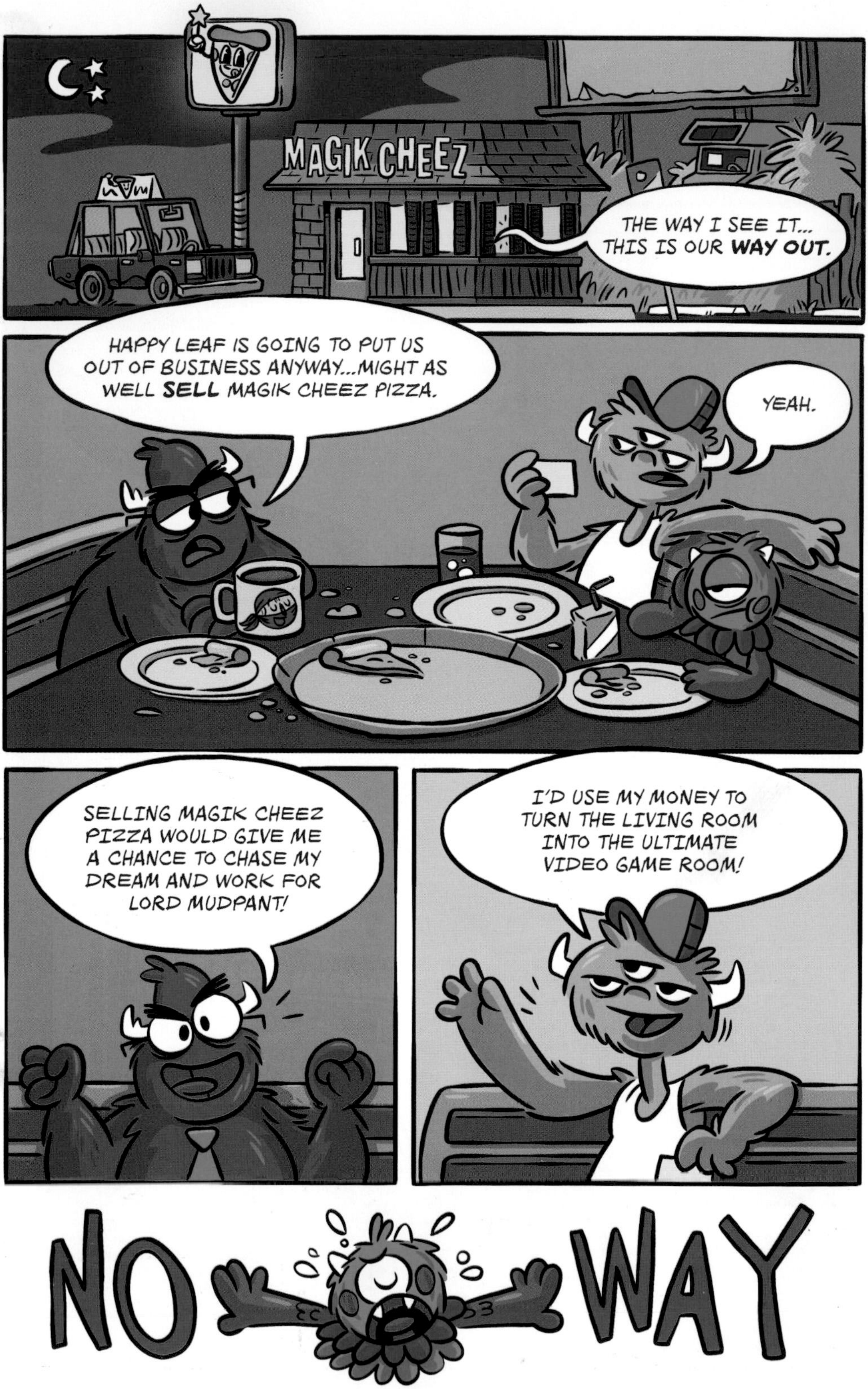
MAGIK CHEEZ
THE WAY I SEE IT... THIS IS OUR **WAY OUT.**
HAPPY LEAF IS GOING TO PUT US OUT OF BUSINESS ANYWAY...MIGHT AS WELL **SELL** MAGIK CHEEZ PIZZA.
YEAH.
SELLING MAGIK CHEEZ PIZZA WOULD GIVE ME A CHANCE TO CHASE MY DREAM AND WORK FOR LORD MUDPANT!
I'D USE MY MONEY TO TURN THE LIVING ROOM INTO THE ULTIMATE VIDEO GAME ROOM!
NO WAY

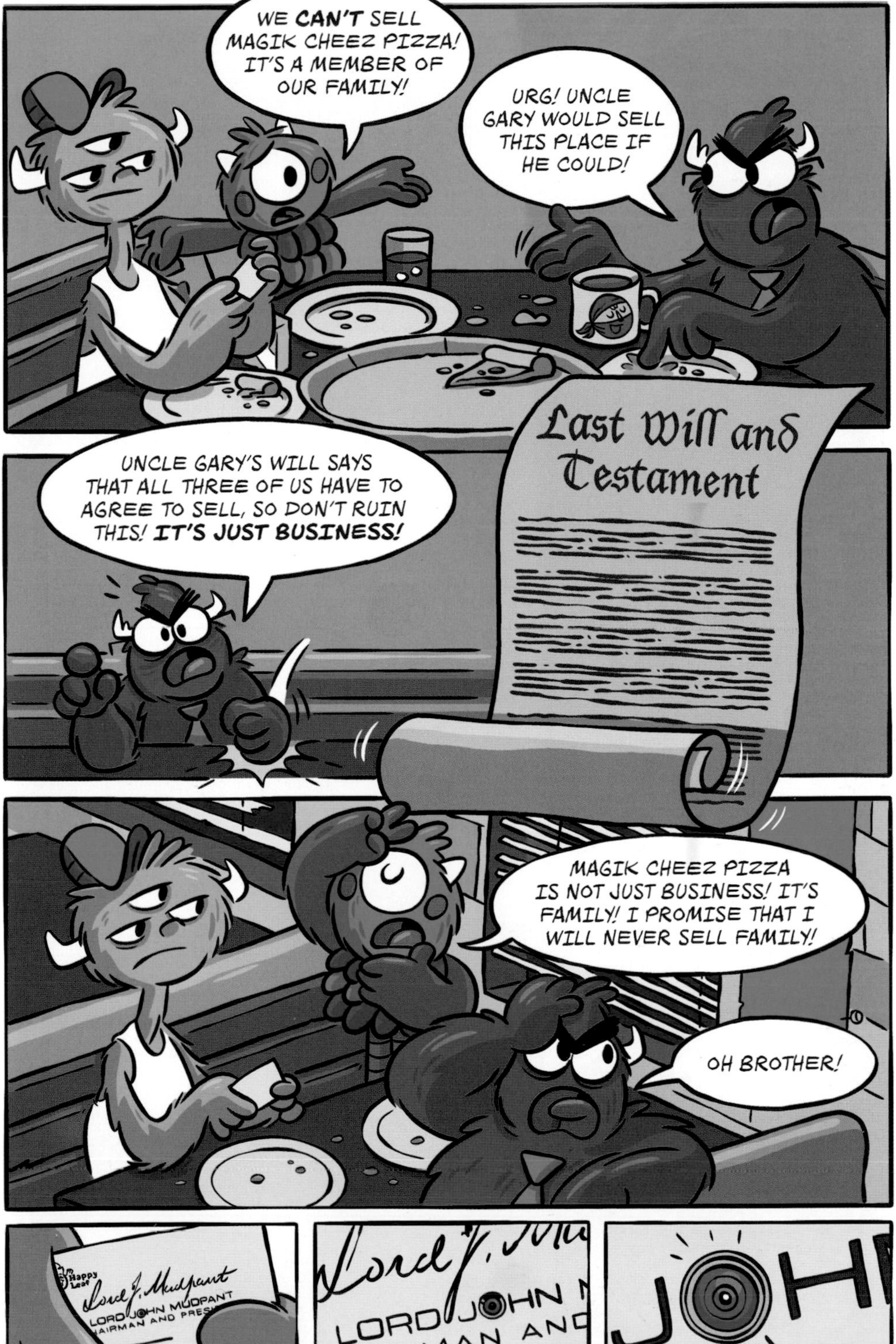
WE **CAN'T** SELL MAGIK CHEEZ PIZZA! IT'S A MEMBER OF OUR FAMILY!
URG! UNCLE GARY WOULD SELL THIS PLACE IF HE COULD!
Last Will and Testament
UNCLE GARY'S WILL SAYS THAT ALL THREE OF US HAVE TO AGREE TO SELL, SO DON'T RUIN THIS! **IT'S JUST BUSINESS!**
MAGIK CHEEZ PIZZA IS NOT JUST BUSINESS! IT'S FAMILY! I PROMISE THAT I WILL NEVER SELL FAMILY!
OH BROTHER!
Happy Leaf
Lord J. Mudpant
LORD JOHN MUDPANT
CHAIRMAN AND PRES
LORD JOHN
CHAIRMAN AND
JOH

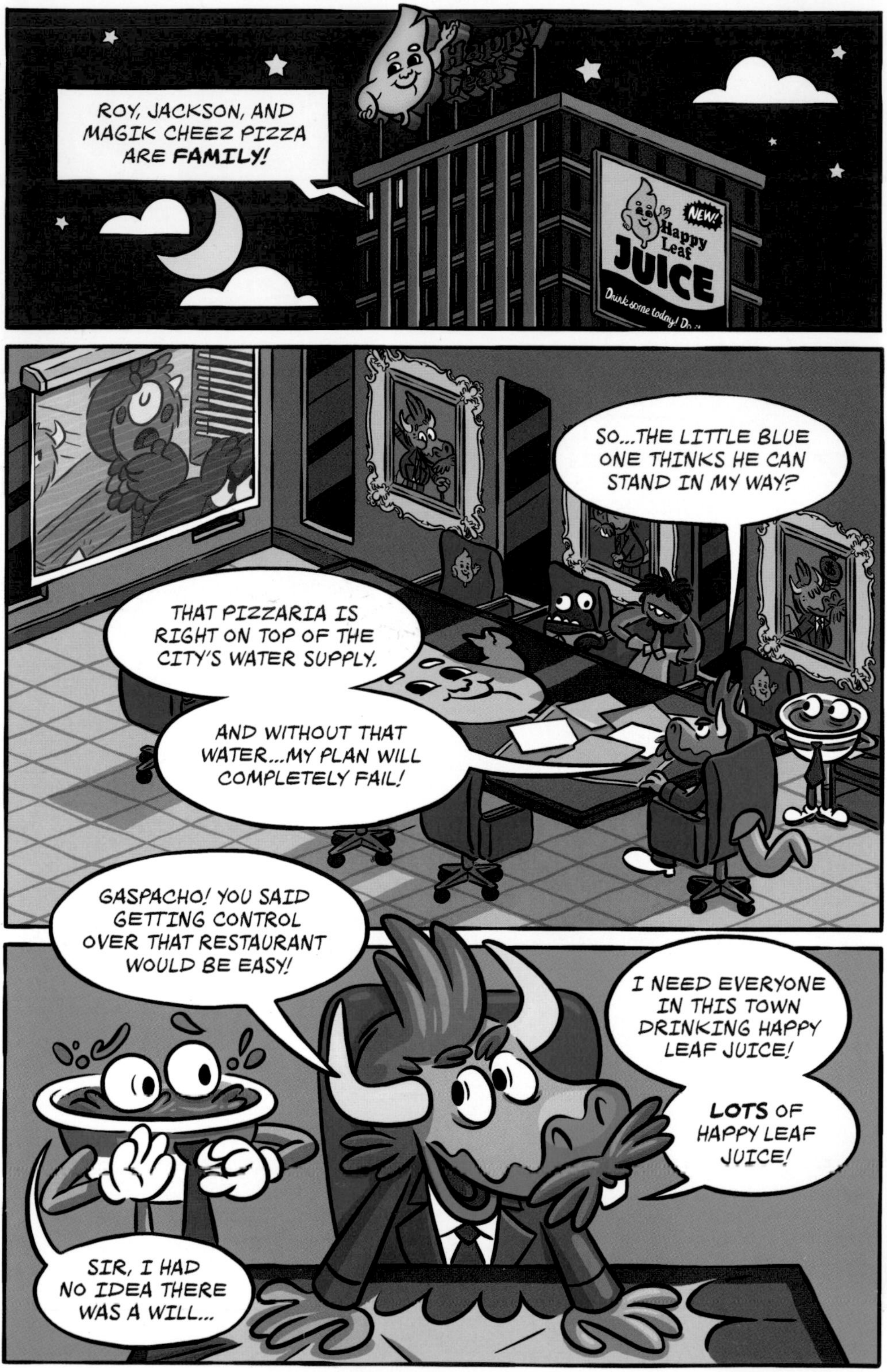

ROY, JACKSON, AND MAGIK CHEEZ PIZZA ARE **FAMILY!**
Happy Leaf
NEW!
Happy Leaf JUICE
SO...THE LITTLE BLUE ONE THINKS HE CAN STAND IN MY WAY?
THAT PIZZARIA IS RIGHT ON TOP OF THE CITY'S WATER SUPPLY.
AND WITHOUT THAT WATER...MY PLAN WILL COMPLETELY FAIL!
GASPACHO! YOU SAID GETTING CONTROL OVER THAT RESTAURANT WOULD BE EASY!
I NEED EVERYONE IN THIS TOWN DRINKING HAPPY LEAF JUICE!
LOTS OF HAPPY LEAF JUICE!
SIR, I HAD NO IDEA THERE WAS A WILL...

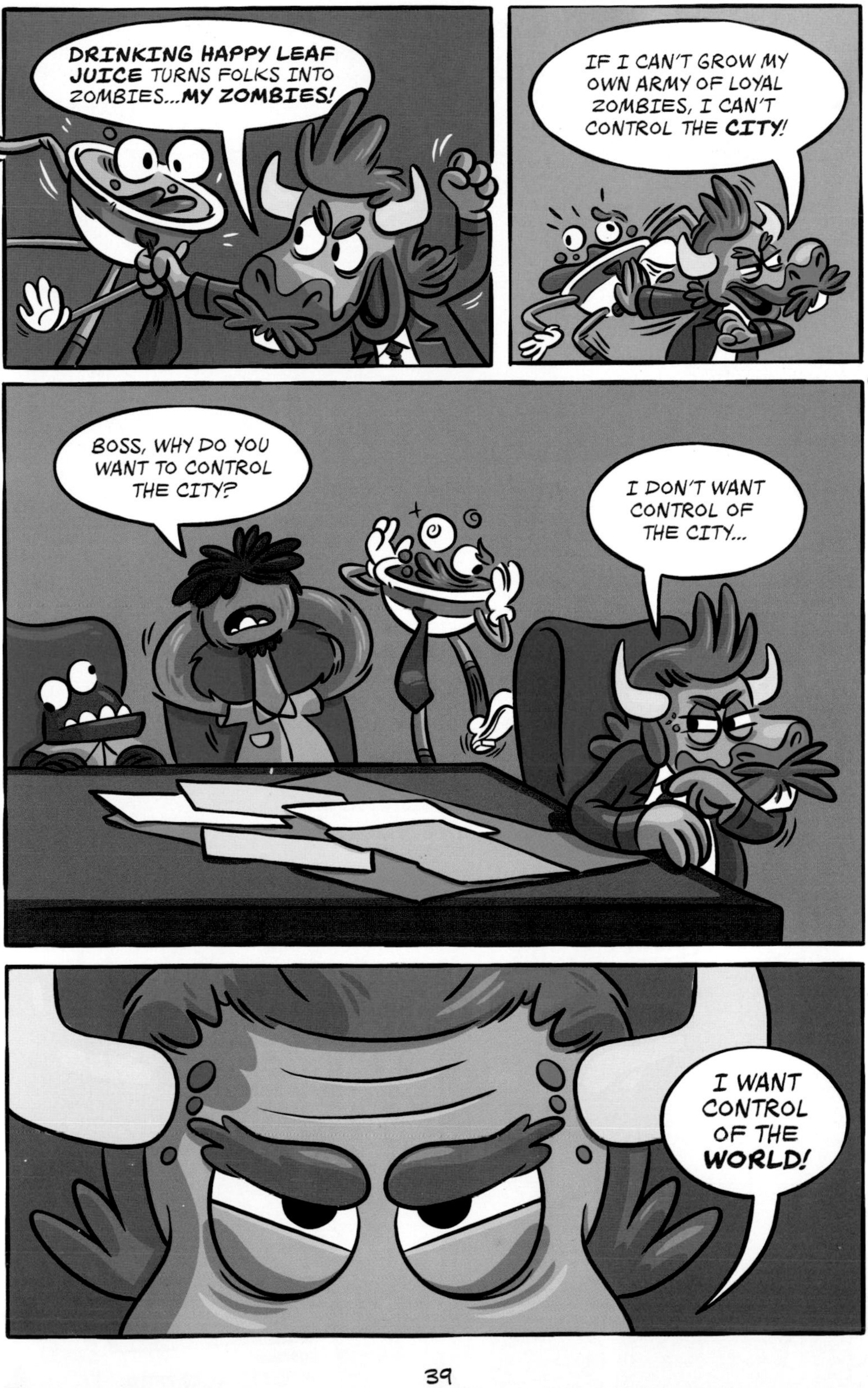
DRINKING HAPPY LEAF JUICE TURNS FOLKS INTO ZOMBIES...MY ZOMBIES!
IF I CAN'T GROW MY OWN ARMY OF LOYAL ZOMBIES, I CAN'T CONTROL THE CITY!
BOSS, WHY DO YOU WANT TO CONTROL THE CITY?
I DON'T WANT CONTROL OF THE CITY...
I WANT CONTROL OF THE WORLD!

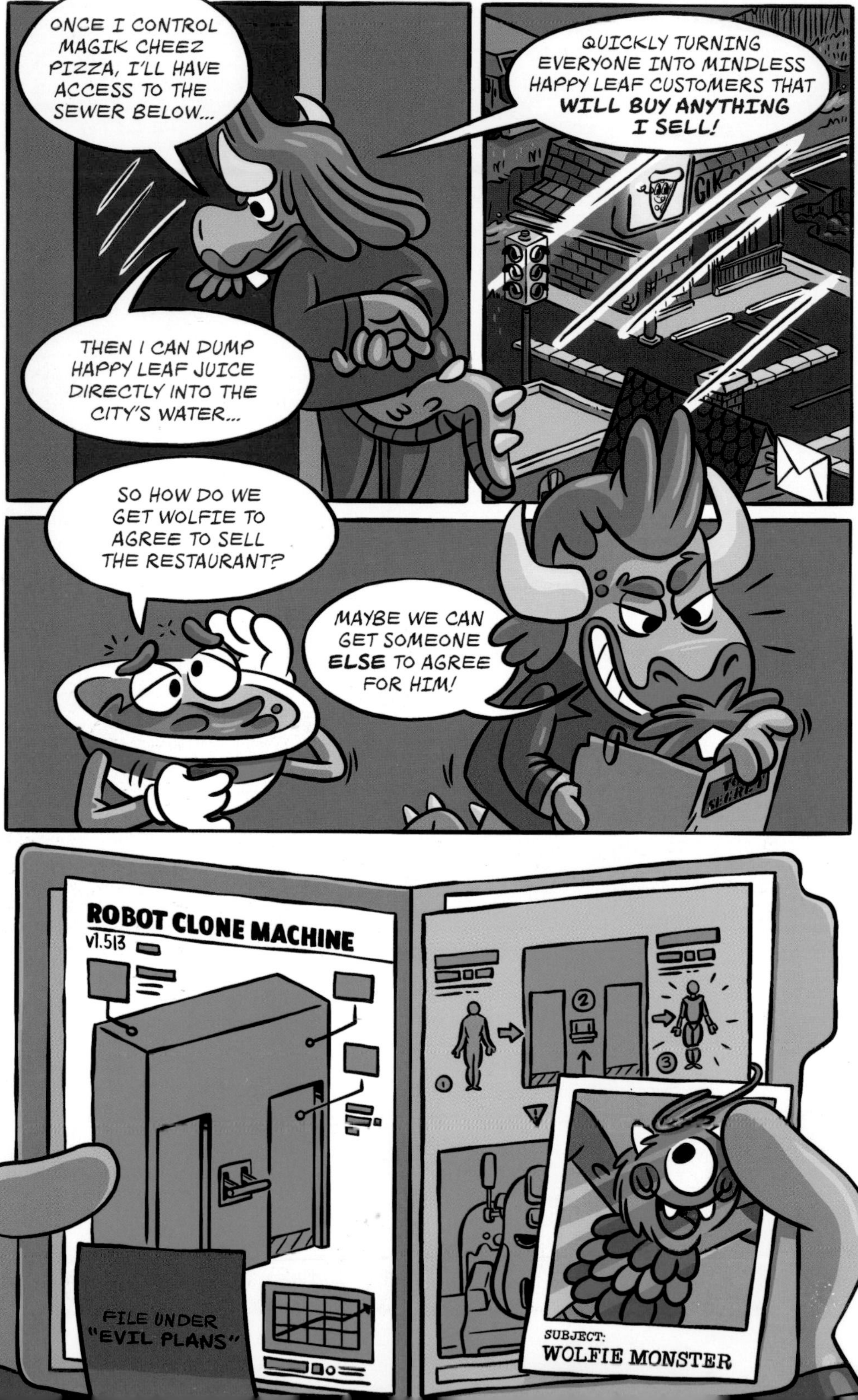
ONCE I CONTROL MAGIK CHEEZ PIZZA, I'LL HAVE ACCESS TO THE SEWER BELOW...
THEN I CAN DUMP HAPPY LEAF JUICE DIRECTLY INTO THE CITY'S WATER...
QUICKLY TURNING EVERYONE INTO MINDLESS HAPPY LEAF CUSTOMERS THAT WILL BUY ANYTHING I SELL!
SO HOW DO WE GET WOLFIE TO AGREE TO SELL THE RESTAURANT?
MAYBE WE CAN GET SOMEONE ELSE TO AGREE FOR HIM!
ROBOT CLONE MACHINE
v1.513
FILE UNDER "EVIL PLANS"
SUBJECT:
WOLFIE MONSTER

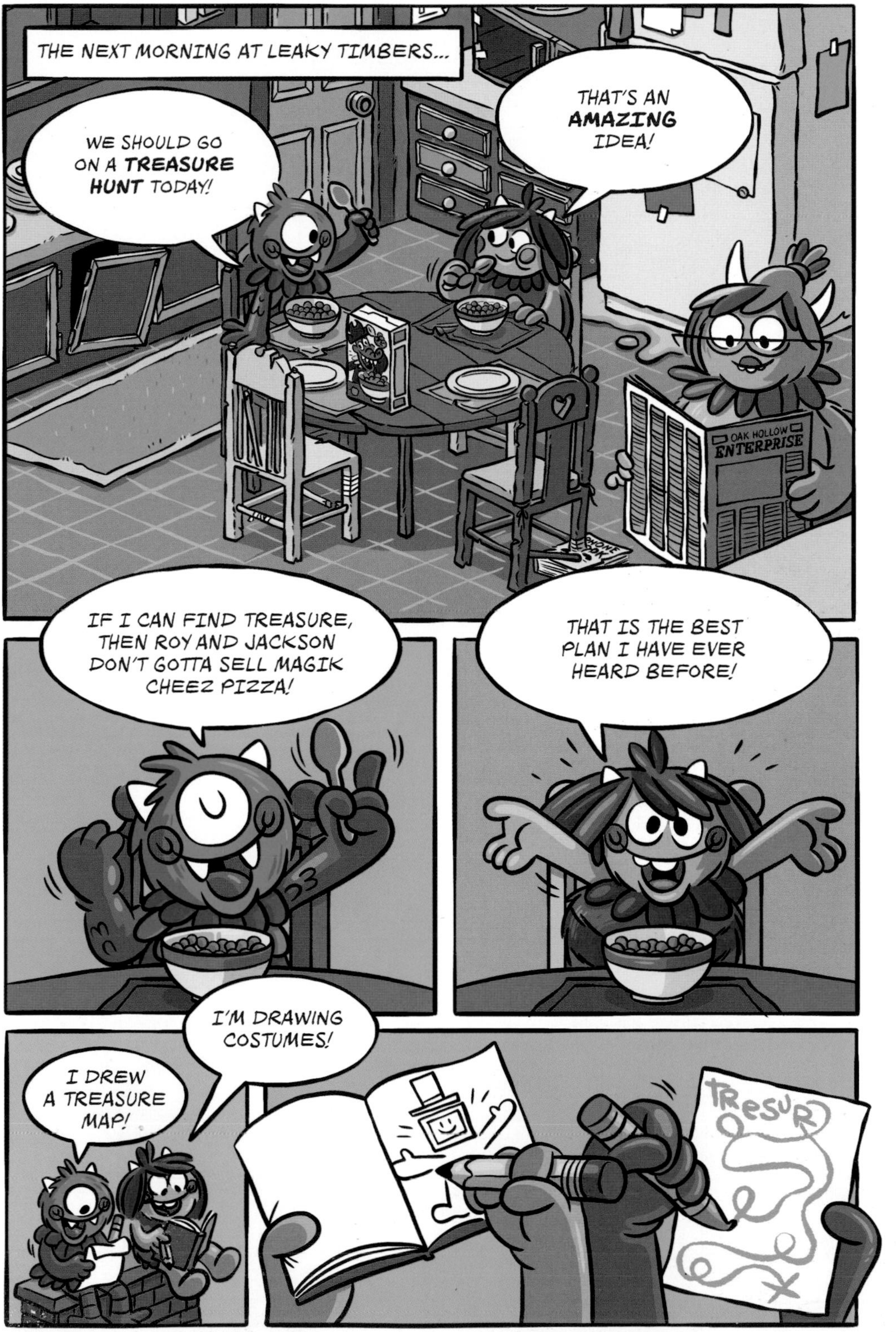
THE NEXT MORNING AT LEAKY TIMBERS...
WE SHOULD GO ON A TREASURE HUNT TODAY!
THAT'S AN AMAZING IDEA!
OAK HOLLOW ENTERPRISE
IF I CAN FIND TREASURE, THEN ROY AND JACKSON DON'T GOTTA SELL MAGIK CHEEZ PIZZA!
THAT IS THE BEST PLAN I HAVE EVER HEARD BEFORE!
I DREW A TREASURE MAP!
I'M DRAWING COSTUMES!
TRESUR

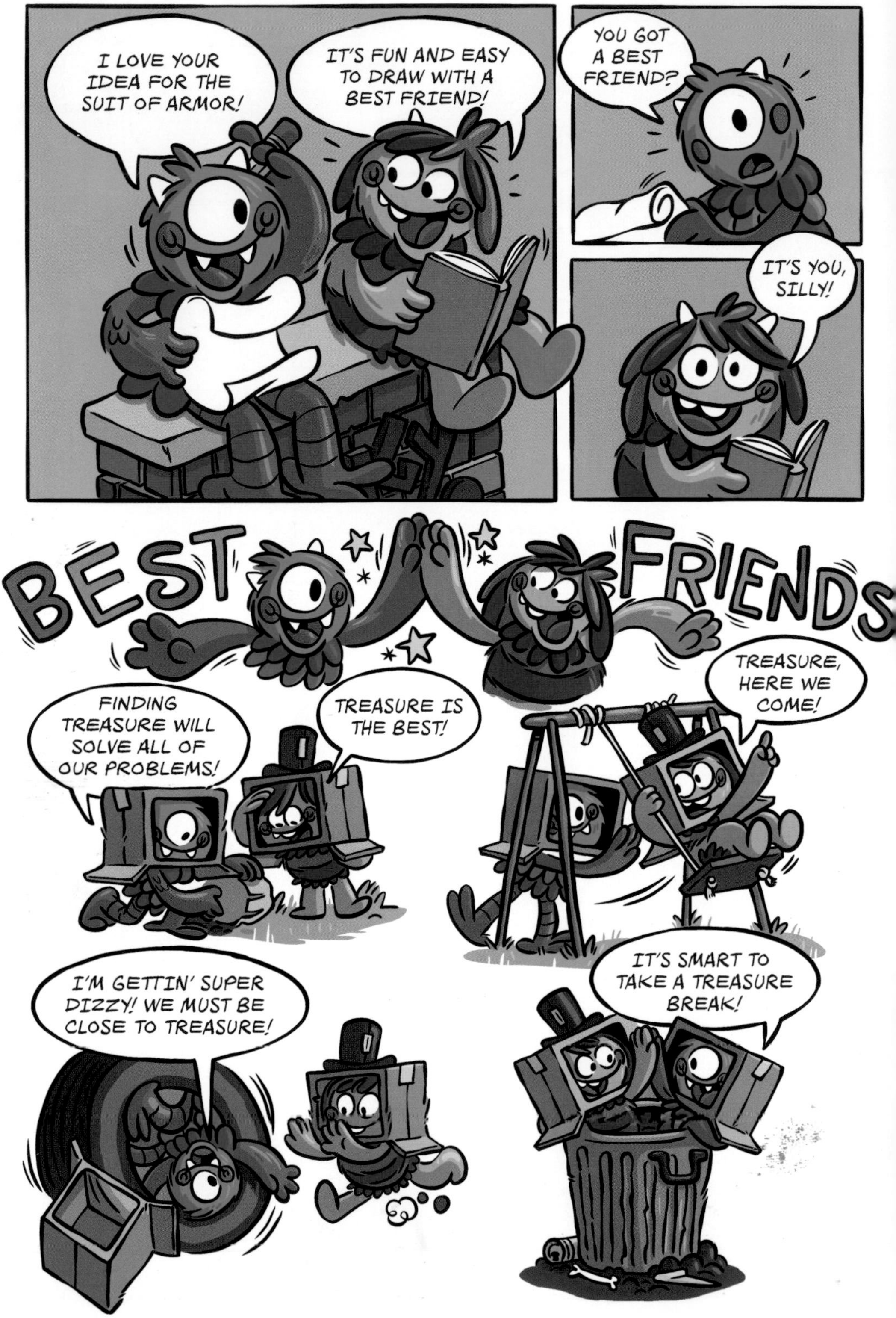
I LOVE YOUR IDEA FOR THE SUIT OF ARMOR!
IT'S FUN AND EASY TO DRAW WITH A BEST FRIEND!
YOU GOT A BEST FRIEND?
IT'S YOU, SILLY!
BEST FRIENDS
FINDING TREASURE WILL SOLVE ALL OF OUR PROBLEMS!
TREASURE IS THE BEST!
TREASURE, HERE WE COME!
I'M GETTIN' SUPER DIZZY! WE MUST BE CLOSE TO TREASURE!
IT'S SMART TO TAKE A TREASURE BREAK!

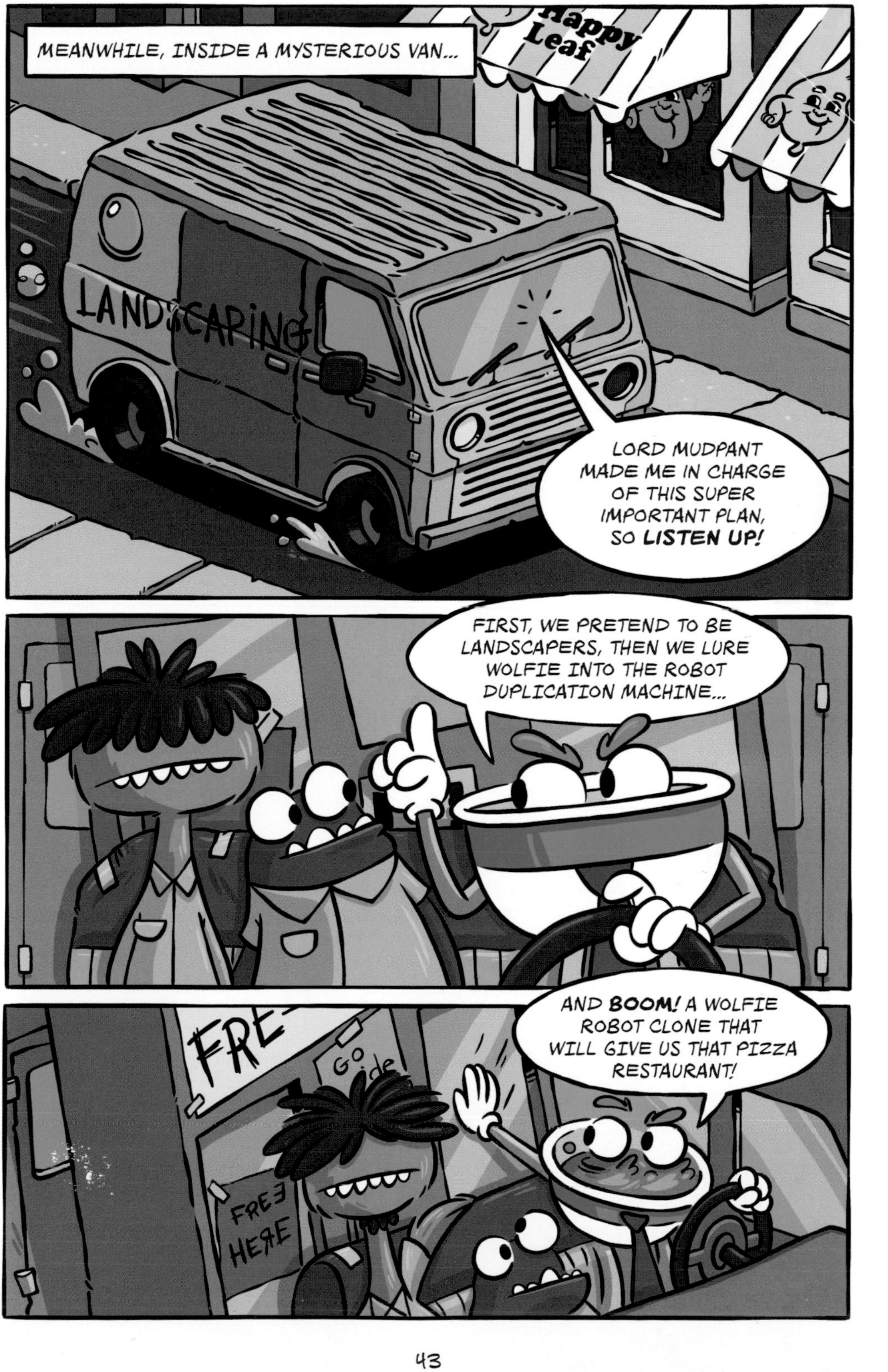
MEANWHILE, INSIDE A MYSTERIOUS VAN...
Happy Leaf
LANDSCAPING
LORD MUDPANT MADE ME IN CHARGE OF THIS SUPER IMPORTANT PLAN, SO LISTEN UP!
FIRST, WE PRETEND TO BE LANDSCAPERS, THEN WE LURE WOLFIE INTO THE ROBOT DUPLICATION MACHINE...
AND BOOM! A WOLFIE ROBOT CLONE THAT WILL GIVE US THAT PIZZA RESTAURANT!
FREE HERE

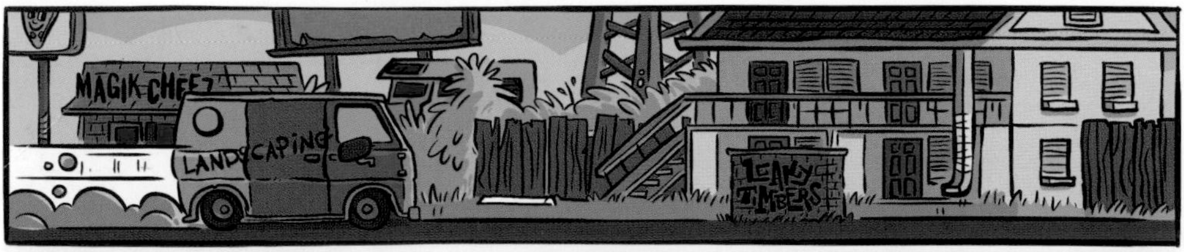
MAGIK CHEF
LANDSCAPING
LEANY TIMBERS

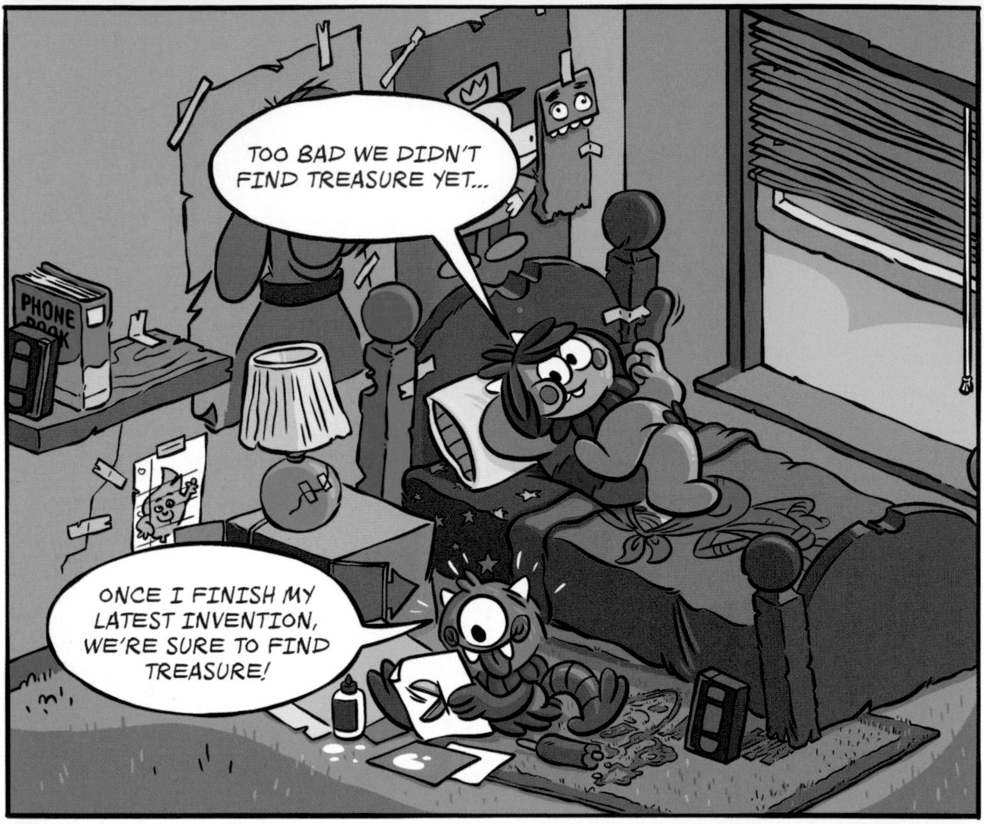
PHONE BOOK
TOO BAD WE DIDN'T FIND TREASURE YET...
ONCE I FINISH MY LATEST INVENTION, WE'RE SURE TO FIND TREASURE!

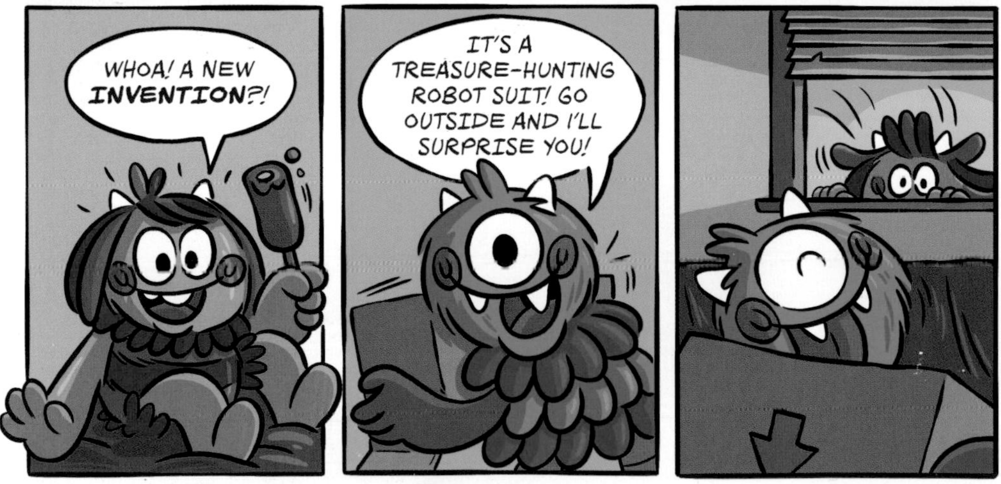
WHOA! A NEW **INVENTION**?!
IT'S A TREASURE-HUNTING ROBOT SUIT! GO OUTSIDE AND I'LL SURPRISE YOU!

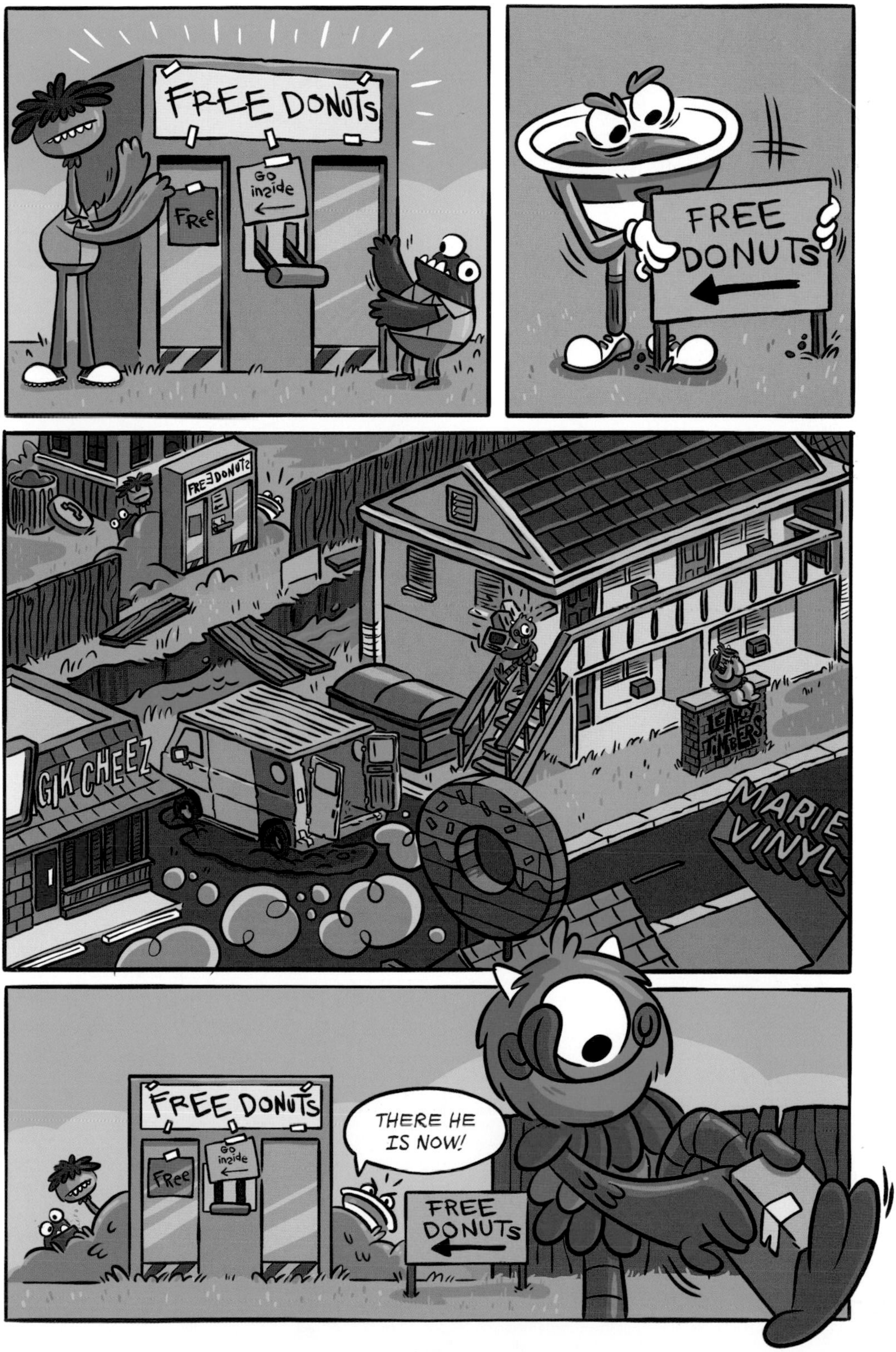

FREE DONUTS
GO inside
Free
FREE DONUTS
FREE DONUTS
GIK CHEEZ
LEAKY TIMBERS
MARIE VINYL
FREE DONUTS
Go inside
Free
FREE DONUTS
THERE HE IS NOW!

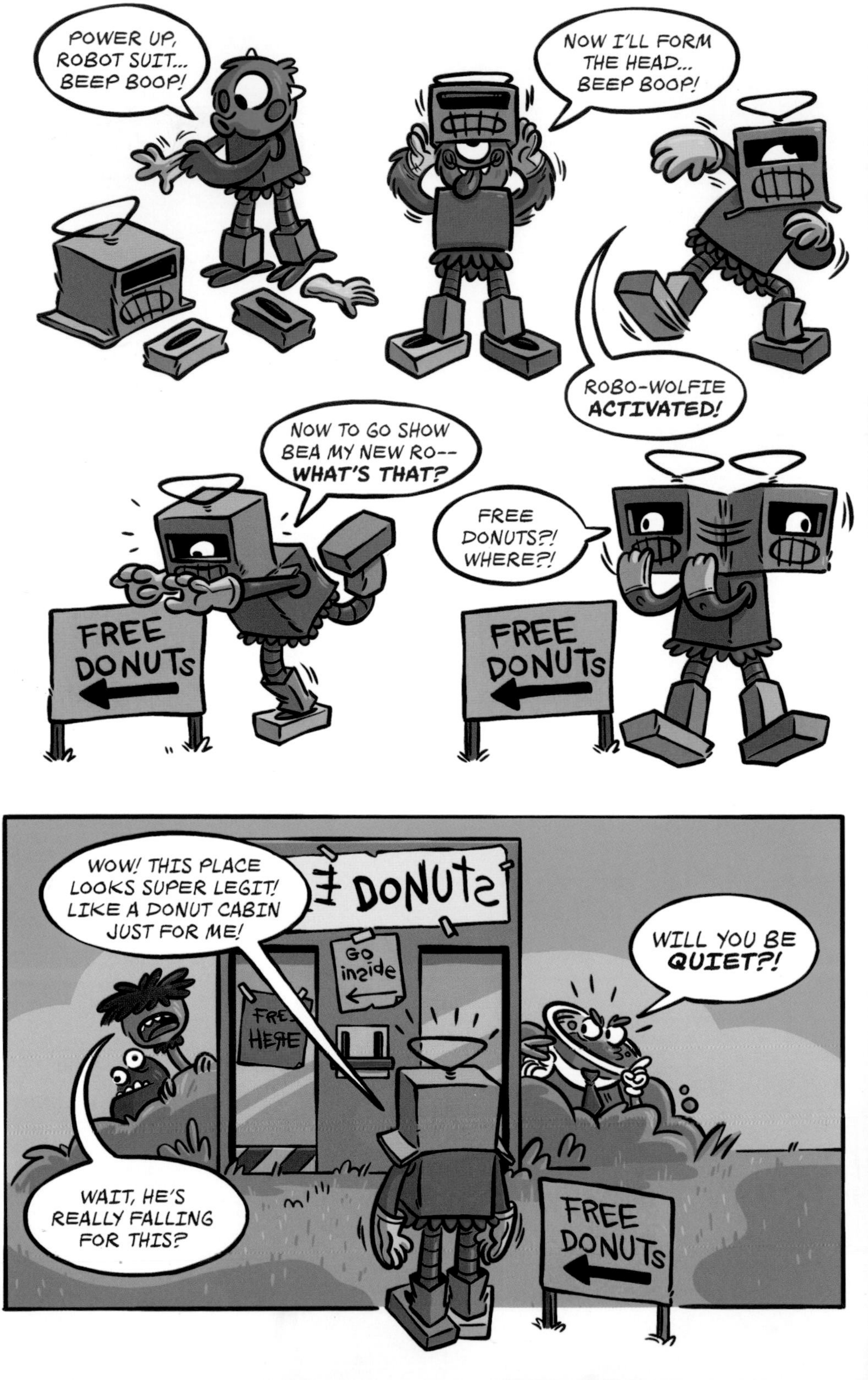
POWER UP, ROBOT SUIT... BEEP BOOP!
NOW I'LL FORM THE HEAD... BEEP BOOP!
ROBO-WOLFIE **ACTIVATED!**
NOW TO GO SHOW BEA MY NEW RO-- **WHAT'S THAT?**
FREE DONUTS
FREE DONUTS?! WHERE?!
FREE DONUTS
WOW! THIS PLACE LOOKS SUPER LEGIT! LIKE A DONUT CABIN JUST FOR ME!
DONUTS
Go inside
HERE
WILL YOU BE **QUIET?!**
WAIT, HE'S REALLY FALLING FOR THIS?
FREE DONUTS

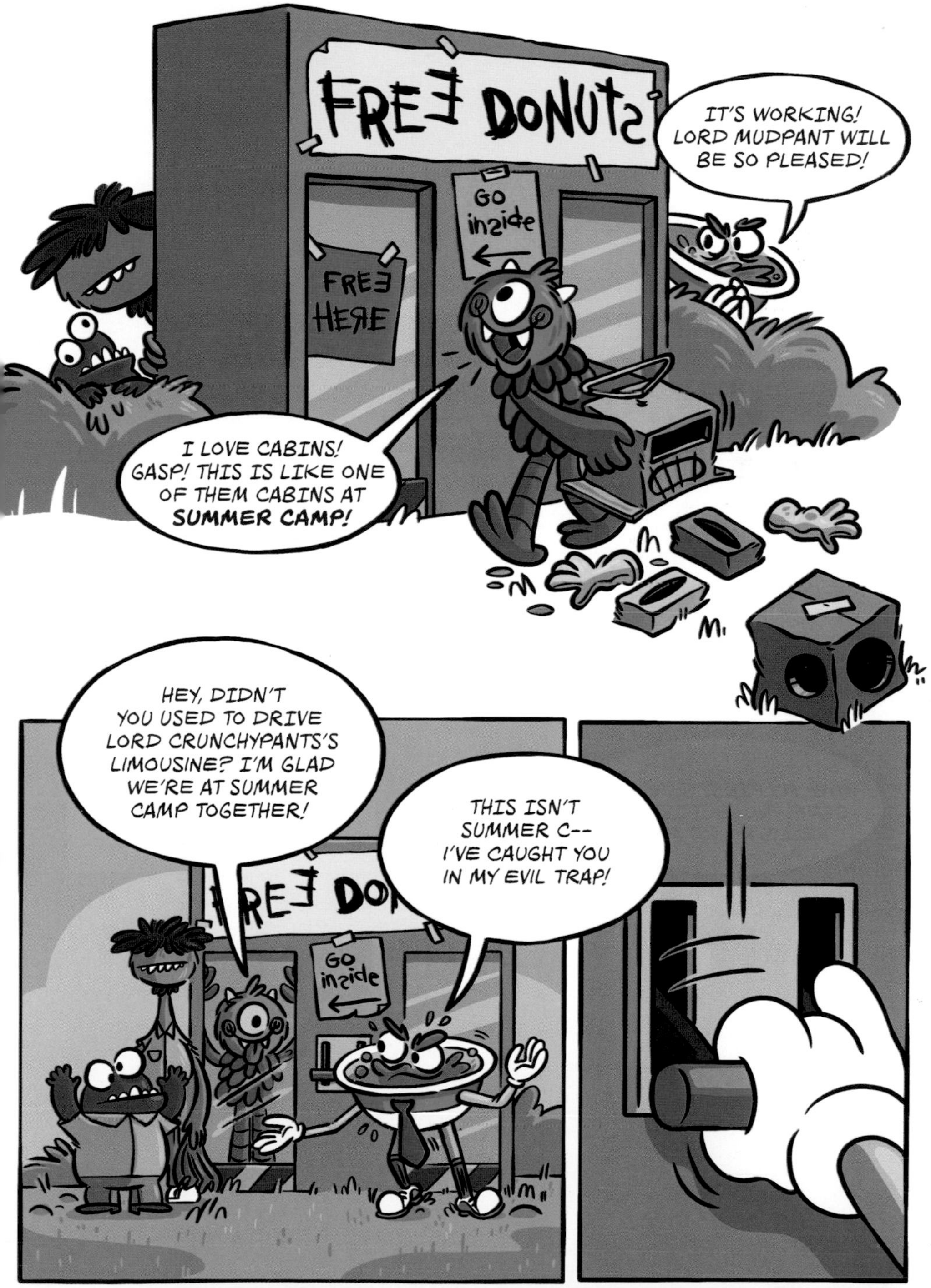
FREƎ DONUTS
GO inside
FREƎ HERE
IT'S WORKING! LORD MUDPANT WILL BE SO PLEASED!
I LOVE CABINS! GASP! THIS IS LIKE ONE OF THEM CABINS AT **SUMMER CAMP!**
HEY, DIDN'T YOU USED TO DRIVE LORD CRUNCHYPANTS'S LIMOUSINE? I'M GLAD WE'RE AT SUMMER CAMP TOGETHER!
THIS ISN'T SUMMER C-- I'VE CAUGHT YOU IN MY EVIL TRAP!
WHRRRRRRRRRRRRRRRRRRRRRRRRRRRRRRRRRRR

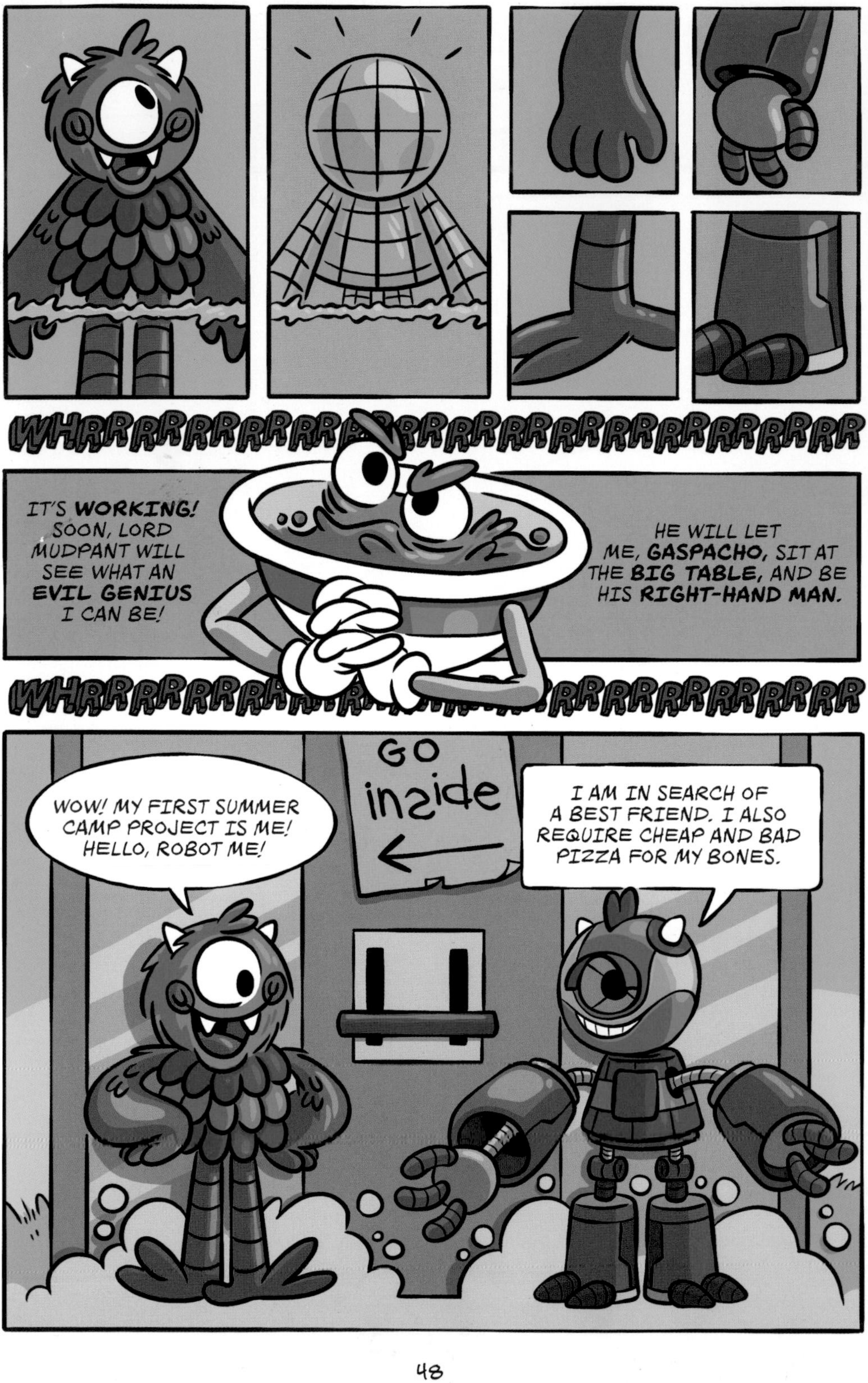
WHRRRRRRRRRRRRRRRRRRRRRRRRRRRRRRRRR
IT'S **WORKING!** SOON, LORD MUDPANT WILL SEE WHAT AN **EVIL GENIUS** I CAN BE!
HE WILL LET ME, **GASPACHO,** SIT AT THE **BIG TABLE,** AND BE HIS **RIGHT-HAND MAN.**
WHRRRRRRRRRRRRRRRRRRRRRRRRRRRRRRRRR
GO inside
WOW! MY FIRST SUMMER CAMP PROJECT IS ME! HELLO, ROBOT ME!
I AM IN SEARCH OF A BEST FRIEND. I ALSO REQUIRE CHEAP AND BAD PIZZA FOR MY BONES.

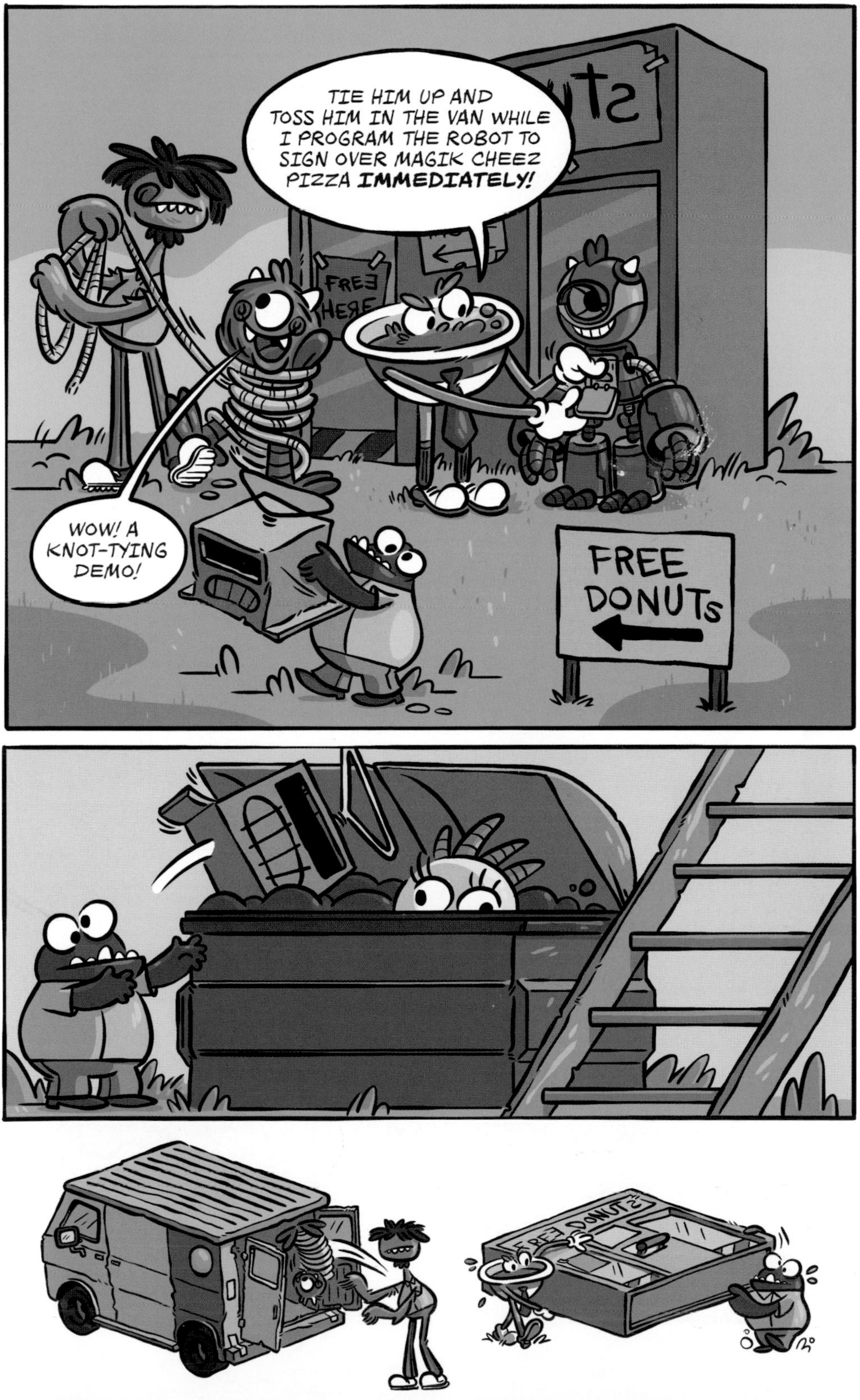
TIE HIM UP AND TOSS HIM IN THE VAN WHILE I PROGRAM THE ROBOT TO SIGN OVER MAGIK CHEEZ PIZZA **IMMEDIATELY!**
FREE HERE
WOW! A KNOT-TYING DEMO!
FREE DONUTs

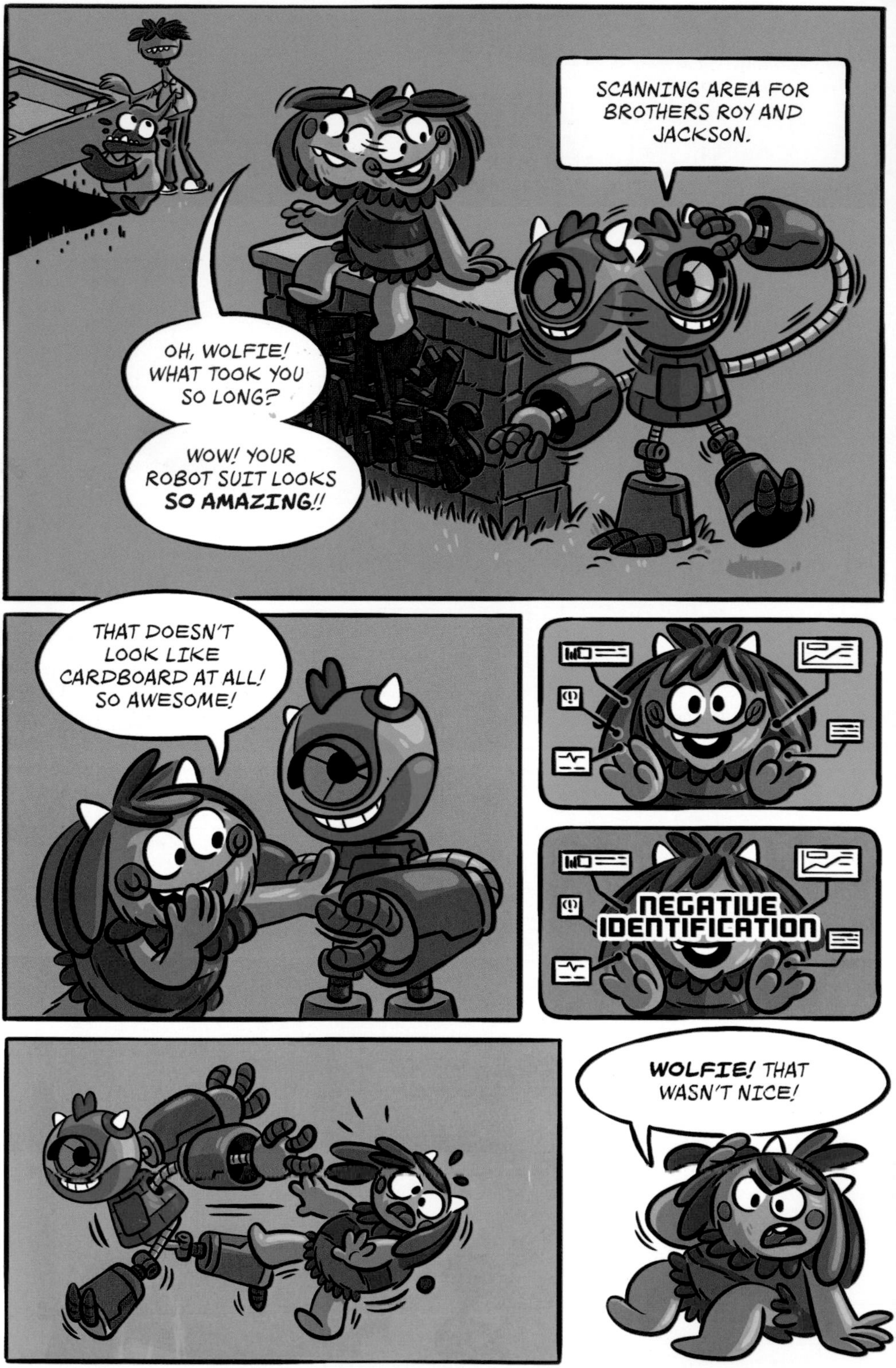
SCANNING AREA FOR BROTHERS ROY AND JACKSON.
OH, WOLFIE! WHAT TOOK YOU SO LONG?
WOW! YOUR ROBOT SUIT LOOKS **SO AMAZING!!**
THAT DOESN'T LOOK LIKE CARDBOARD AT ALL! SO AWESOME!
NEGATIVE IDENTIFICATION
WOLFIE! THAT WASN'T NICE!

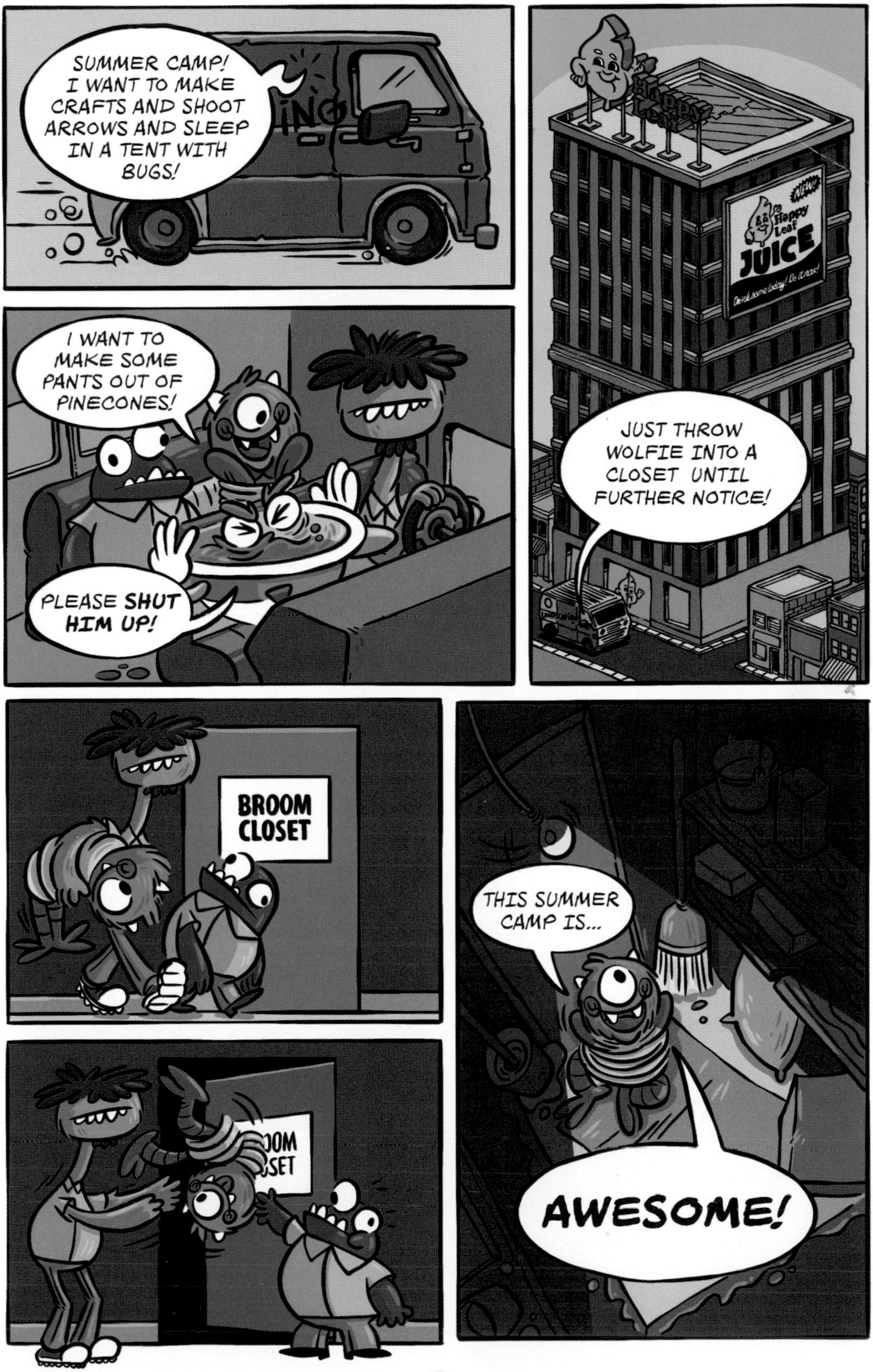
SUMMER CAMP! I WANT TO MAKE CRAFTS AND SHOOT ARROWS AND SLEEP IN A TENT WITH BUGS!
I WANT TO MAKE SOME PANTS OUT OF PINECONES!
PLEASE SHUT HIM UP!
JUST THROW WOLFIE INTO A CLOSET UNTIL FURTHER NOTICE!
BROOM CLOSET
THIS SUMMER CAMP IS...
AWESOME!

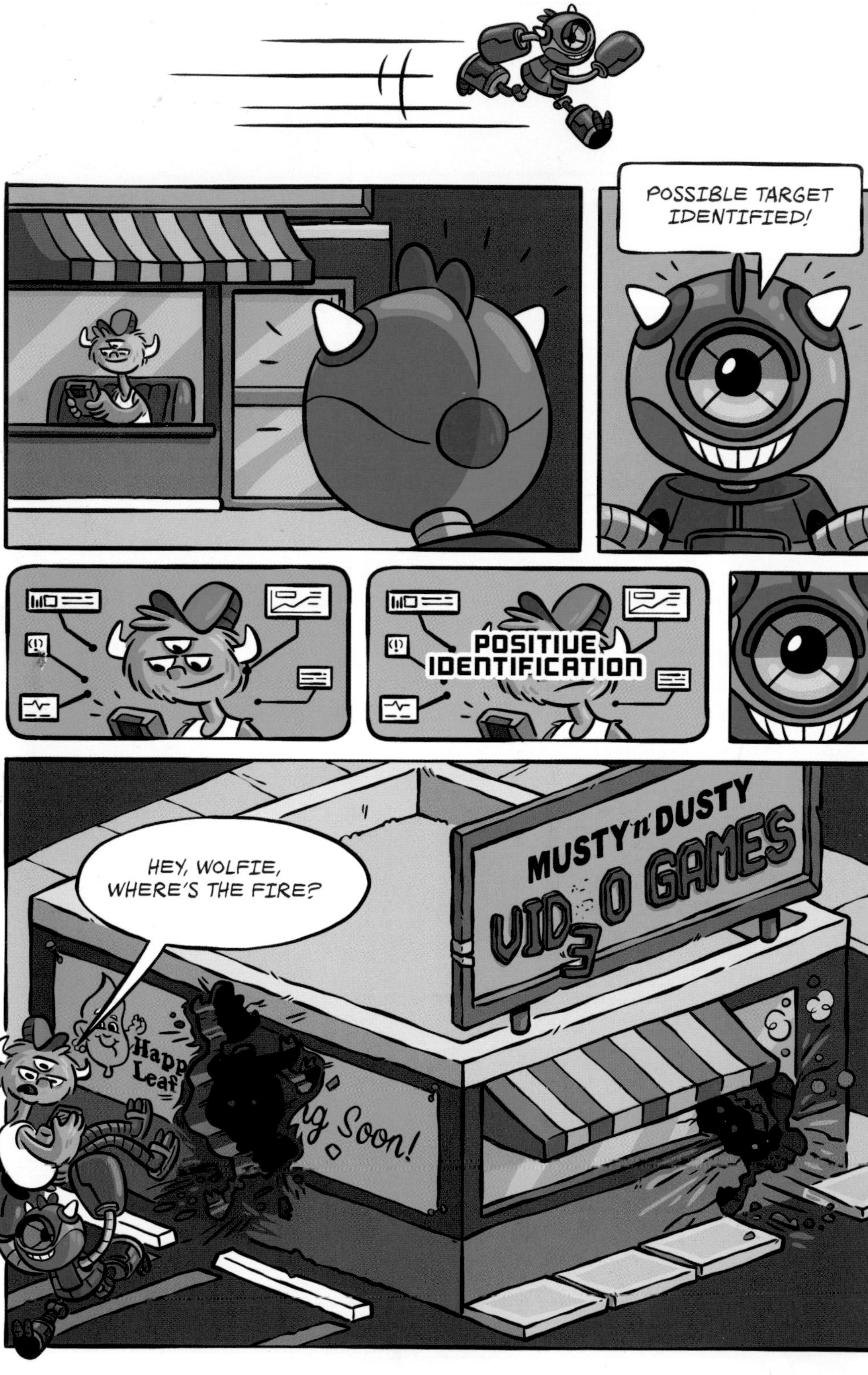
POSSIBLE TARGET IDENTIFIED!
POSITIVE IDENTIFICATION
MUSTY 'n' DUSTY
VID3O GAMES
HEY, WOLFIE, WHERE'S THE FIRE?
Happ
Leaf
g Soon!

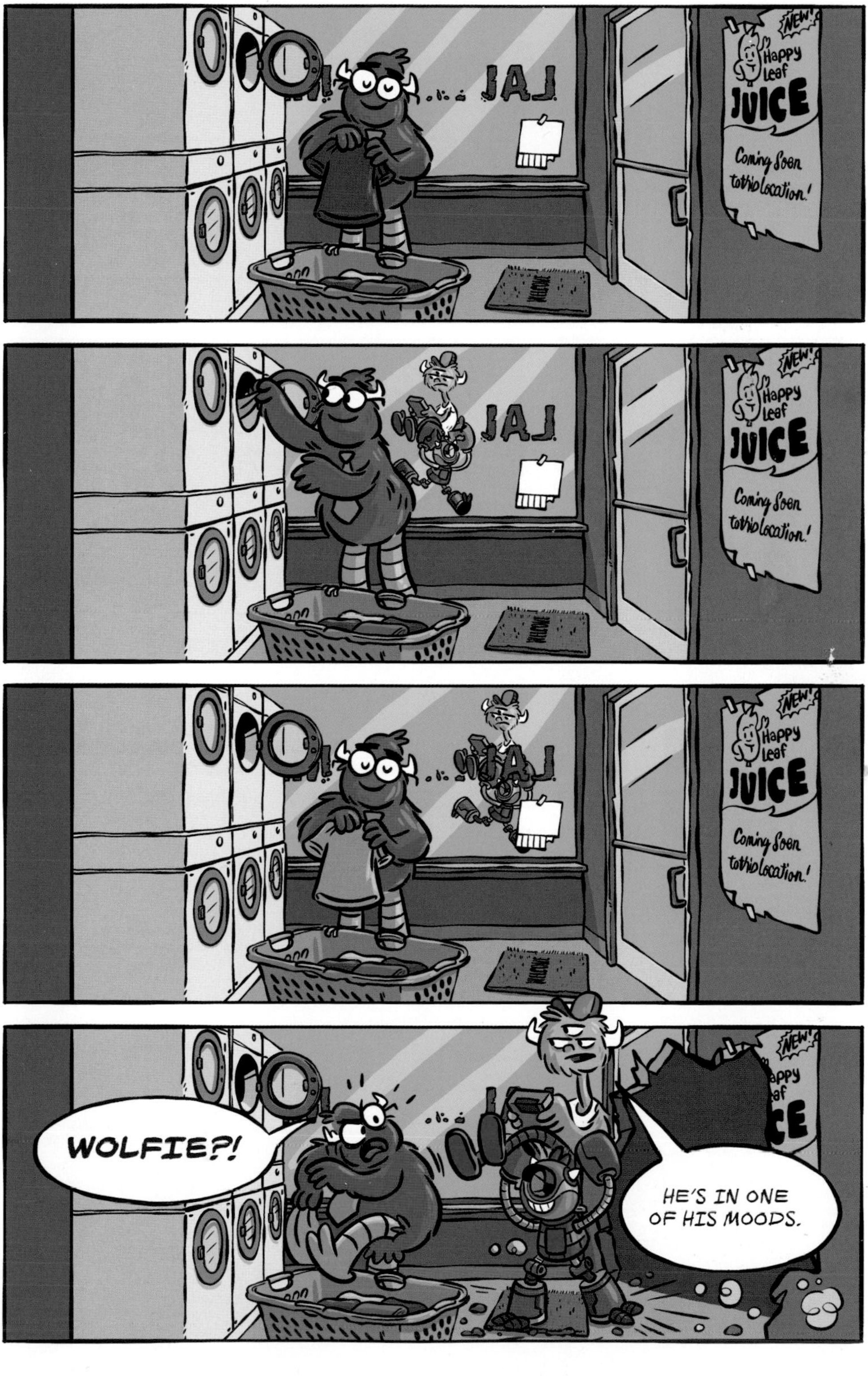
NEW!
Happy Leaf
JUICE
Coming Soon to this location!
WOLFIE?!
HE'S IN ONE OF HIS MOODS.

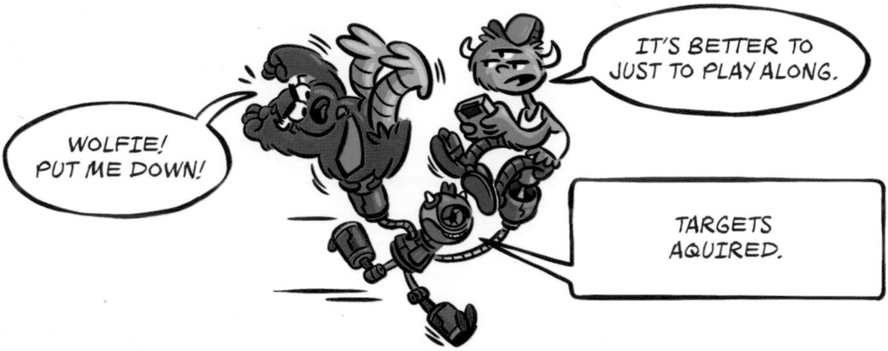
WOLFIE! PUT ME DOWN!
IT'S BETTER TO JUST TO PLAY ALONG.
TARGETS AQUIRED.

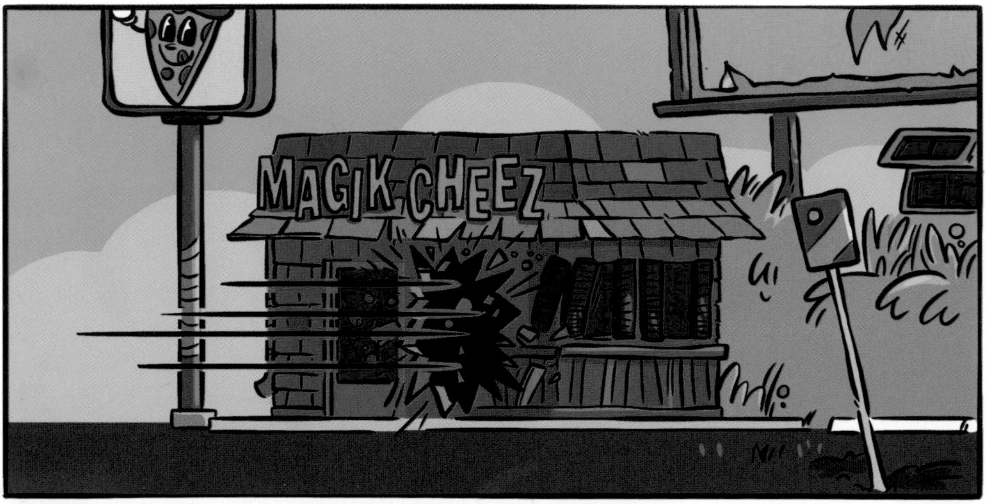
MAGIK CHEEZ

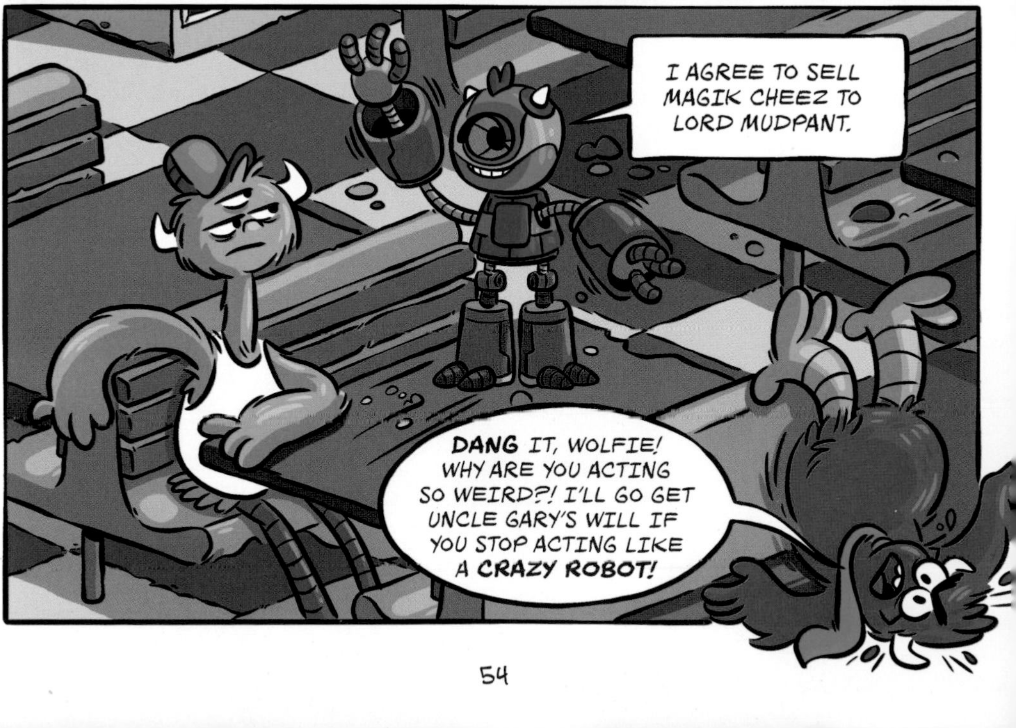
I AGREE TO SELL MAGIK CHEEZ TO LORD MUDPANT.
DANG IT, WOLFIE! WHY ARE YOU ACTING SO WEIRD?! I'LL GO GET UNCLE GARY'S WILL IF YOU STOP ACTING LIKE A CRAZY ROBOT!

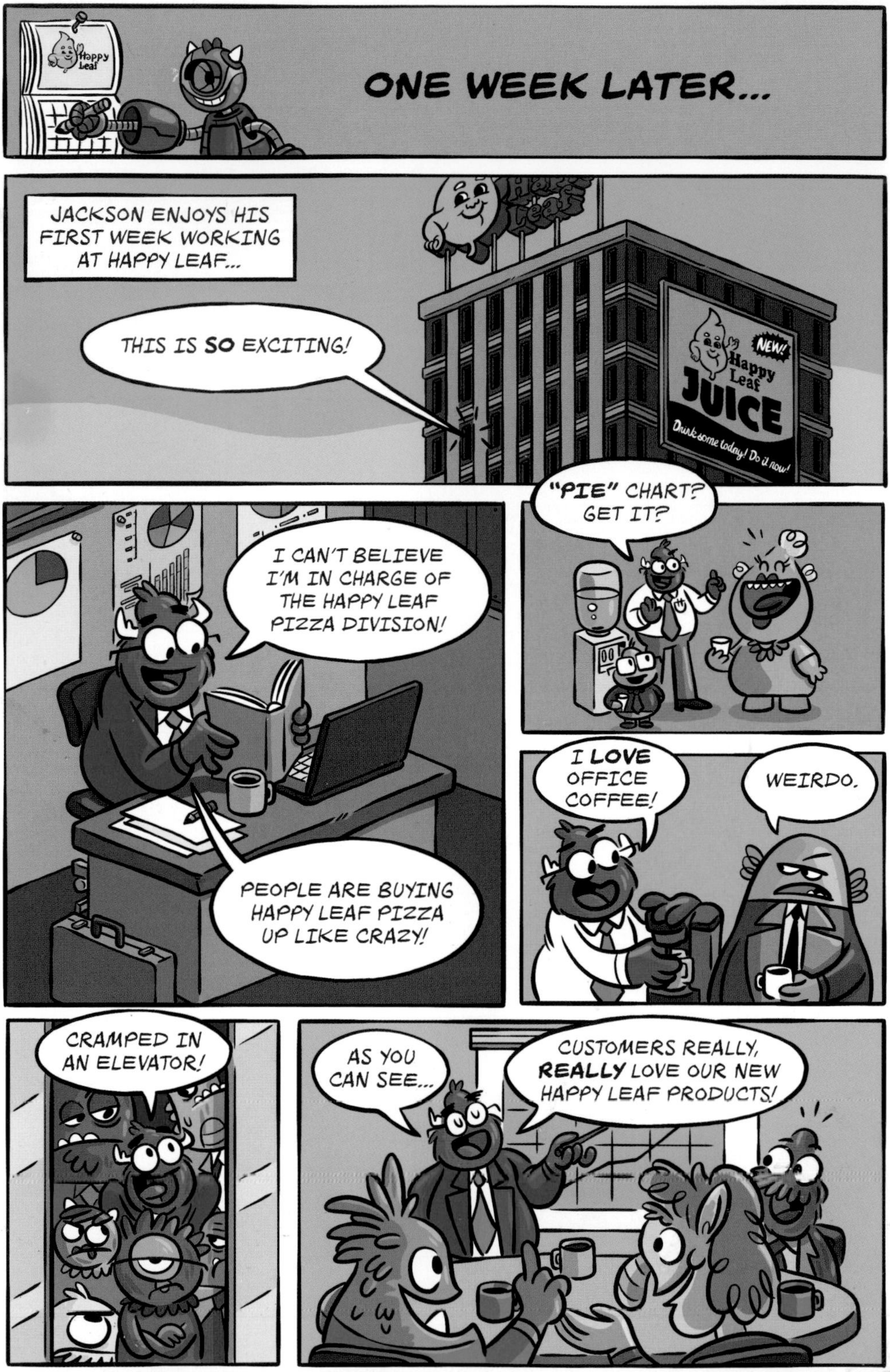
Happy Leaf
ONE WEEK LATER...
JACKSON ENJOYS HIS FIRST WEEK WORKING AT HAPPY LEAF...
THIS IS SO EXCITING!
NEW!
Happy Leaf
JUICE
Drink some today! Do it now!
I CAN'T BELIEVE I'M IN CHARGE OF THE HAPPY LEAF PIZZA DIVISION!
PEOPLE ARE BUYING HAPPY LEAF PIZZA UP LIKE CRAZY!
"PIE" CHART? GET IT?
I LOVE OFFICE COFFEE!
WEIRDO.
CRAMPED IN AN ELEVATOR!
AS YOU CAN SEE...
CUSTOMERS REALLY, REALLY LOVE OUR NEW HAPPY LEAF PRODUCTS!

57

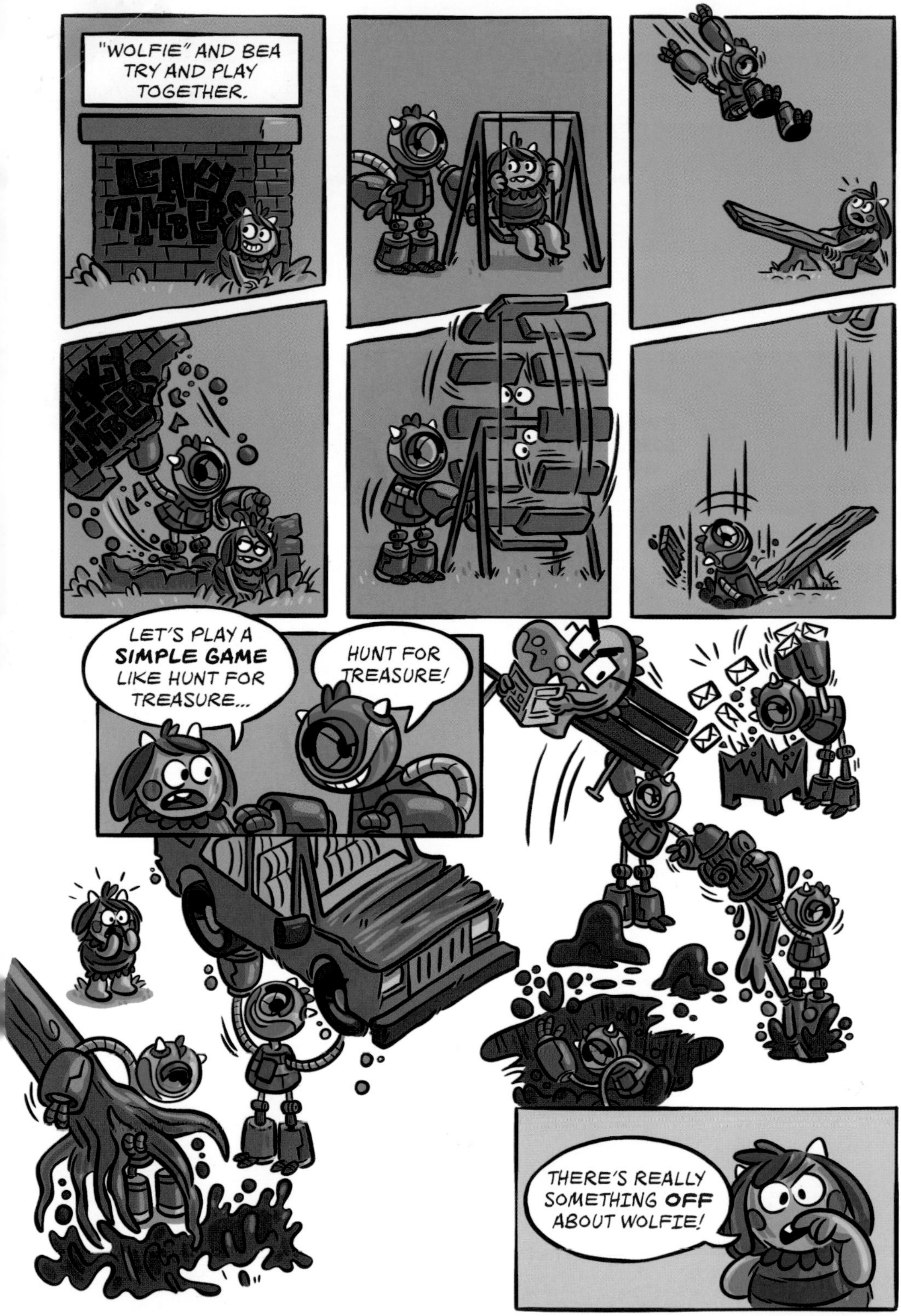
"WOLFIE" AND BEA TRY AND PLAY TOGETHER.
LEAKY TIMBERS
LET'S PLAY A **SIMPLE GAME** LIKE HUNT FOR TREASURE...
HUNT FOR TREASURE!
THERE'S REALLY SOMETHING **OFF** ABOUT WOLFIE!

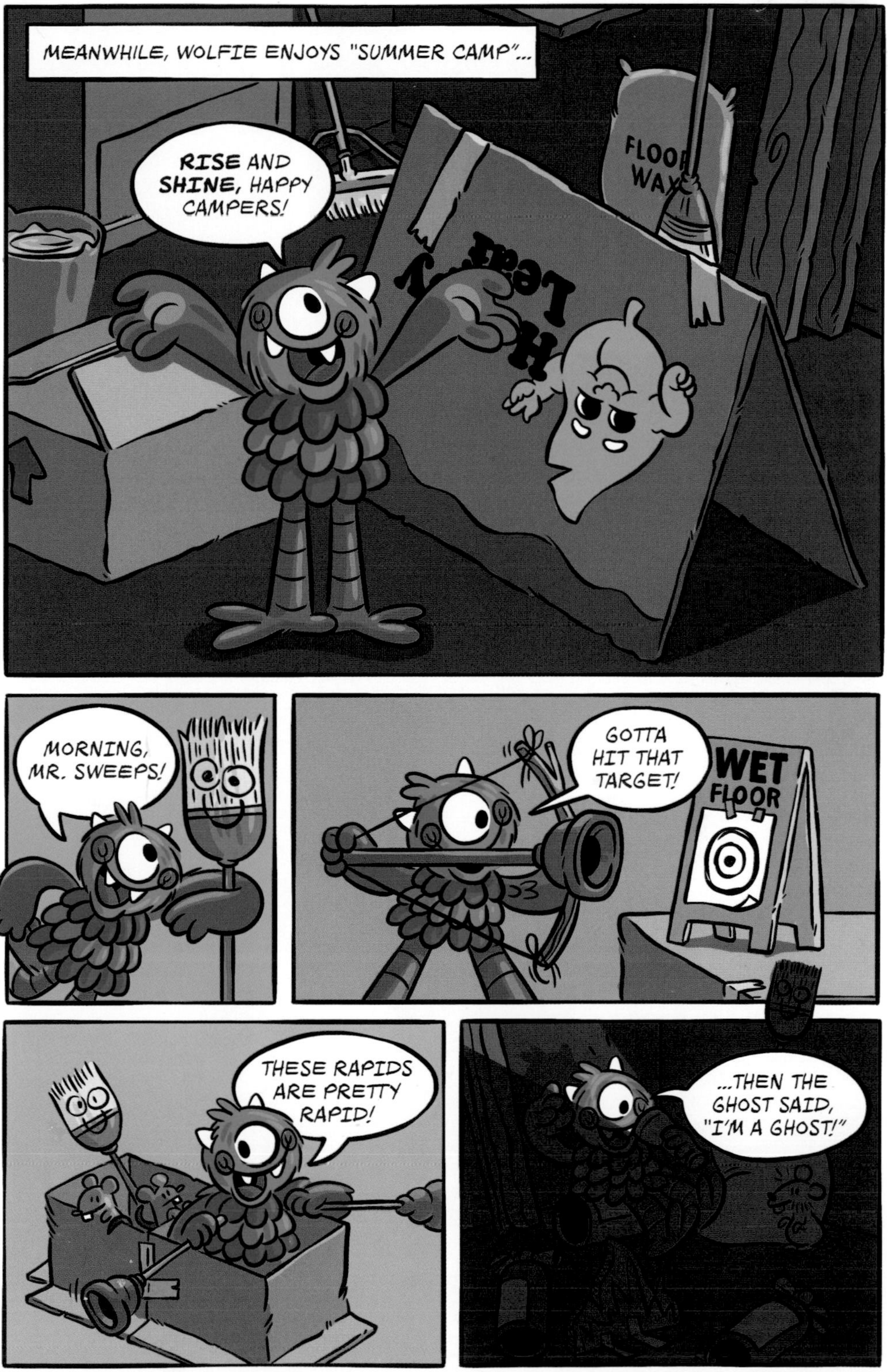
MEANWHILE, WOLFIE ENJOYS "SUMMER CAMP"...
RISE AND SHINE, HAPPY CAMPERS!
FLOOR WAX
MORNING, MR. SWEEPS!
GOTTA HIT THAT TARGET!
WET FLOOR
THESE RAPIDS ARE PRETTY RAPID!
...THEN THE GHOST SAID, "I'M A GHOST!"

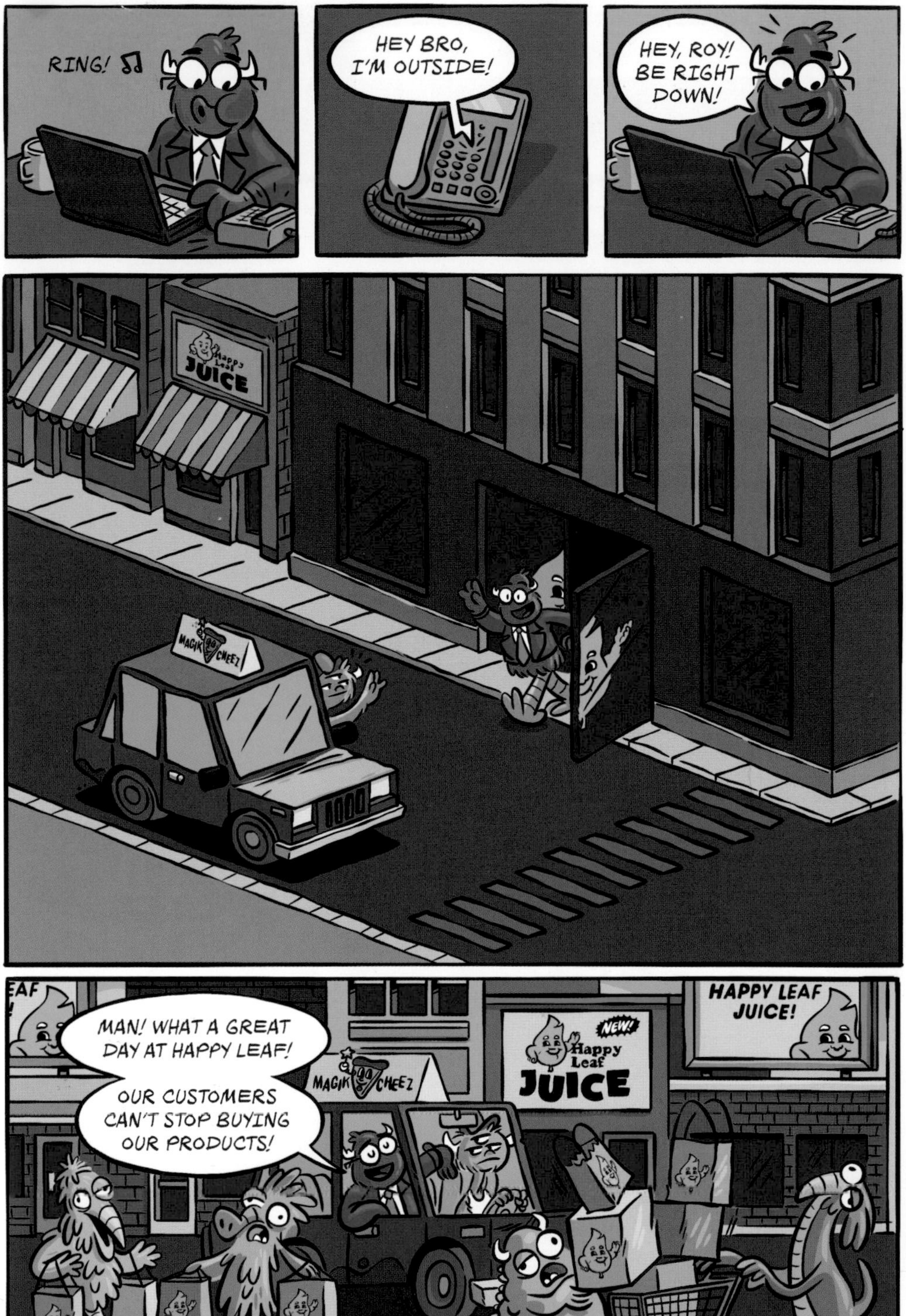
RING!
HEY BRO, I'M OUTSIDE!
HEY, ROY! BE RIGHT DOWN!
Happy Leaf JUICE
MAGIK CHEEZ
MAN! WHAT A GREAT DAY AT HAPPY LEAF!
OUR CUSTOMERS CAN'T STOP BUYING OUR PRODUCTS!
HAPPY LEAF JUICE!
NEW! Happy Leaf JUICE

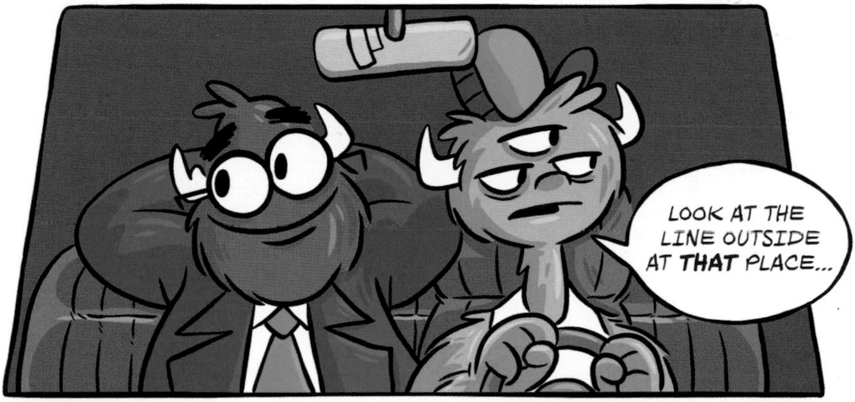
LOOK AT THE LINE OUTSIDE AT THAT PLACE...

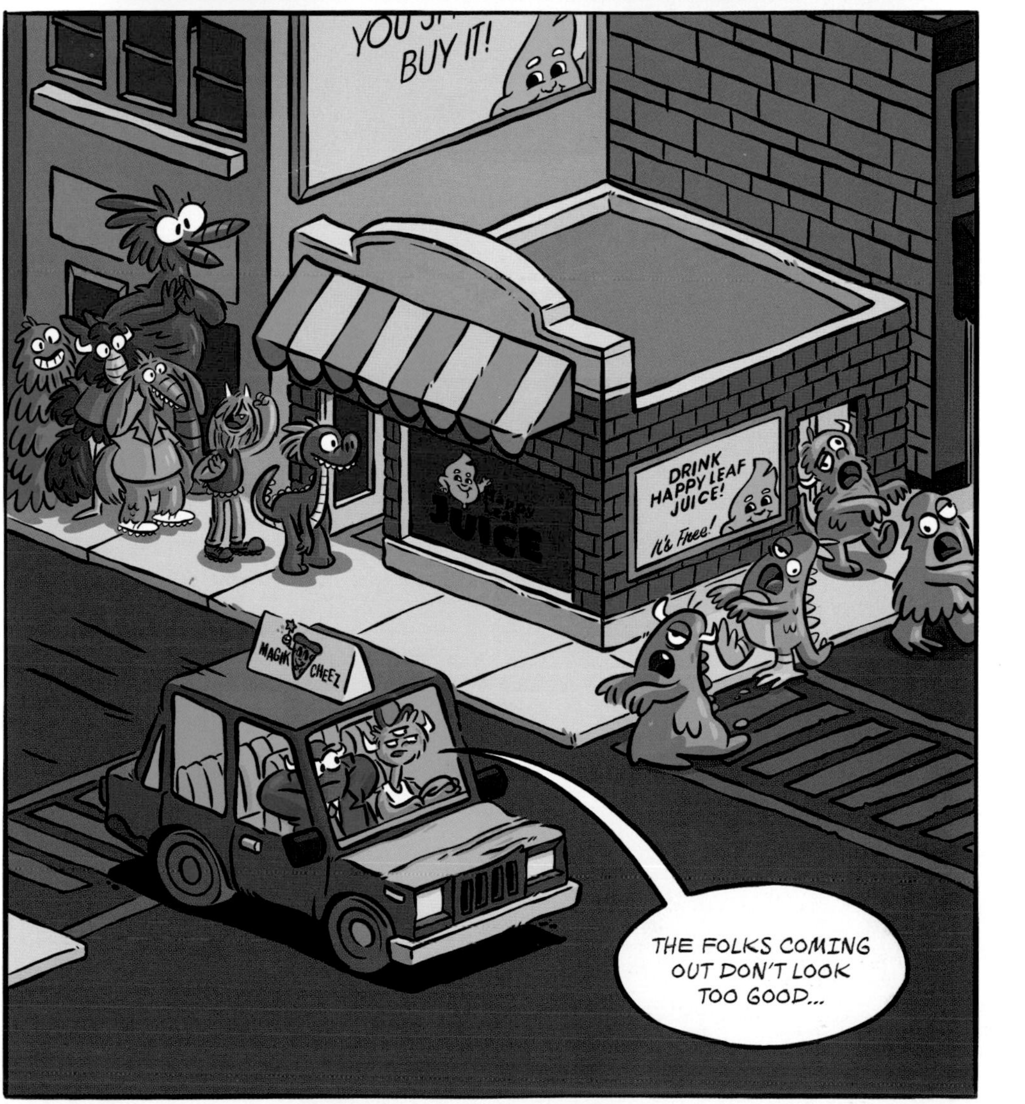
BUY IT!
DRINK HAPPY LEAF JUICE!
It's Free!
JUICE
MAGIK CHEEZ
THE FOLKS COMING OUT DON'T LOOK TOO GOOD...

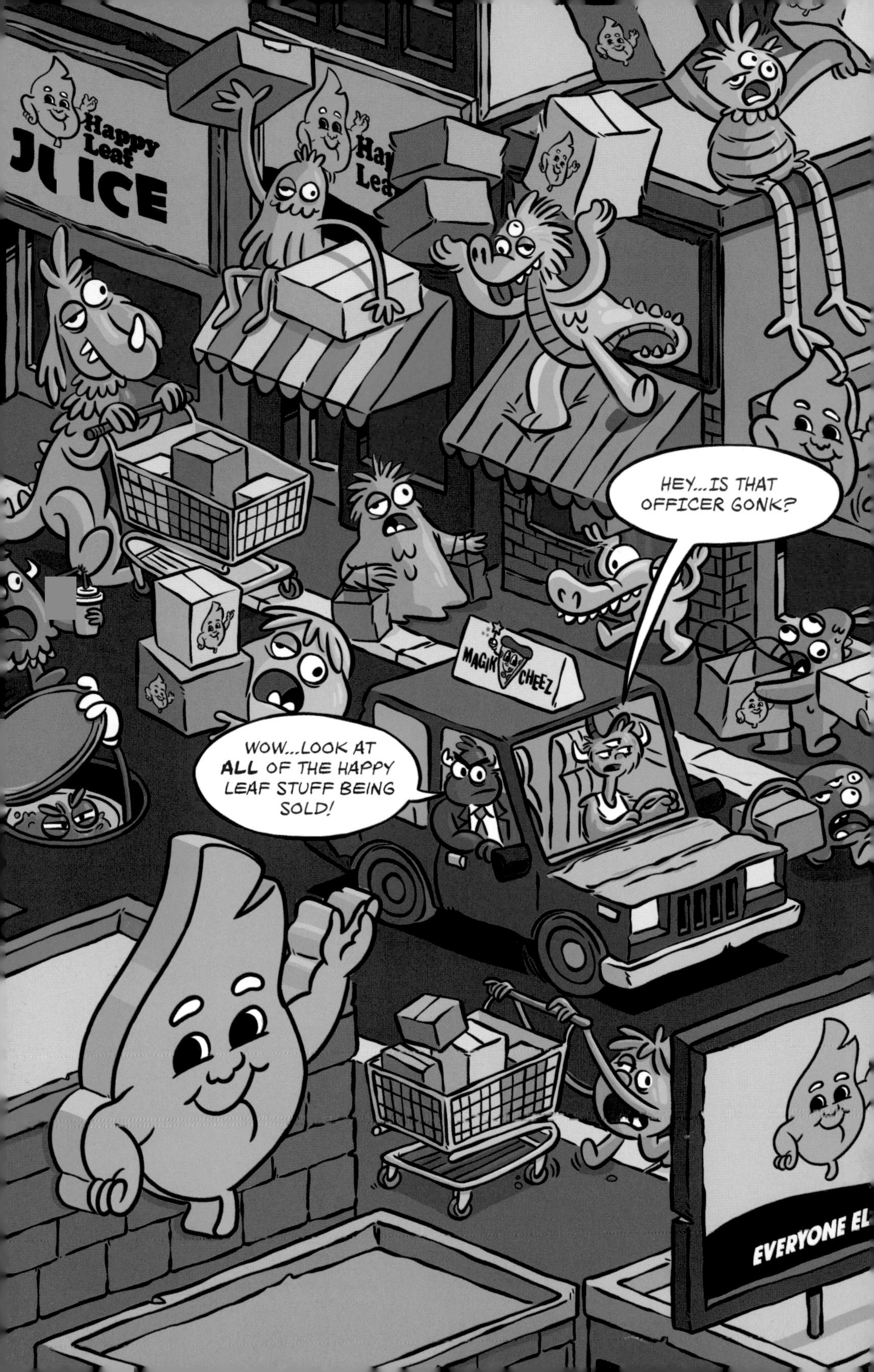
Happy Leaf
MAGIK CHEEZ
WOW...LOOK AT **ALL** OF THE HAPPY LEAF STUFF BEING SOLD!
HEY...IS THAT OFFICER GONK?
EVERYONE EL

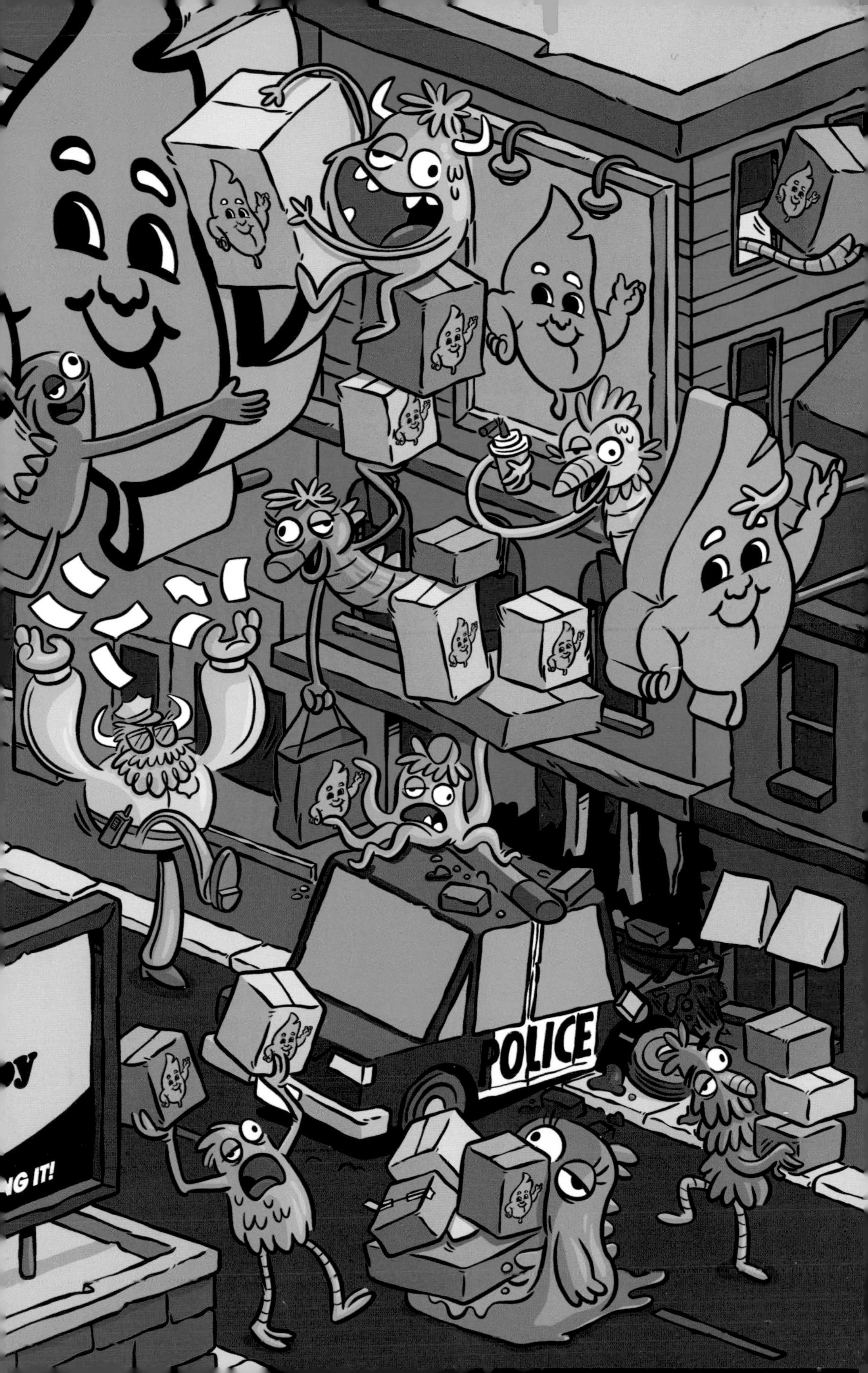
POLICE
NG IT!

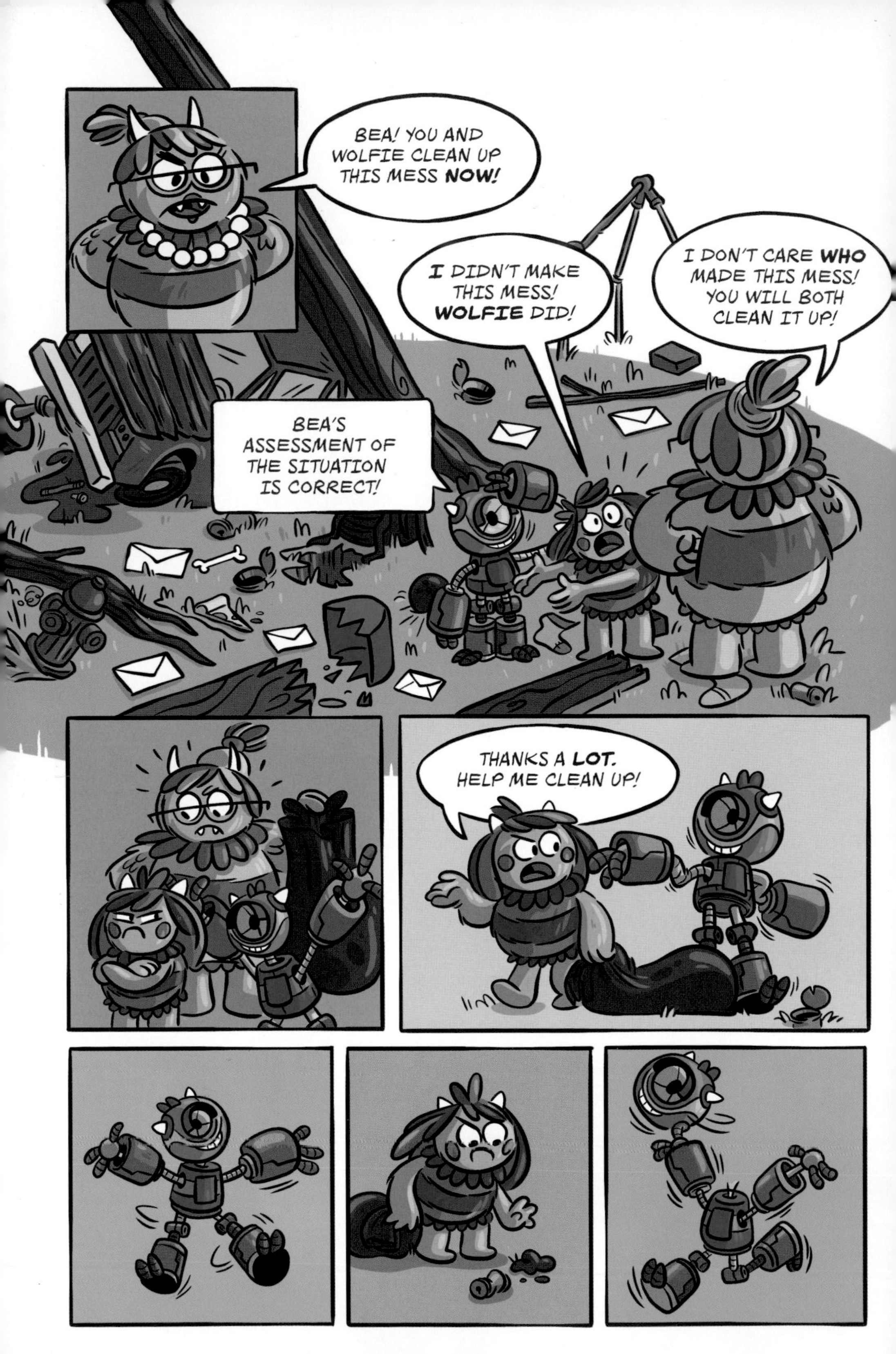
BEA! YOU AND WOLFIE CLEAN UP THIS MESS **NOW!**
I DIDN'T MAKE THIS MESS! **WOLFIE** DID!
I DON'T CARE **WHO** MADE THIS MESS! YOU WILL BOTH CLEAN IT UP!
BEA'S ASSESSMENT OF THE SITUATION IS CORRECT!
THANKS A **LOT.** HELP ME CLEAN UP!

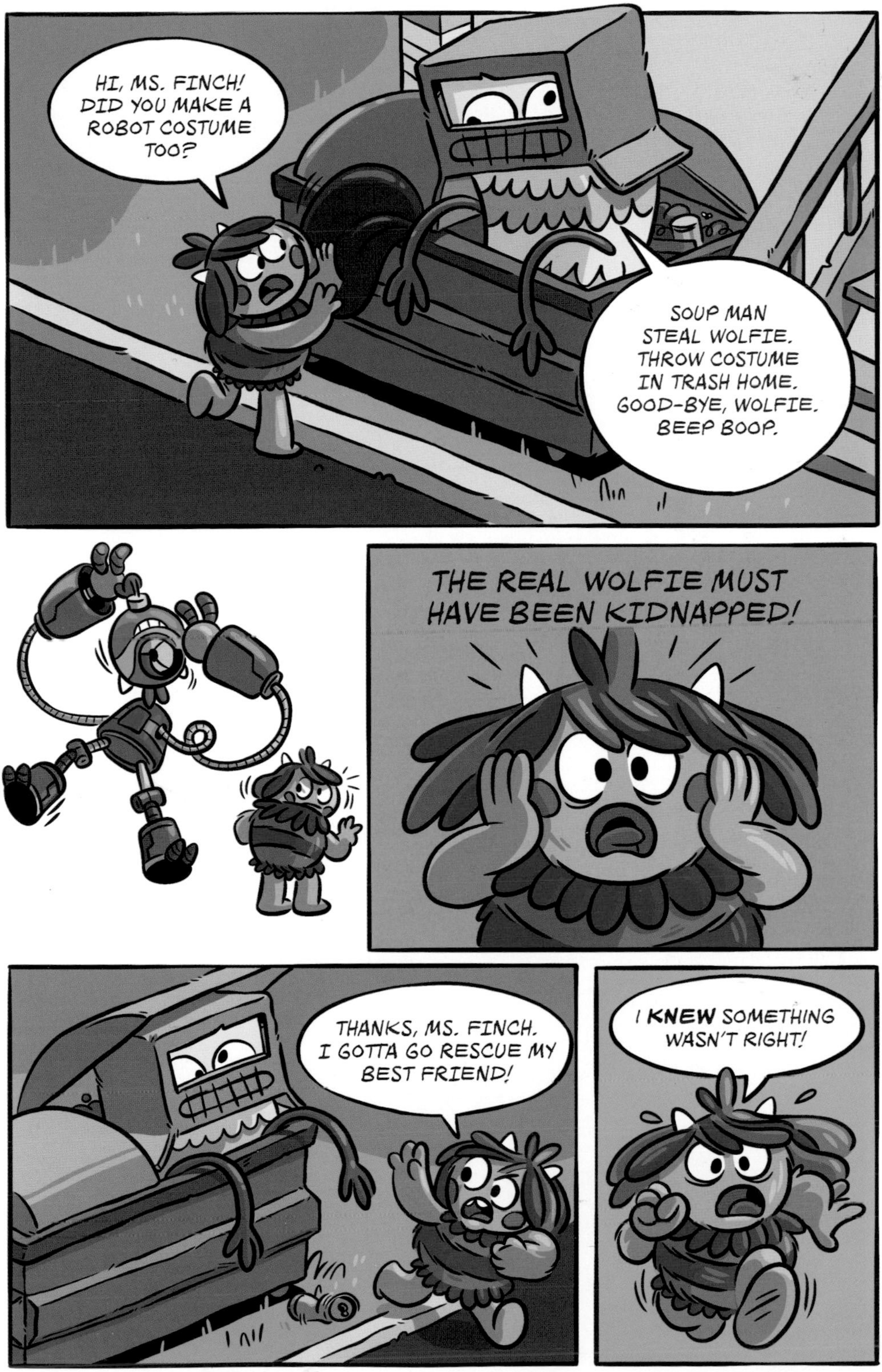
HI, MS. FINCH! DID YOU MAKE A ROBOT COSTUME TOO?
SOUP MAN STEAL WOLFIE. THROW COSTUME IN TRASH HOME. GOOD-BYE, WOLFIE. BEEP BOOP.
THE REAL WOLFIE MUST HAVE BEEN KIDNAPPED!
THANKS, MS. FINCH. I GOTTA GO RESCUE MY BEST FRIEND!
I **KNEW** SOMETHING WASN'T RIGHT!

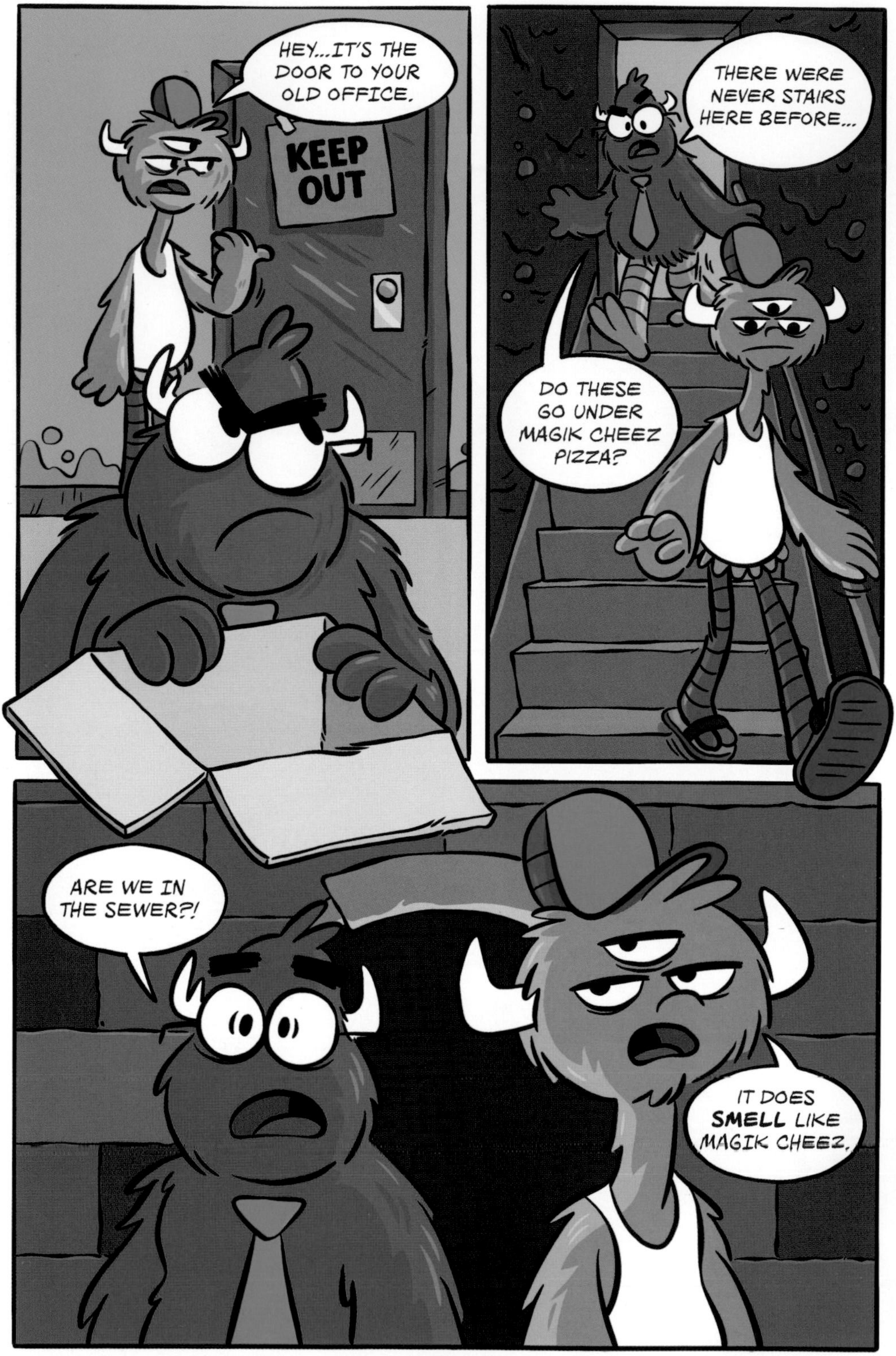
HEY...IT'S THE DOOR TO YOUR OLD OFFICE.
KEEP OUT
THERE WERE NEVER STAIRS HERE BEFORE...
DO THESE GO UNDER MAGIK CHEEZ PIZZA?
ARE WE IN THE SEWER?!
IT DOES **SMELL** LIKE MAGIK CHEEZ.

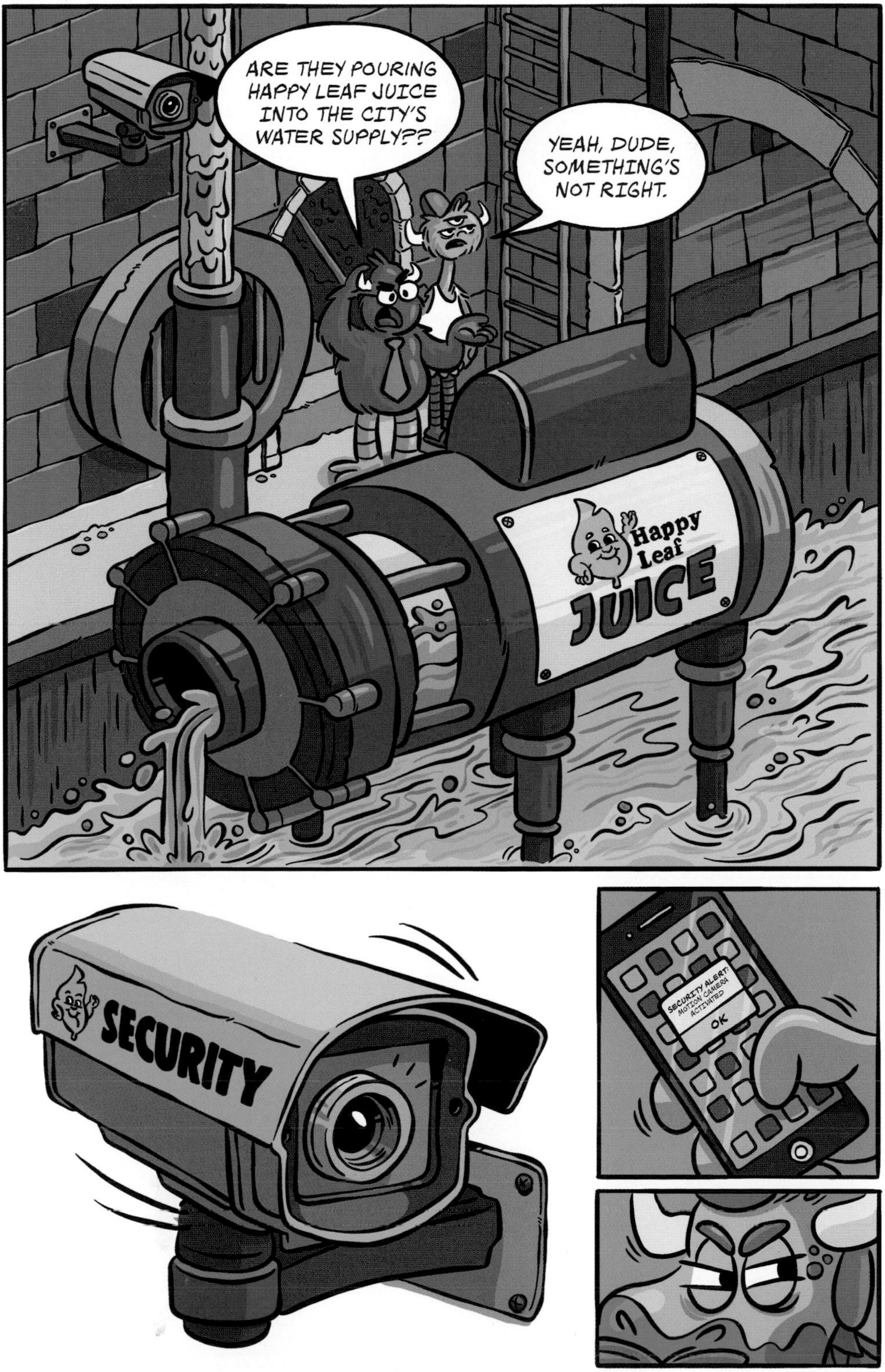
ARE THEY POURING HAPPY LEAF JUICE INTO THE CITY'S WATER SUPPLY??
YEAH, DUDE, SOMETHING'S NOT RIGHT.
Happy Leaf JUICE
SECURITY
SECURITY ALERT: MOTION CAMERA ACTIVATED
OK

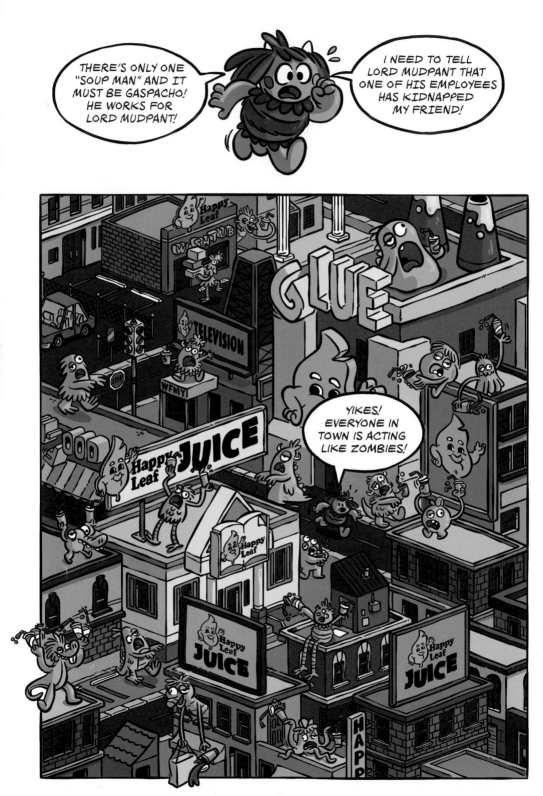

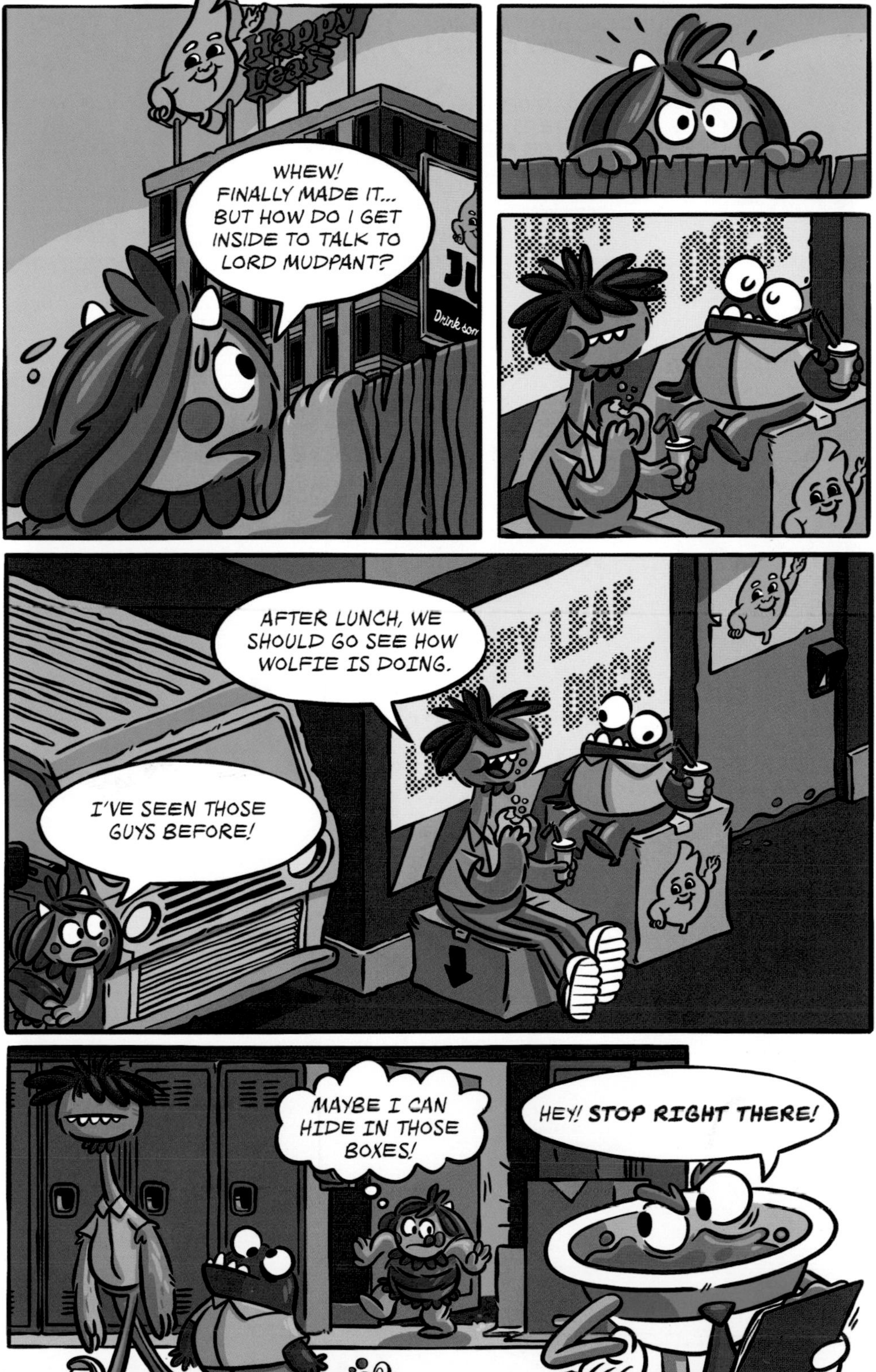
Happy Leaf
WHEW! FINALLY MADE IT... BUT HOW DO I GET INSIDE TO TALK TO LORD MUDPANT?
AFTER LUNCH, WE SHOULD GO SEE HOW WOLFIE IS DOING.
I'VE SEEN THOSE GUYS BEFORE!
MAYBE I CAN HIDE IN THOSE BOXES!
HEY! **STOP RIGHT THERE!**

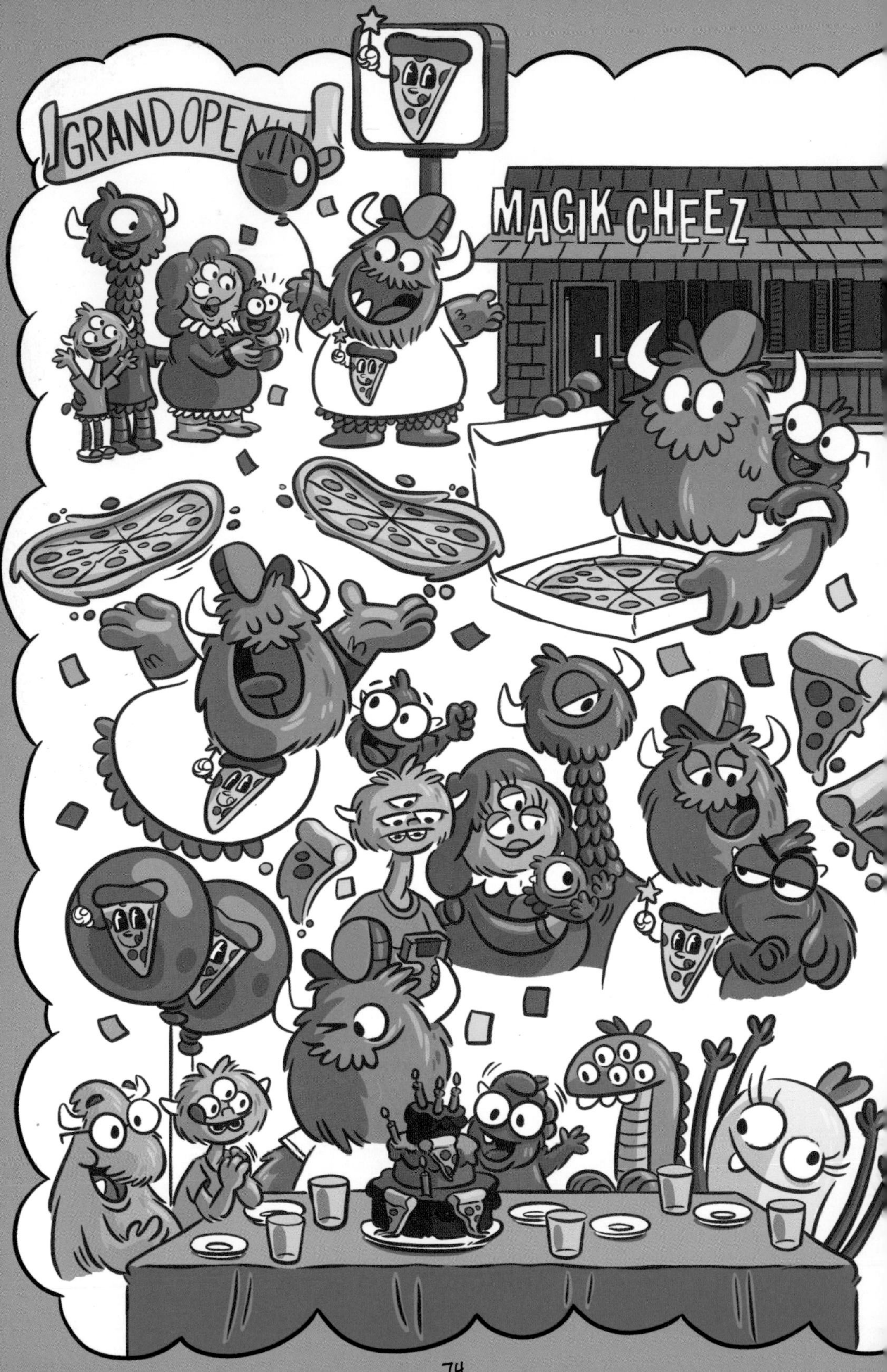
MAGIK CHEEZ

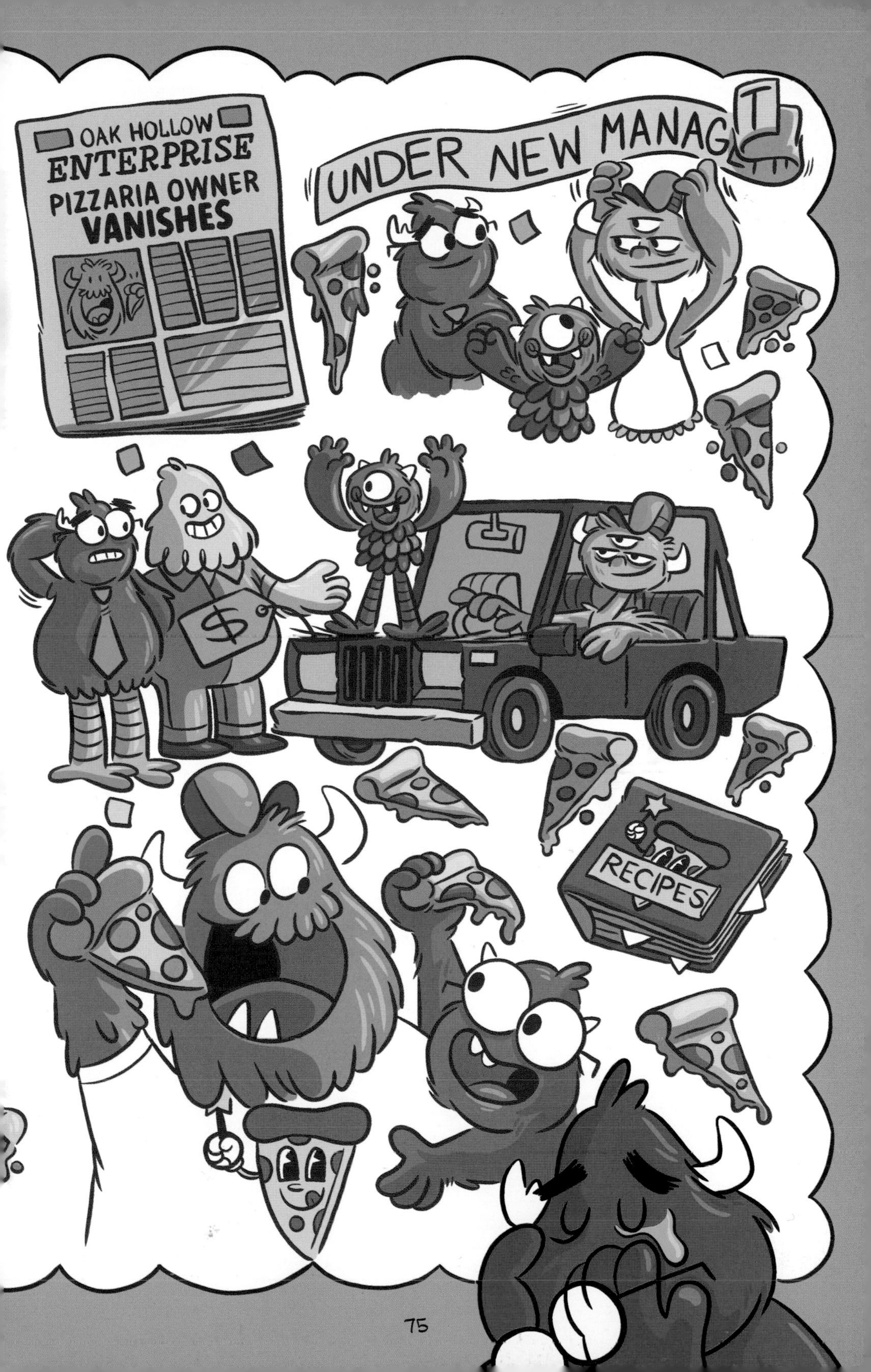
OAK HOLLOW
ENTERPRISE
PIZZARIA OWNER
VANISHES
UNDER NEW MANAG
RECIPES

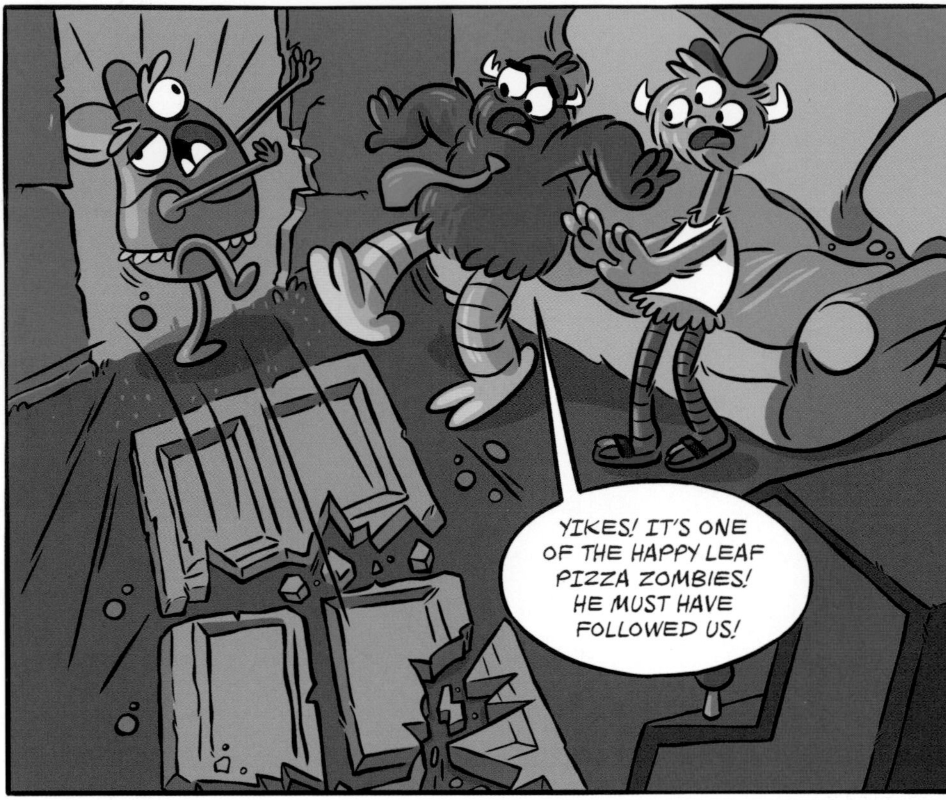
YIKES! IT'S ONE OF THE HAPPY LEAF PIZZA ZOMBIES! HE MUST HAVE FOLLOWED US!

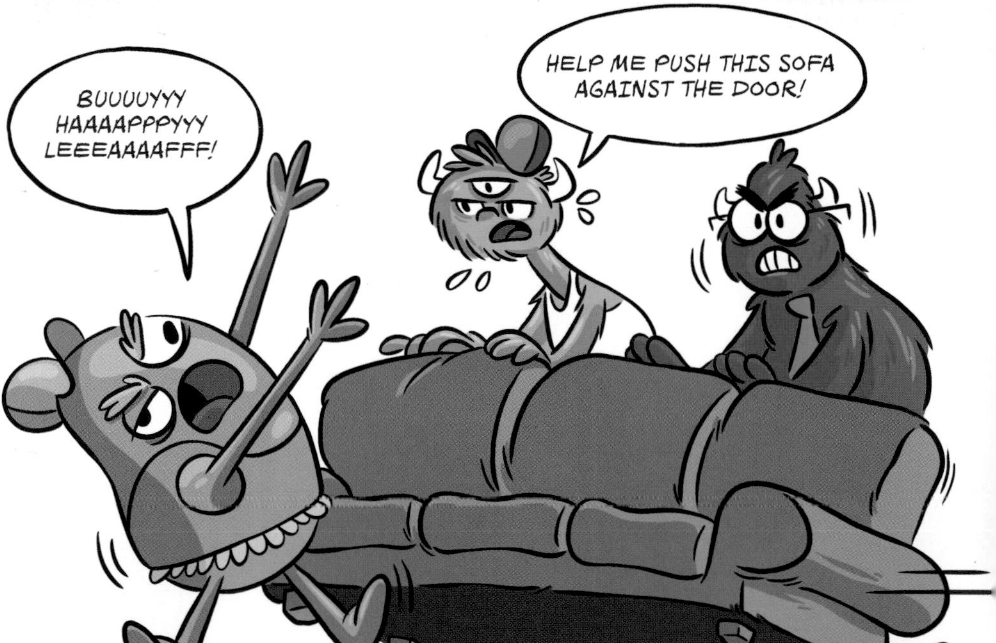
BUUUUYYY HAAAAPPPYYY LEEEAAAAFFF!
HELP ME PUSH THIS SOFA AGAINST THE DOOR!

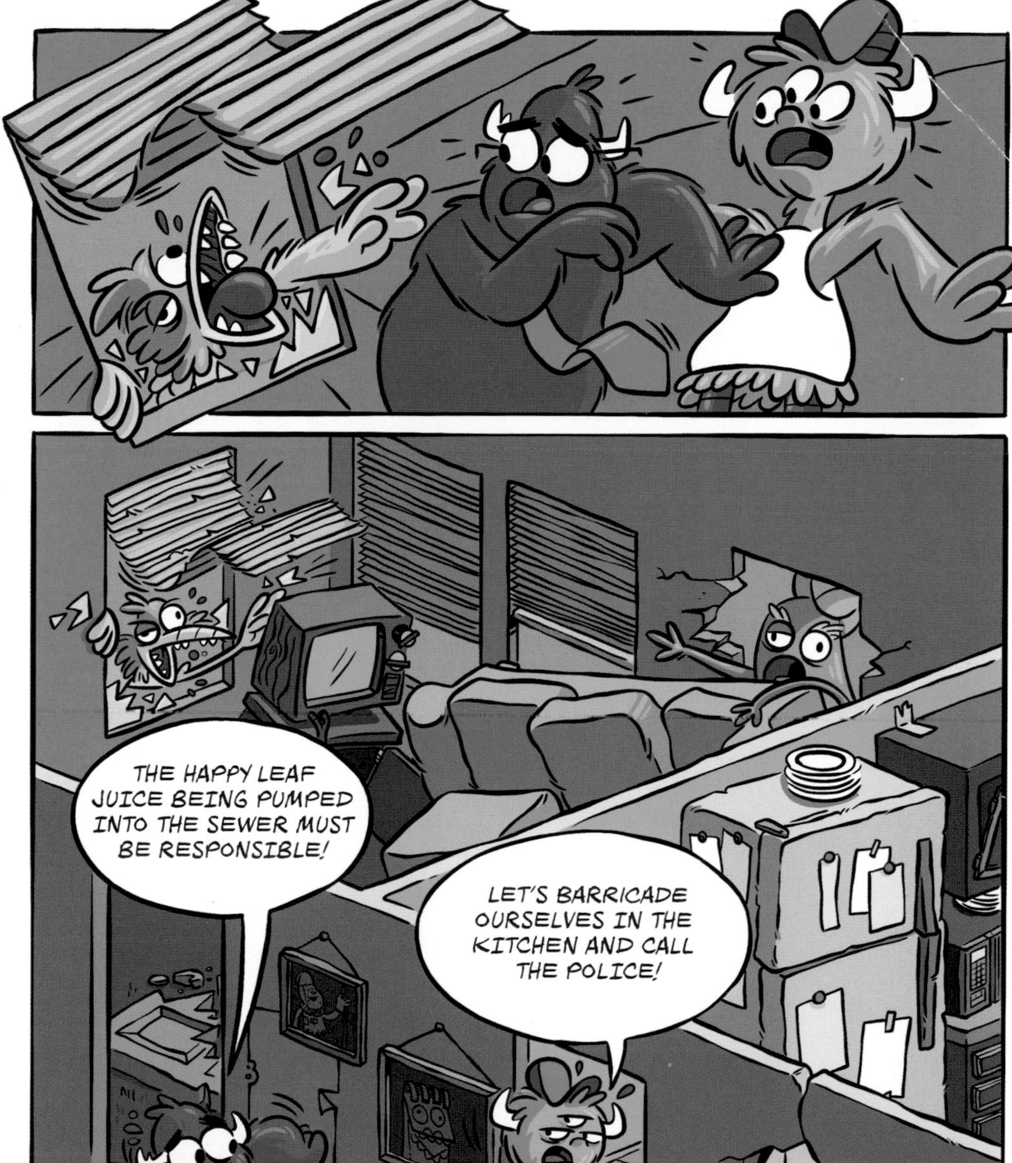
THE HAPPY LEAF JUICE BEING PUMPED INTO THE SEWER MUST BE RESPONSIBLE!
LET'S BARRICADE OURSELVES IN THE KITCHEN AND CALL THE POLICE!

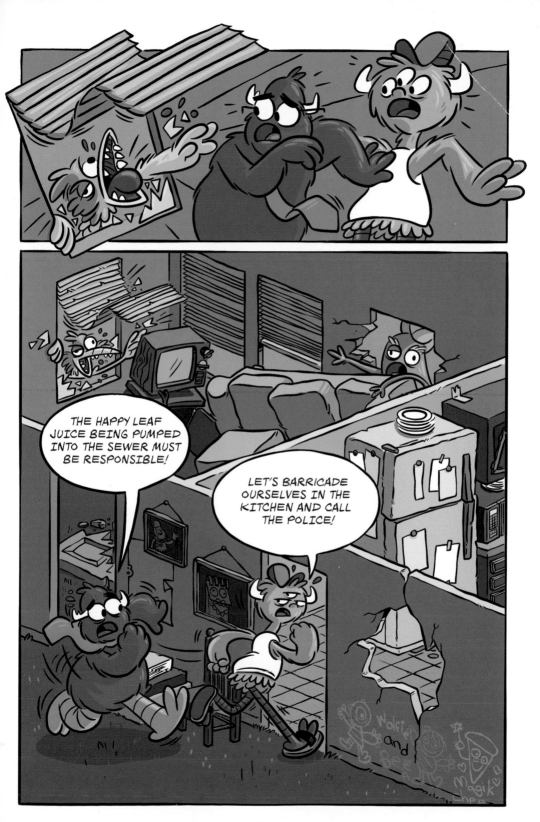

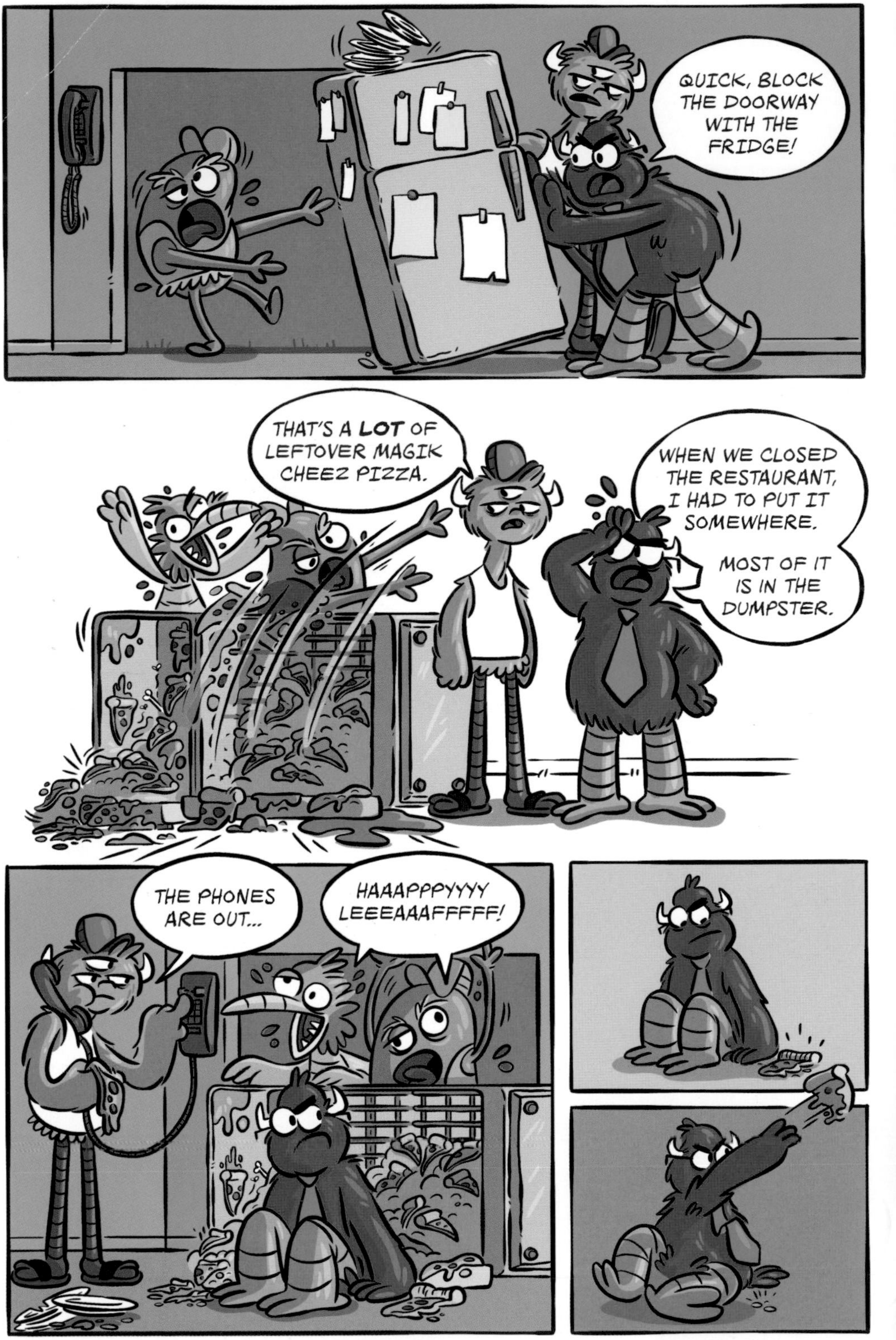
QUICK, BLOCK THE DOORWAY WITH THE FRIDGE!
THAT'S A **LOT** OF LEFTOVER MAGIK CHEEZ PIZZA.
WHEN WE CLOSED THE RESTAURANT, I HAD TO PUT IT SOMEWHERE.
MOST OF IT IS IN THE DUMPSTER.
THE PHONES ARE OUT...
HAAAPPPYYYY LEEEAAAFFFFF!

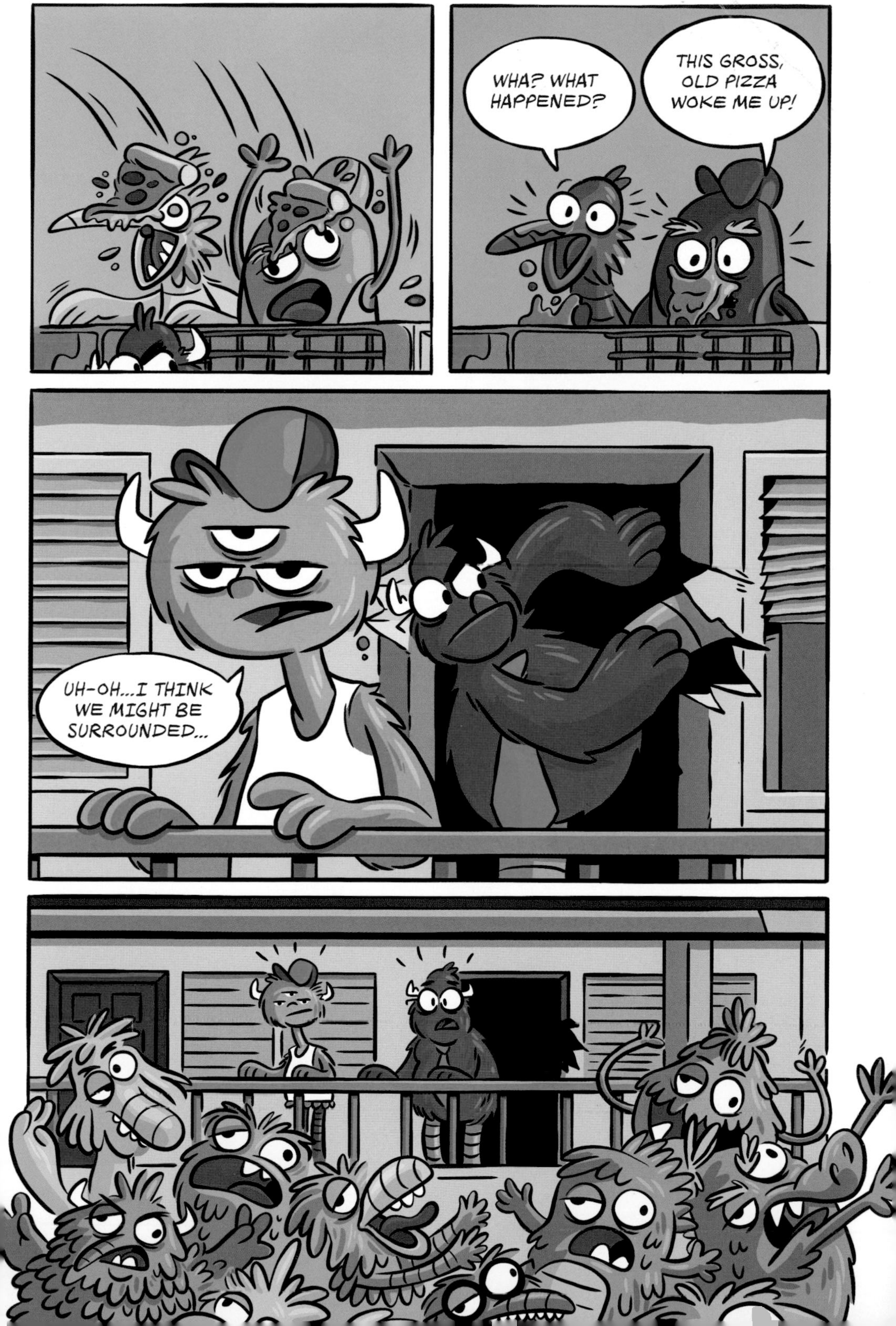
WHA? WHAT HAPPENED?
THIS GROSS, OLD PIZZA WOKE ME UP!
UH-OH...I THINK WE MIGHT BE SURROUNDED...

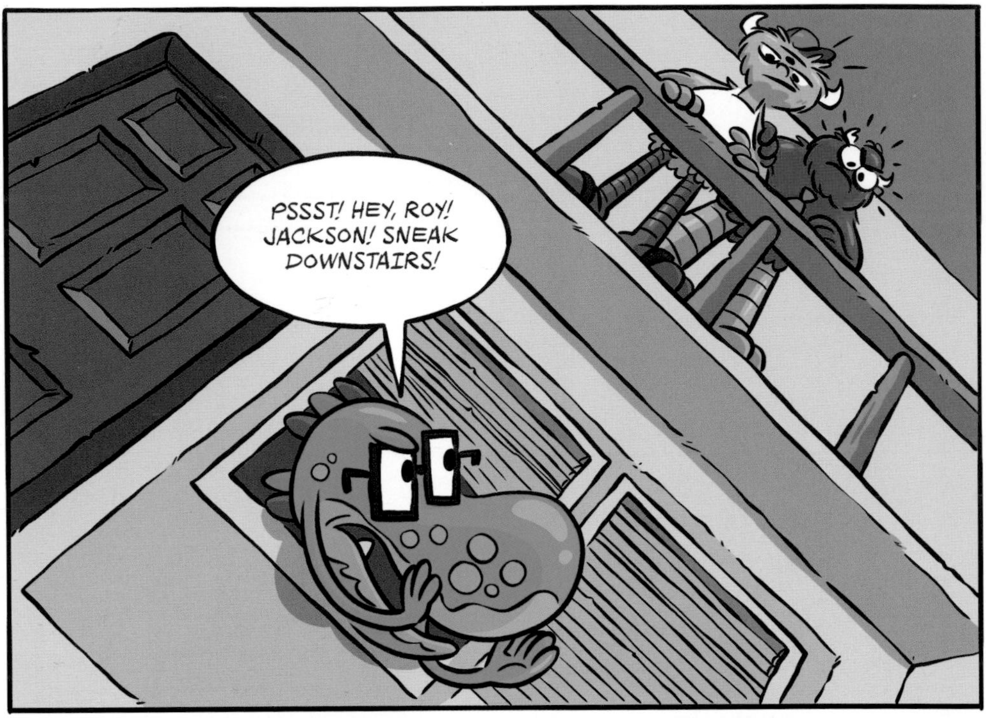
PSSST! HEY, ROY! JACKSON! SNEAK DOWNSTAIRS!

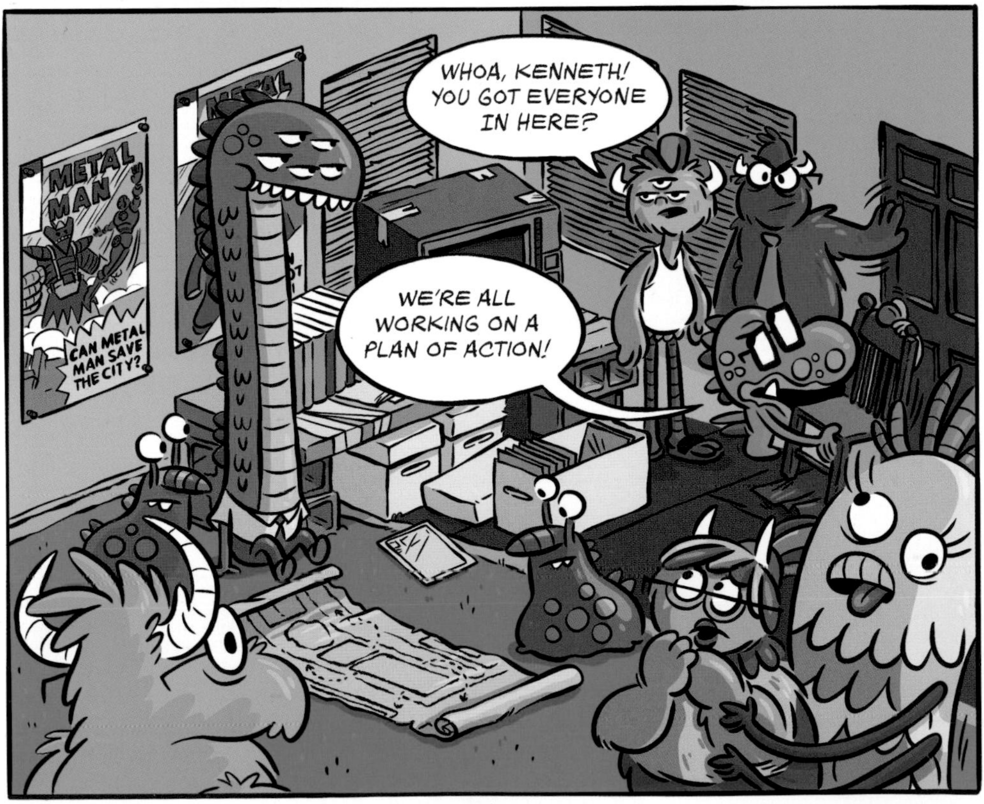
METAL MAN
CAN METAL MAN SAVE THE CITY?
WHOA, KENNETH! YOU GOT EVERYONE IN HERE?
WE'RE ALL WORKING ON A PLAN OF ACTION!

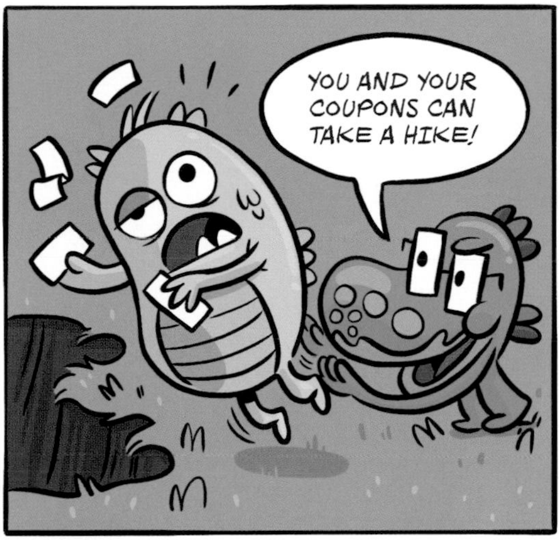
YOU AND YOUR COUPONS CAN TAKE A HIKE!

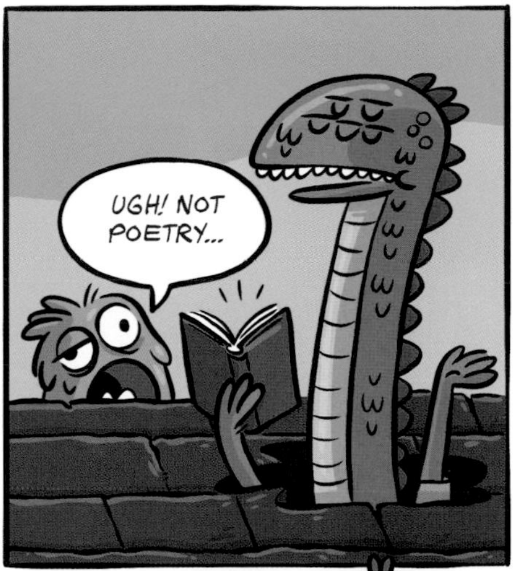
UGH! NOT POETRY...

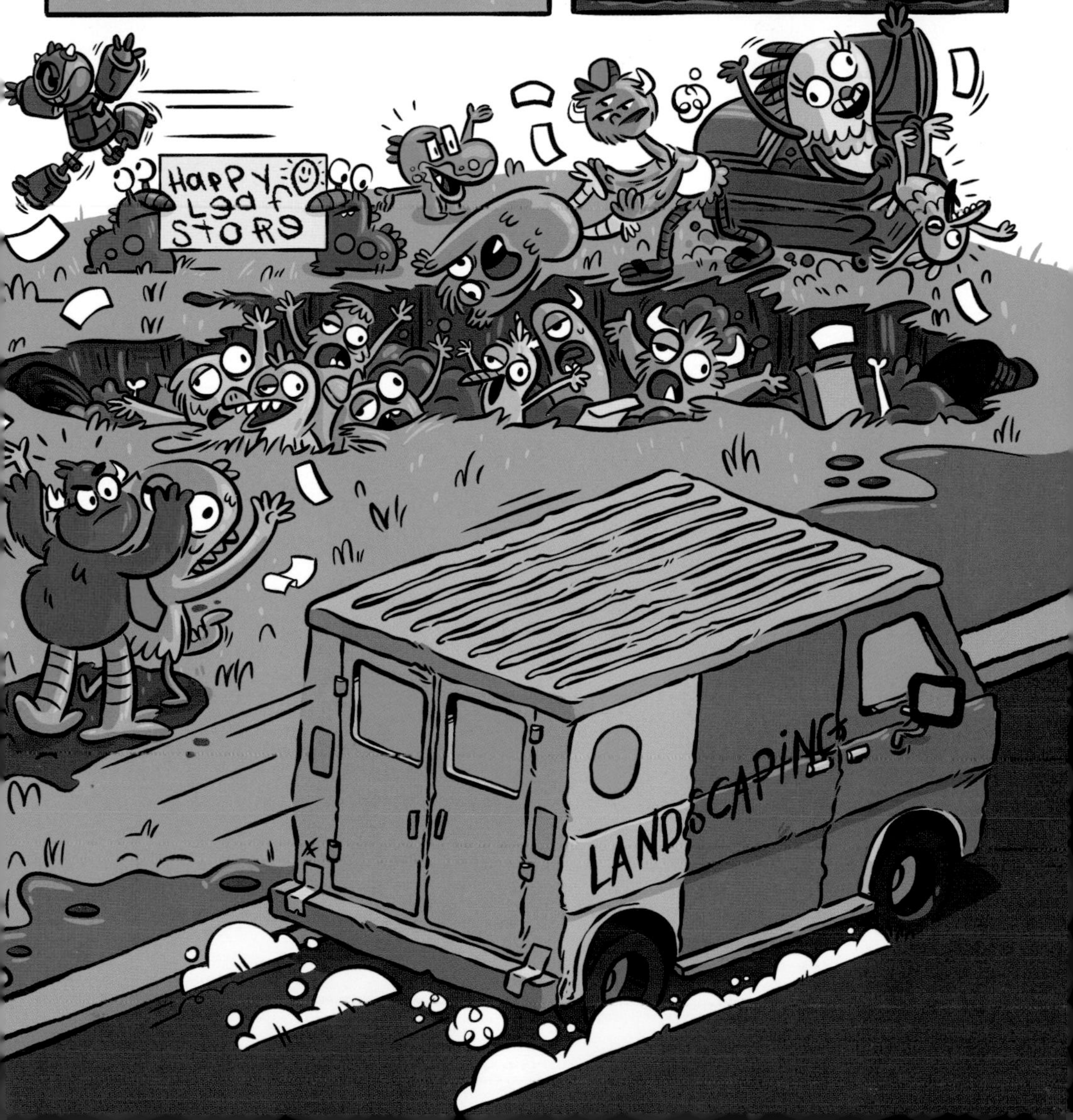
Happy Leaf STORE
LANDSCAPING

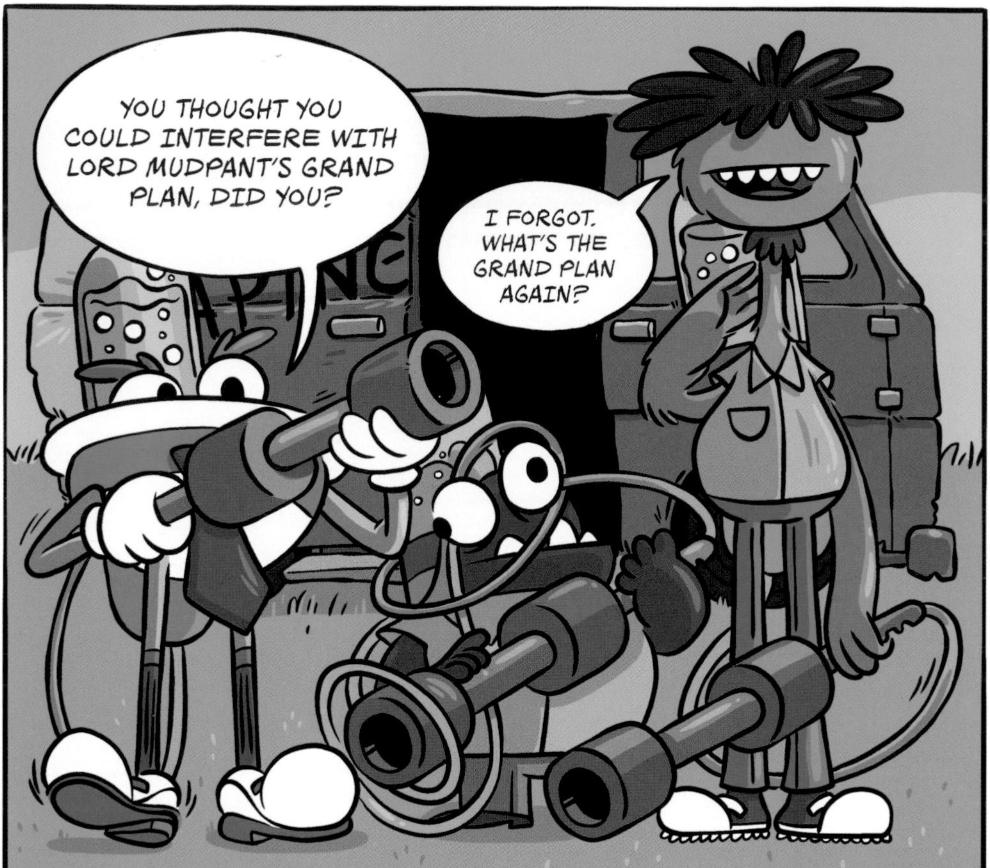
YOU THOUGHT YOU COULD INTERFERE WITH LORD MUDPANT'S GRAND PLAN, DID YOU?
I FORGOT. WHAT'S THE GRAND PLAN AGAIN?
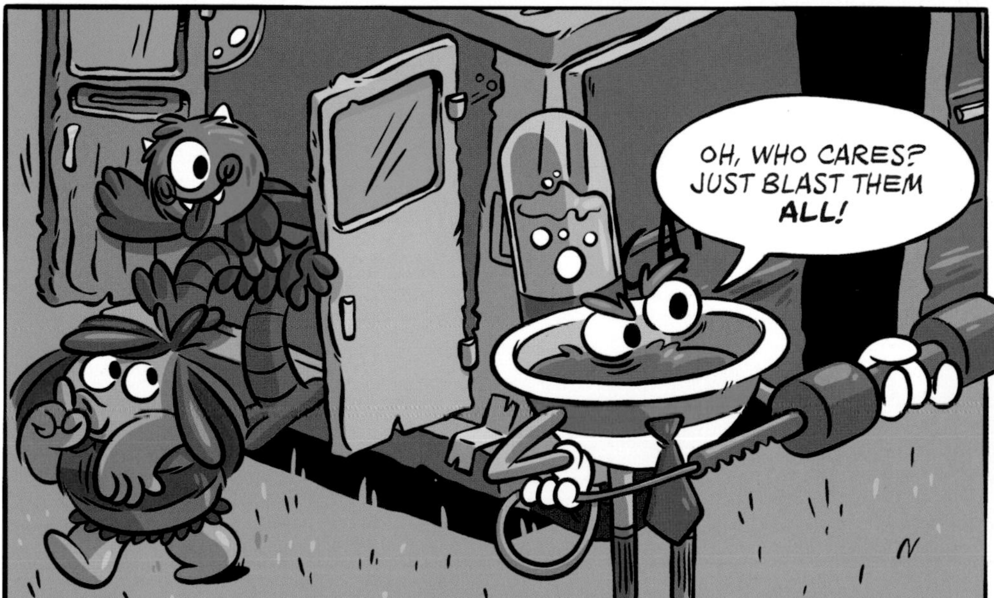
OH, WHO CARES? JUST BLAST THEM **ALL!**

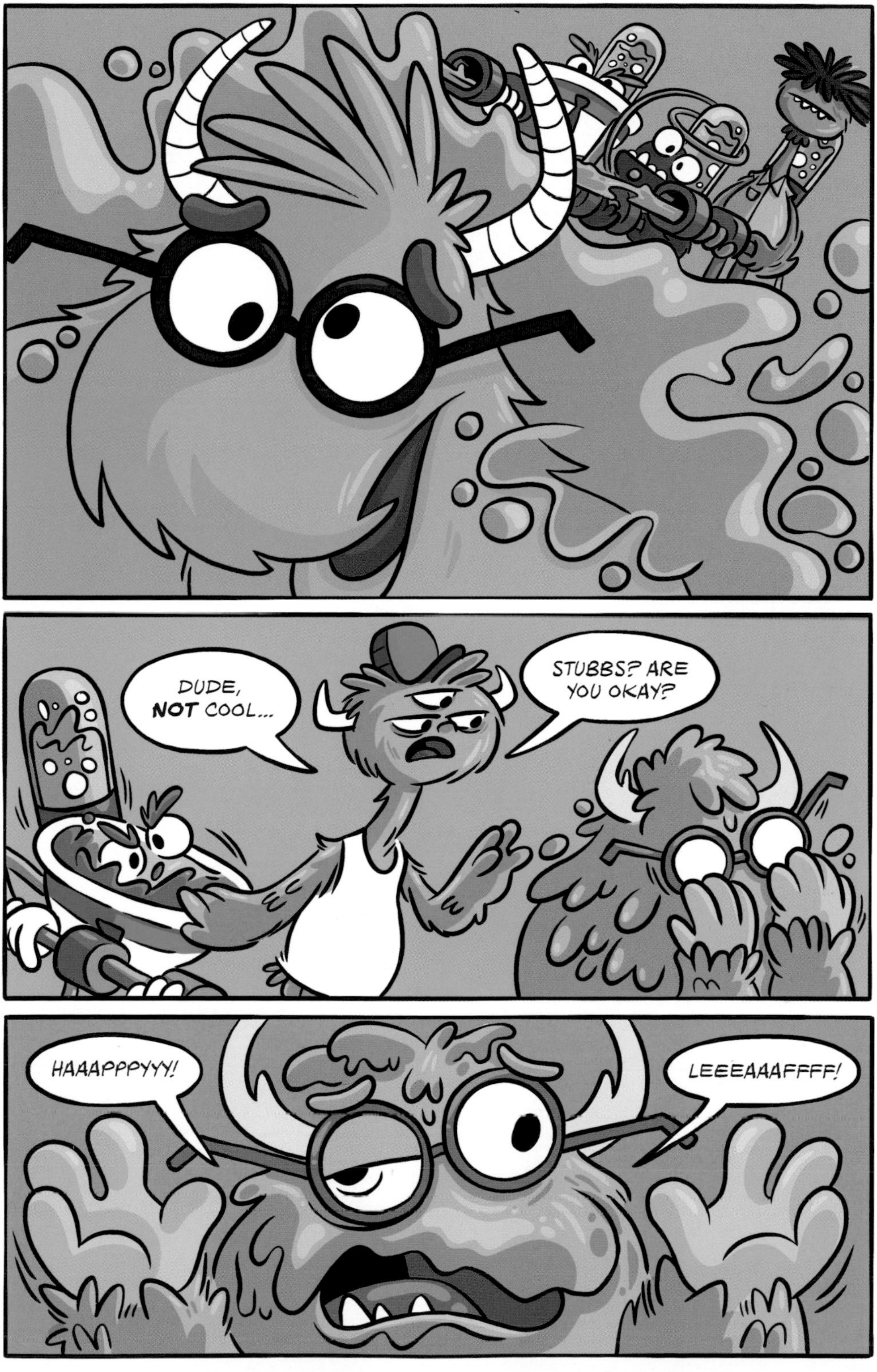
DUDE, NOT COOL...
STUBBS? ARE YOU OKAY?
HAAAPPPYYY!
LEEEAAAFFFF!

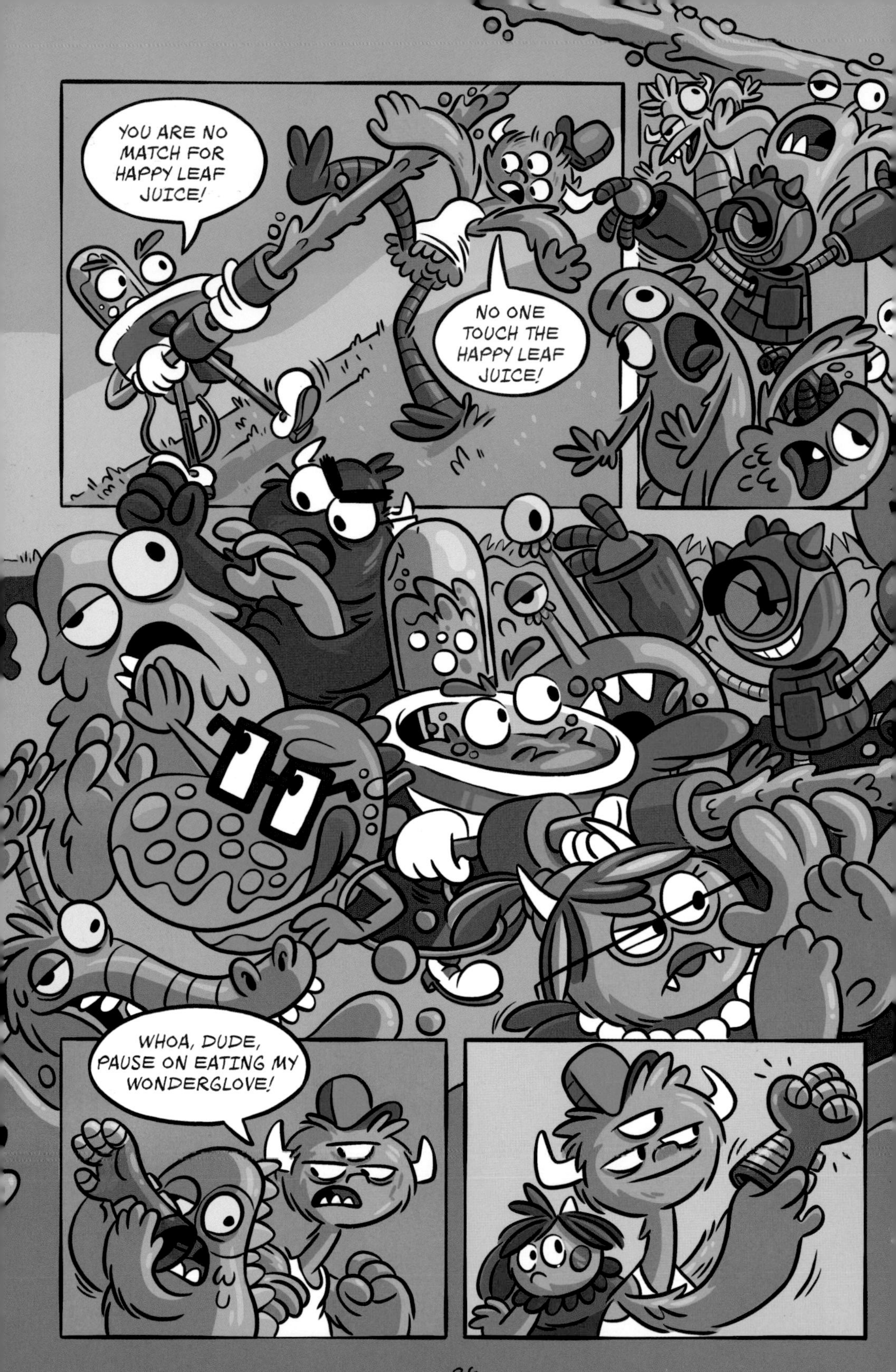
YOU ARE NO MATCH FOR HAPPY LEAF JUICE!
NO ONE TOUCH THE HAPPY LEAF JUICE!
WHOA, DUDE, PAUSE ON EATING MY WONDERGLOVE!

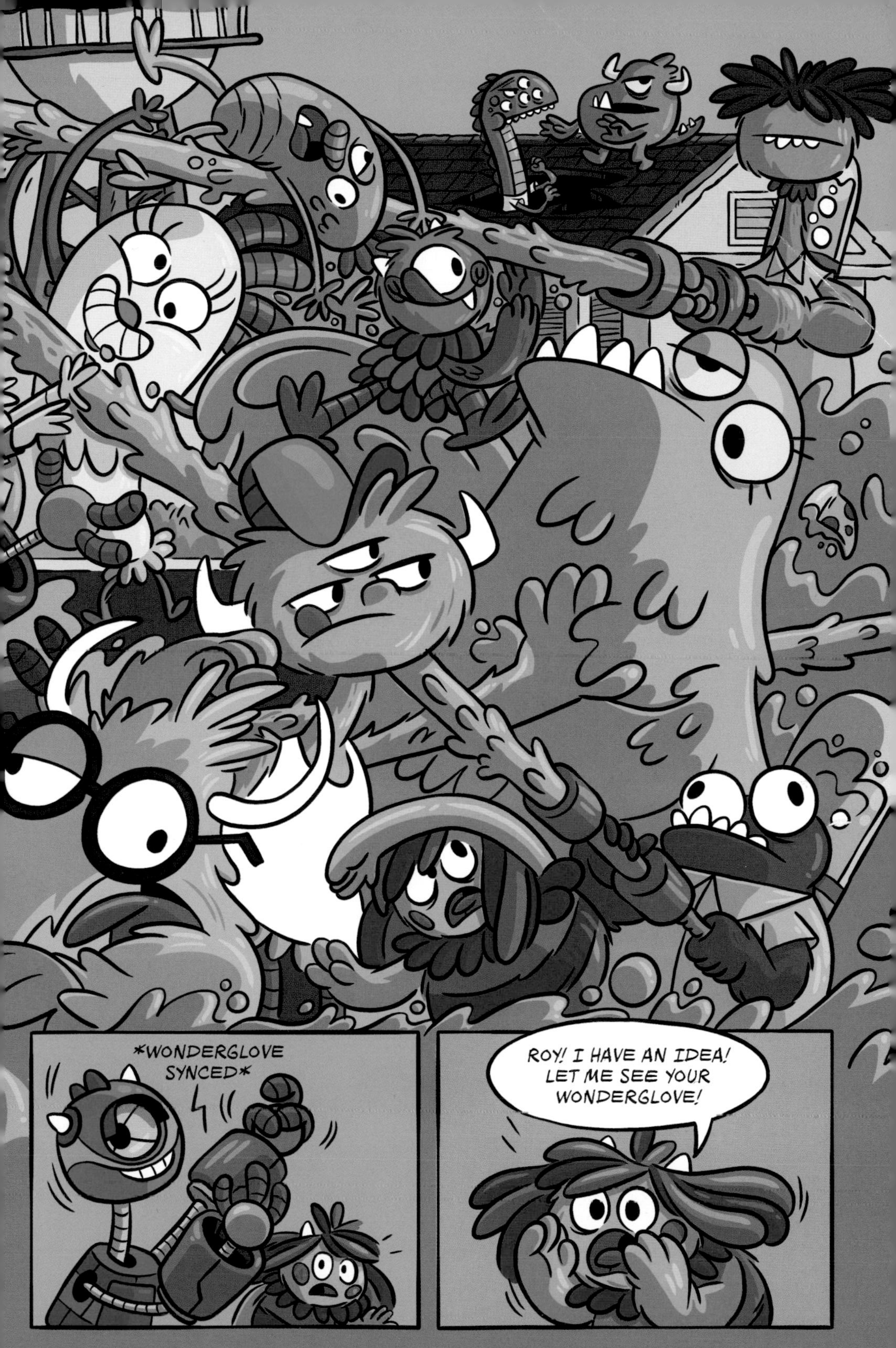
*WONDERGLOVE
SYNCED*
ROY! I HAVE AN IDEA!
LET ME SEE YOUR
WONDERGLOVE!

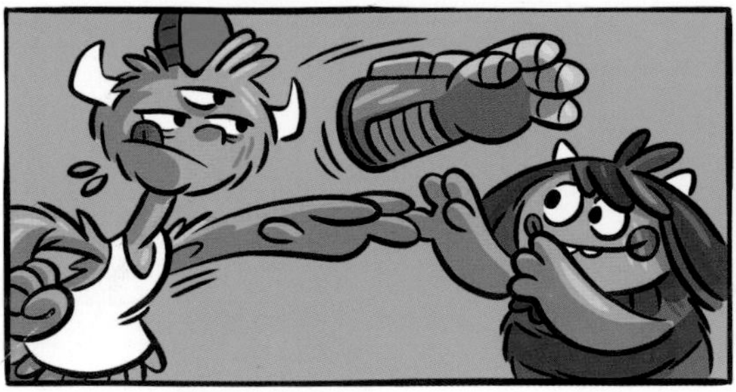

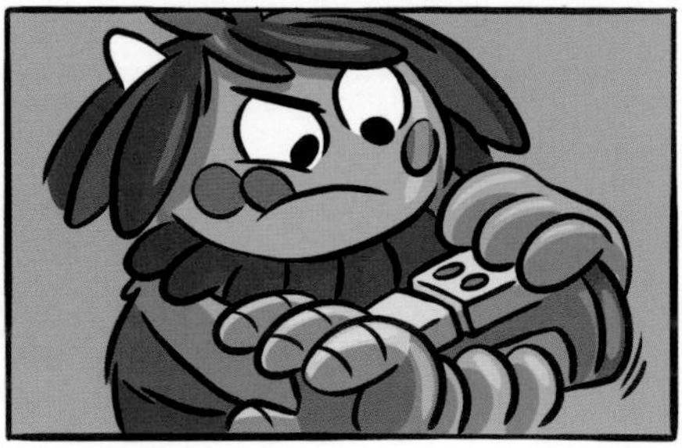

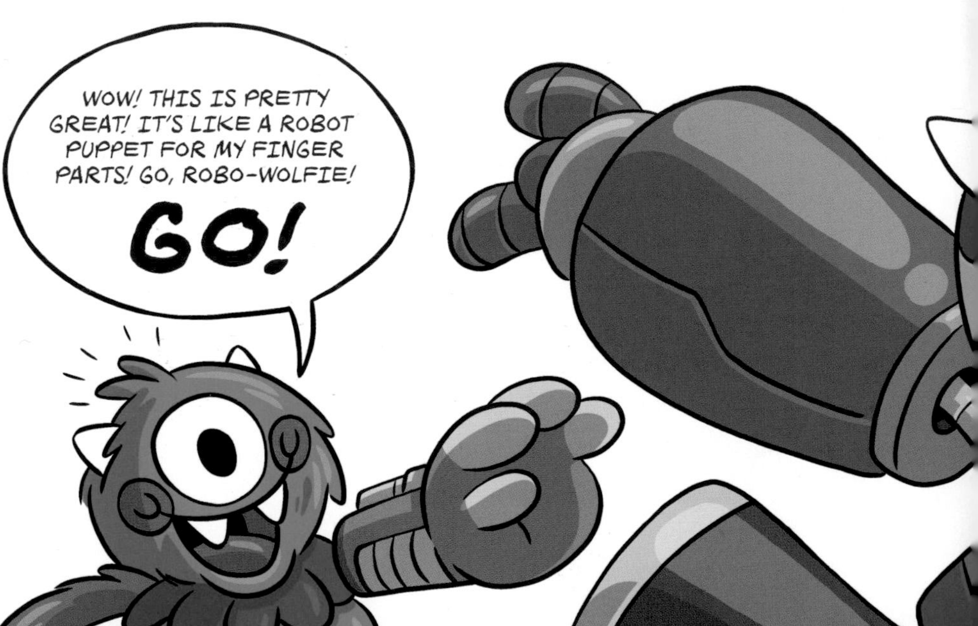
WOW! THIS IS PRETTY GREAT! IT'S LIKE A ROBOT PUPPET FOR MY FINGER PARTS! GO, ROBO-WOLFIE!
GO!

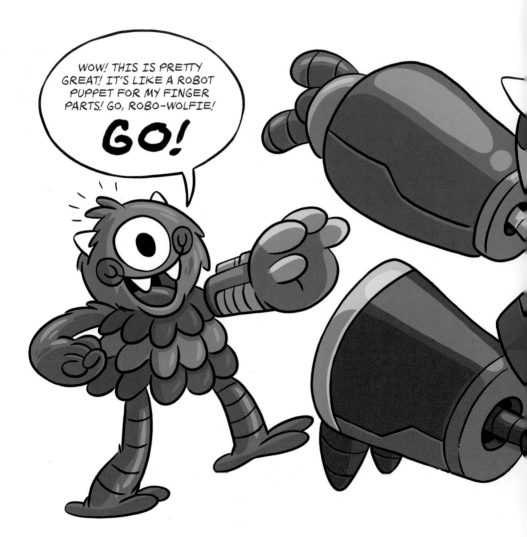

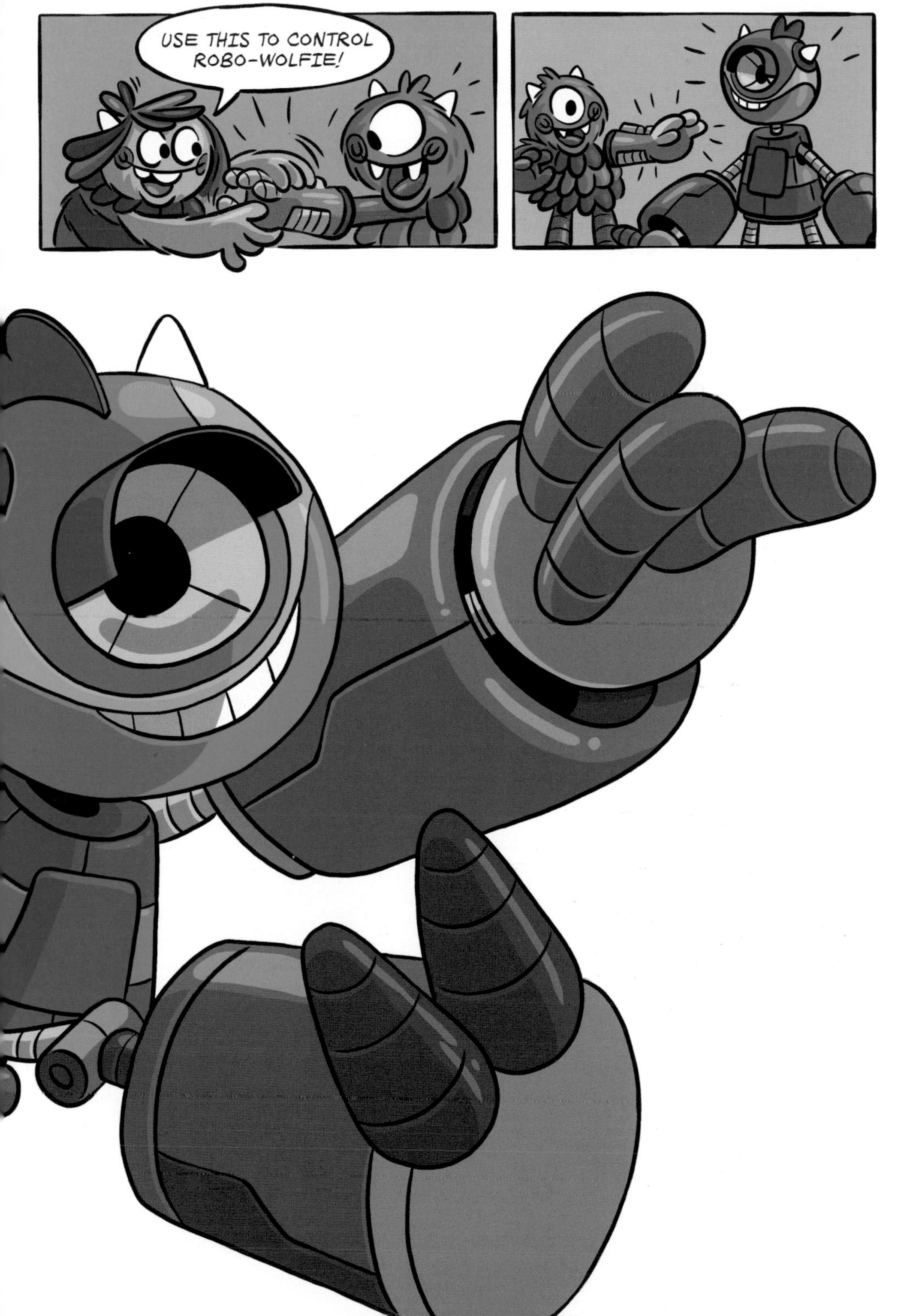
USE THIS TO CONTROL ROBO-WOLFIE!

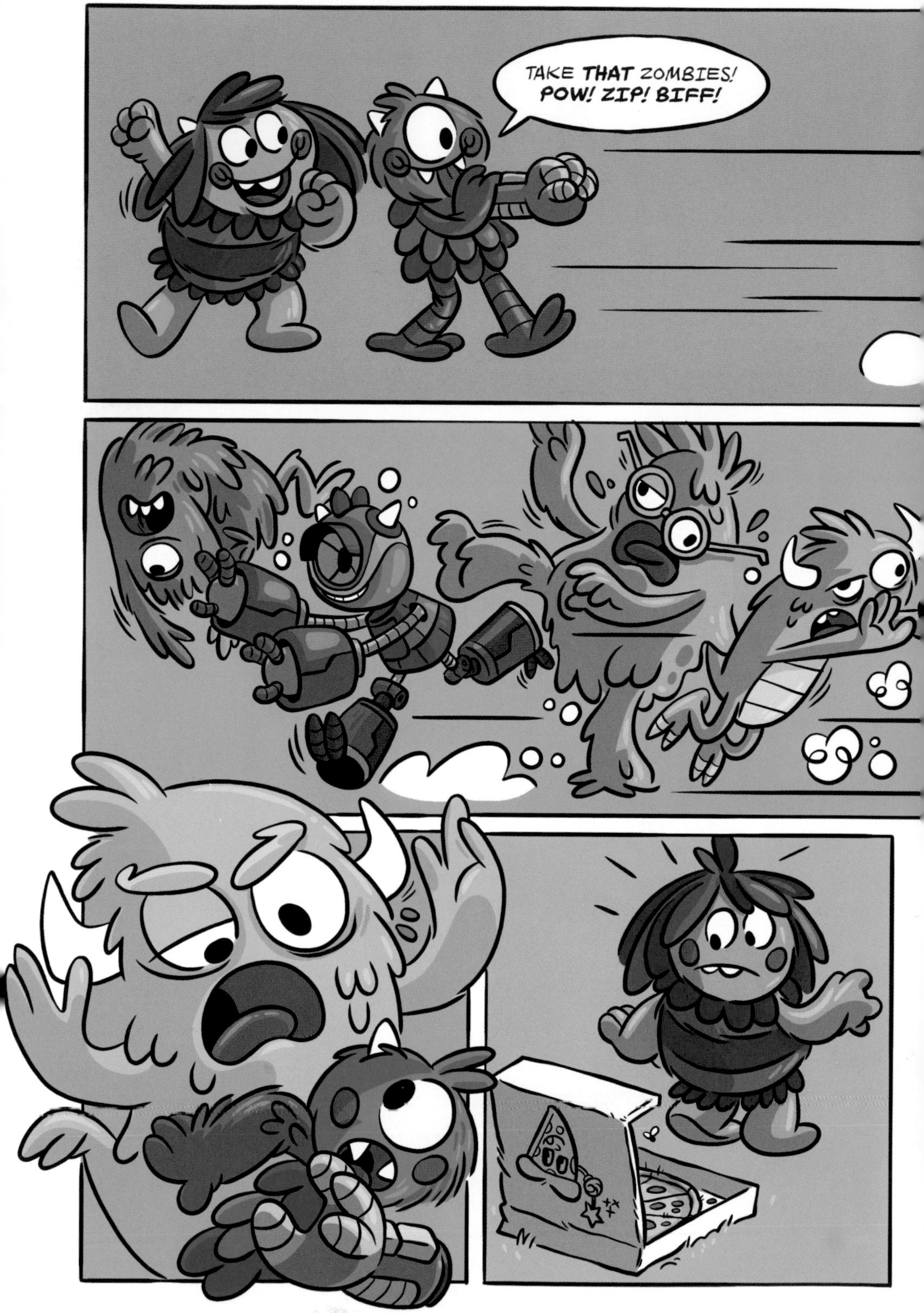
TAKE **THAT** ZOMBIES!
POW! ZIP! BIFF!

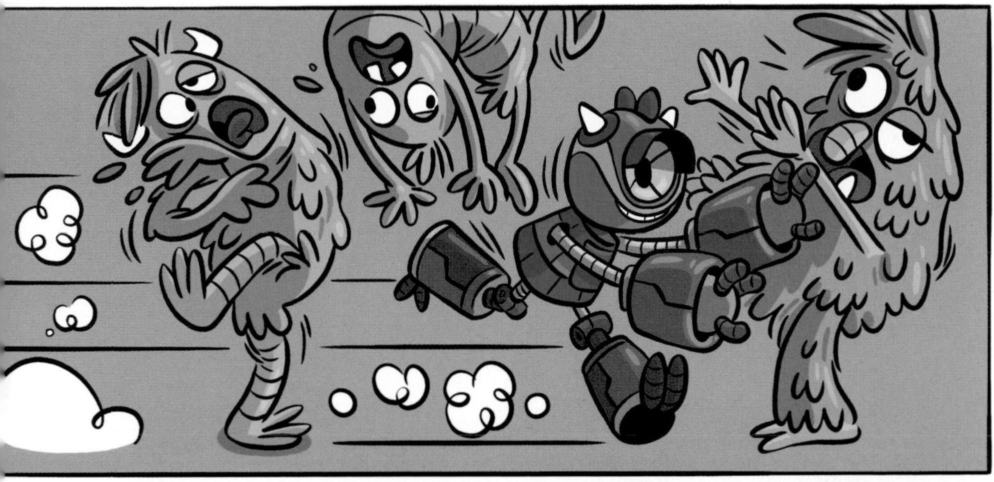

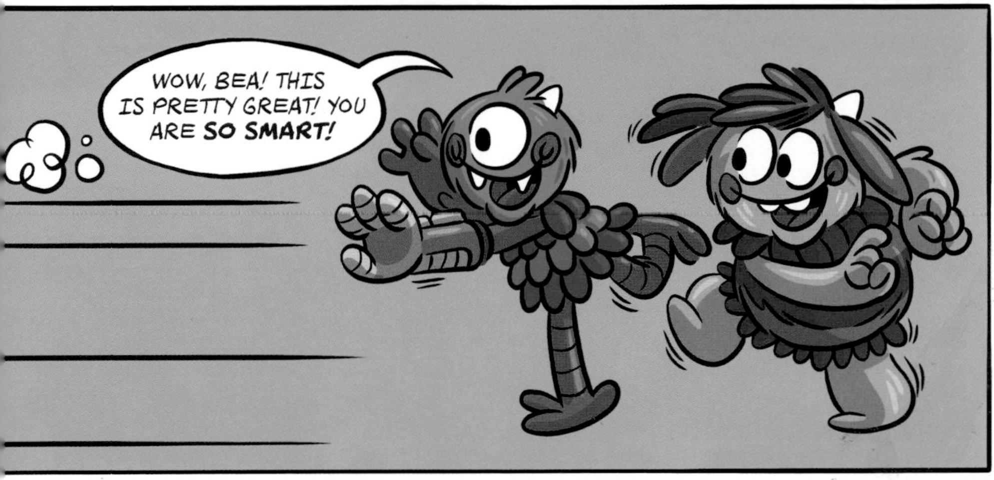
WOW, BEA! THIS IS PRETTY GREAT! YOU ARE **SO SMART!**

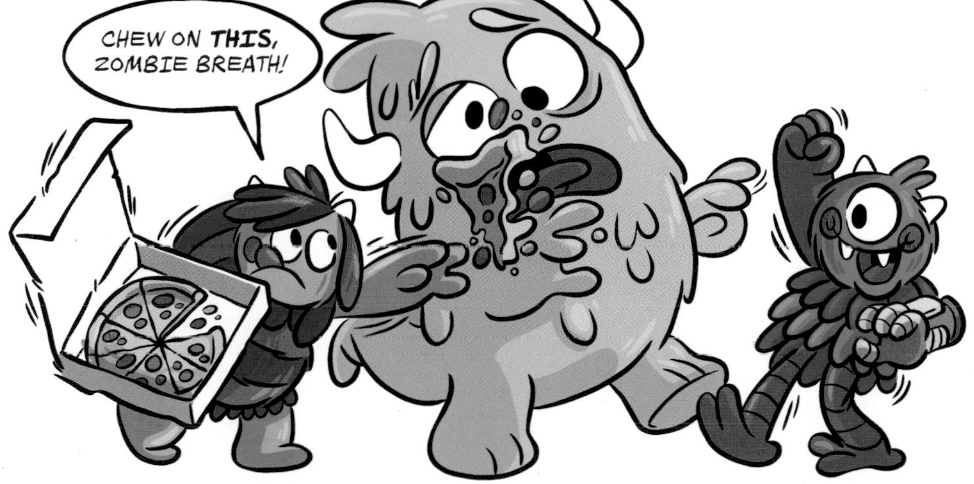
CHEW ON **THIS,** ZOMBIE BREATH!

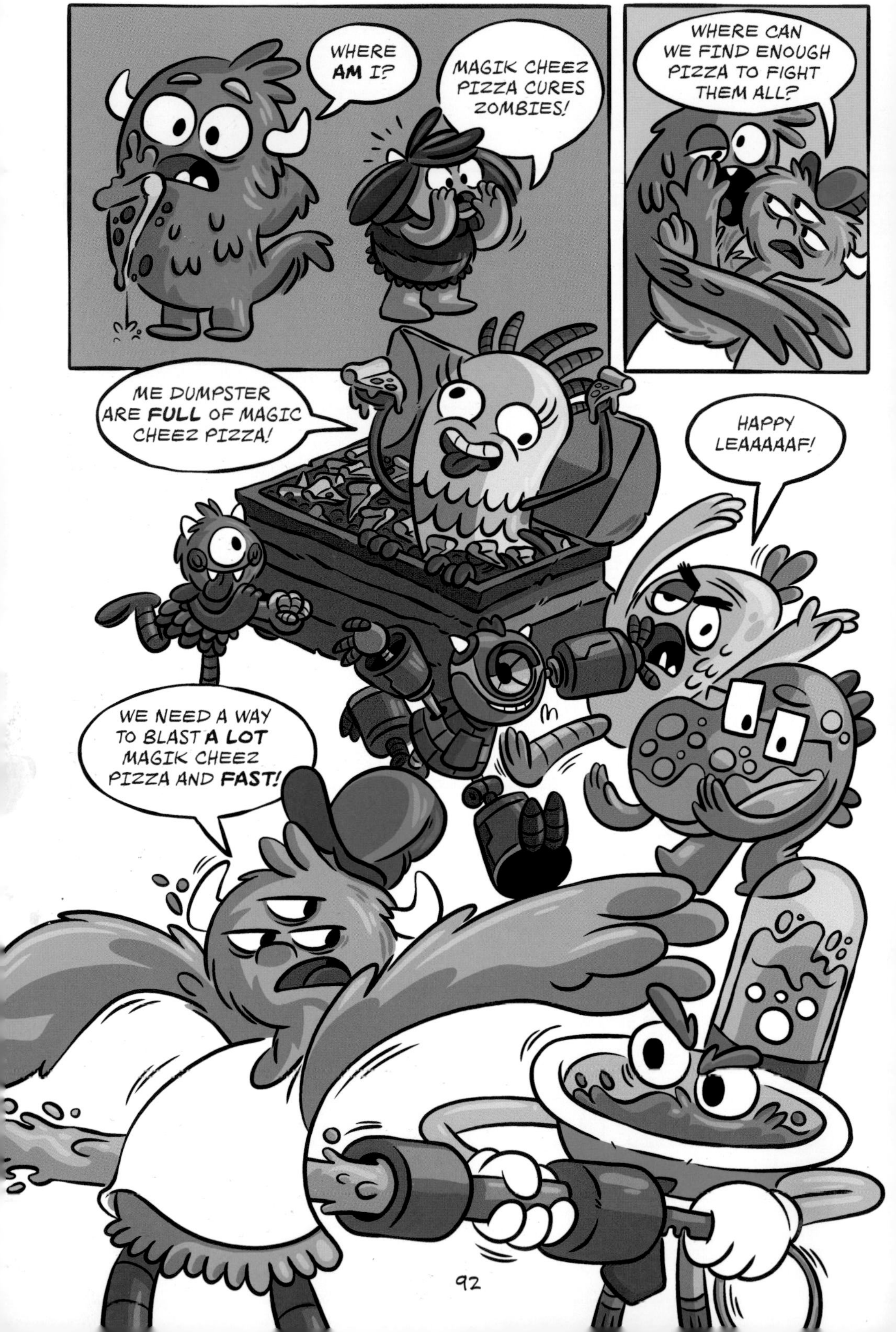
WHERE AM I?
MAGIK CHEEZ PIZZA CURES ZOMBIES!
WHERE CAN WE FIND ENOUGH PIZZA TO FIGHT THEM ALL?
ME DUMPSTER ARE FULL OF MAGIC CHEEZ PIZZA!
HAPPY LEAAAAAF!
WE NEED A WAY TO BLAST A LOT MAGIK CHEEZ PIZZA AND FAST!

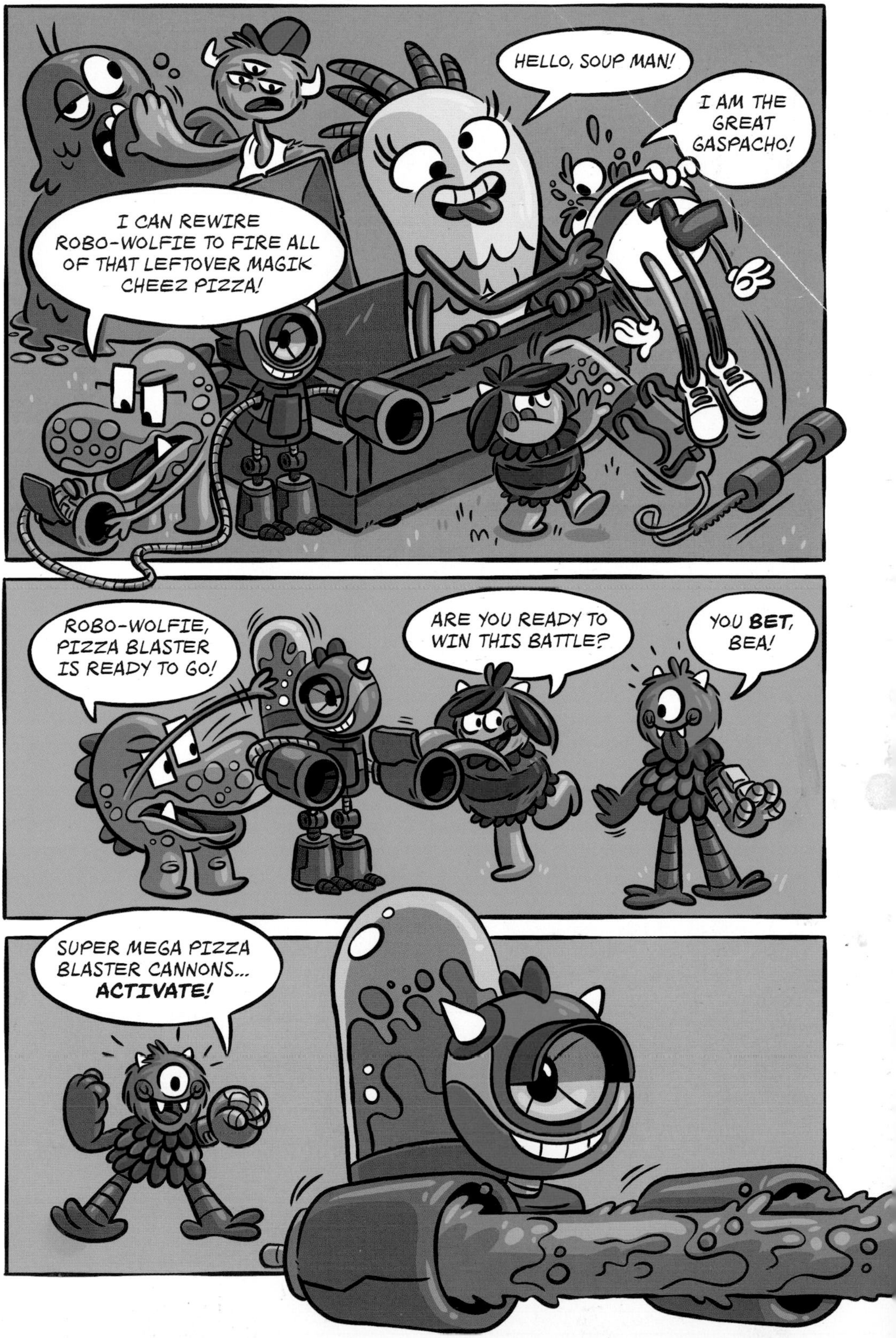
I CAN REWIRE ROBO-WOLFIE TO FIRE ALL OF THAT LEFTOVER MAGIK CHEEZ PIZZA!
HELLO, SOUP MAN!
I AM THE GREAT GASPACHO!
ROBO-WOLFIE, PIZZA BLASTER IS READY TO GO!
ARE YOU READY TO WIN THIS BATTLE?
YOU BET, BEA!
SUPER MEGA PIZZA BLASTER CANNONS... ACTIVATE!

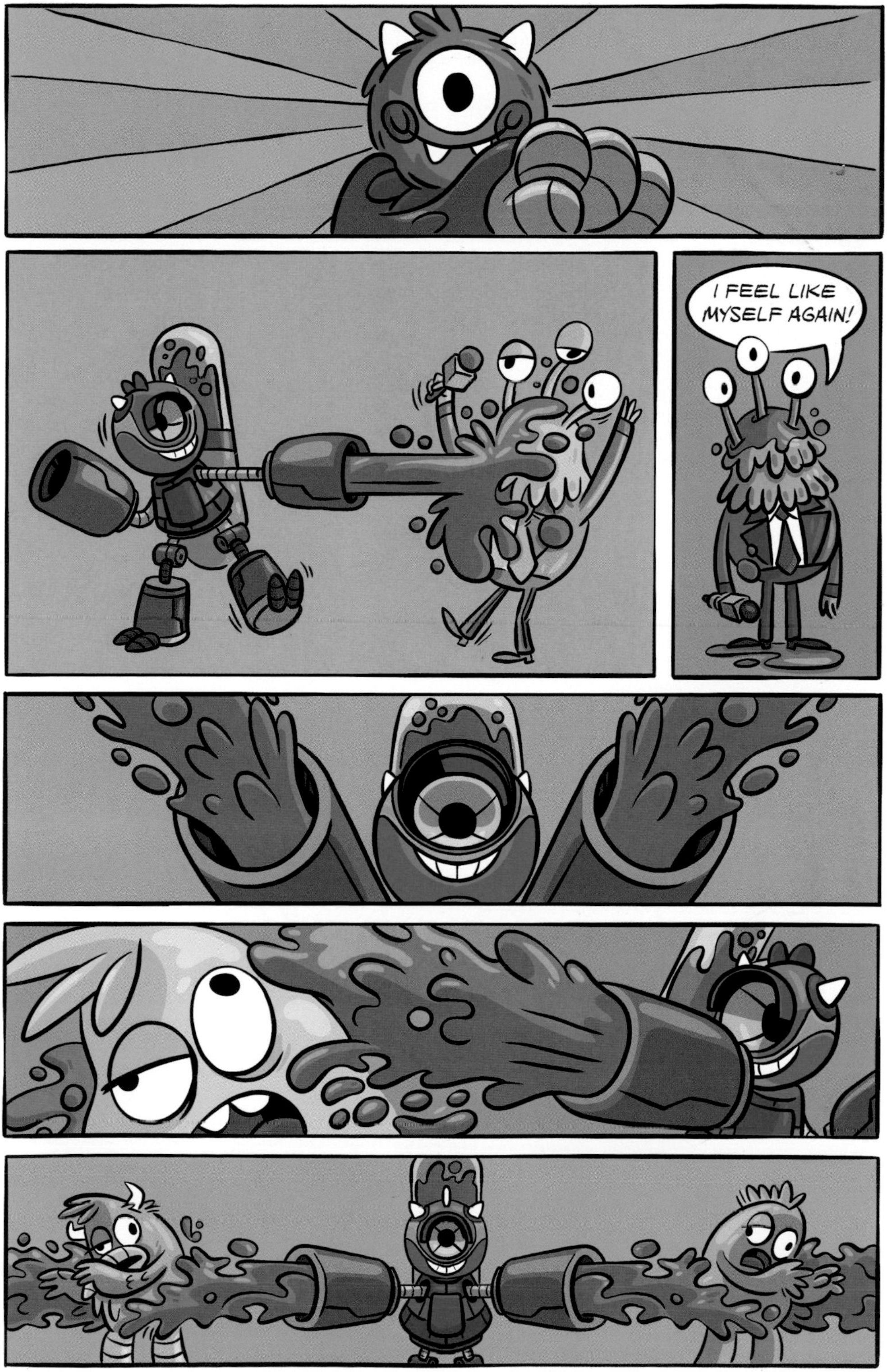
I FEEL LIKE MYSELF AGAIN!

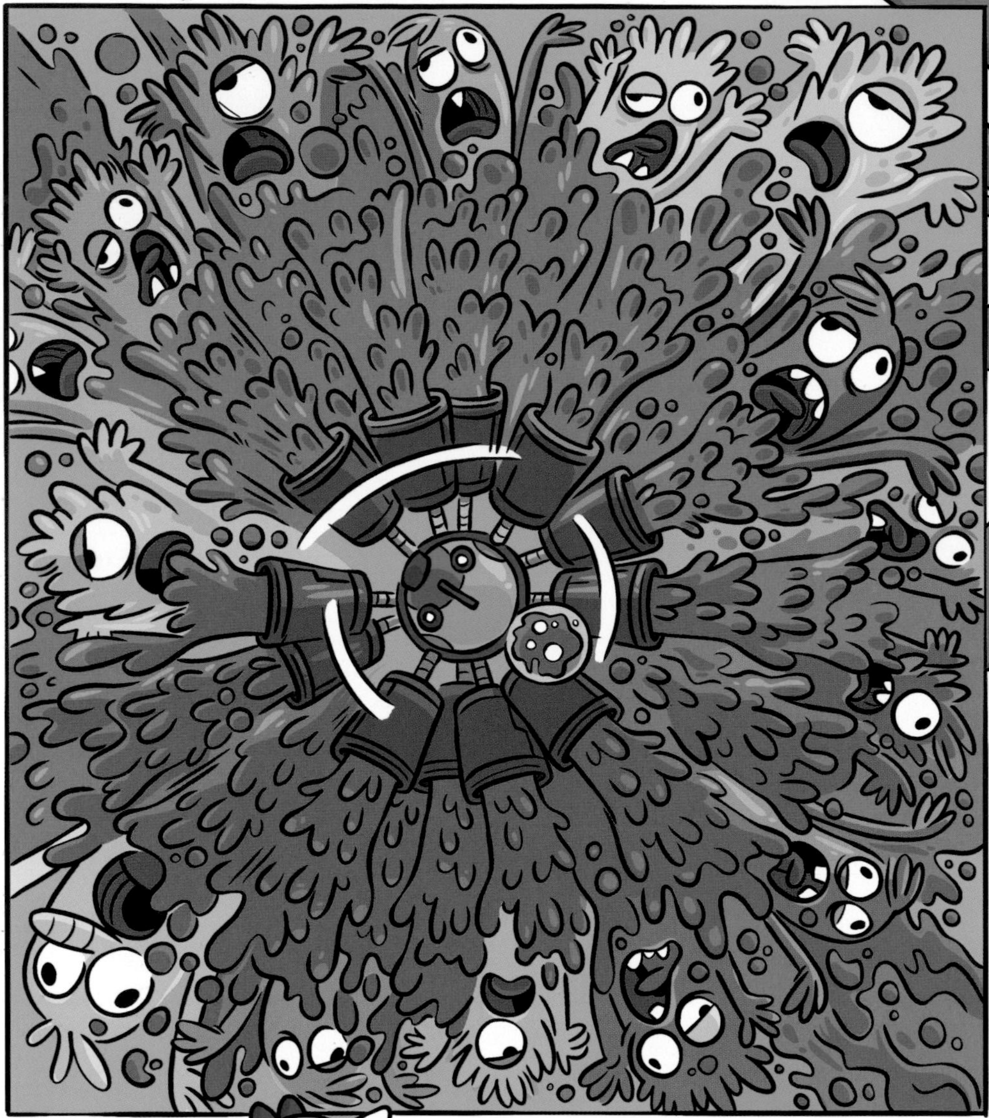

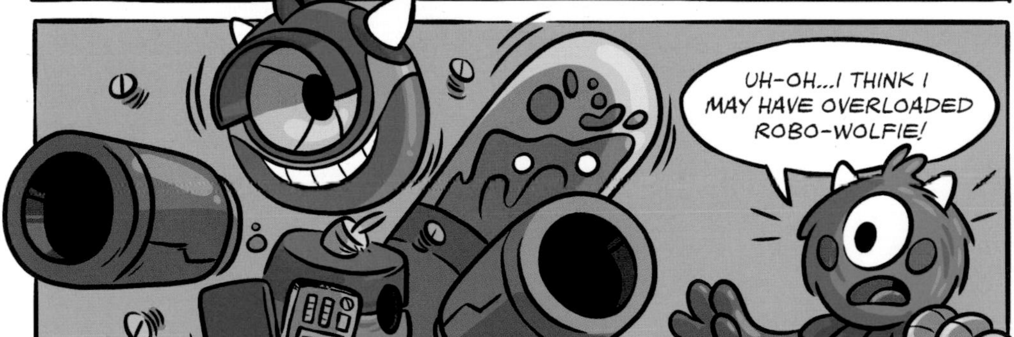
UH-OH...I THINK I MAY HAVE OVERLOADED ROBO-WOLFIE!

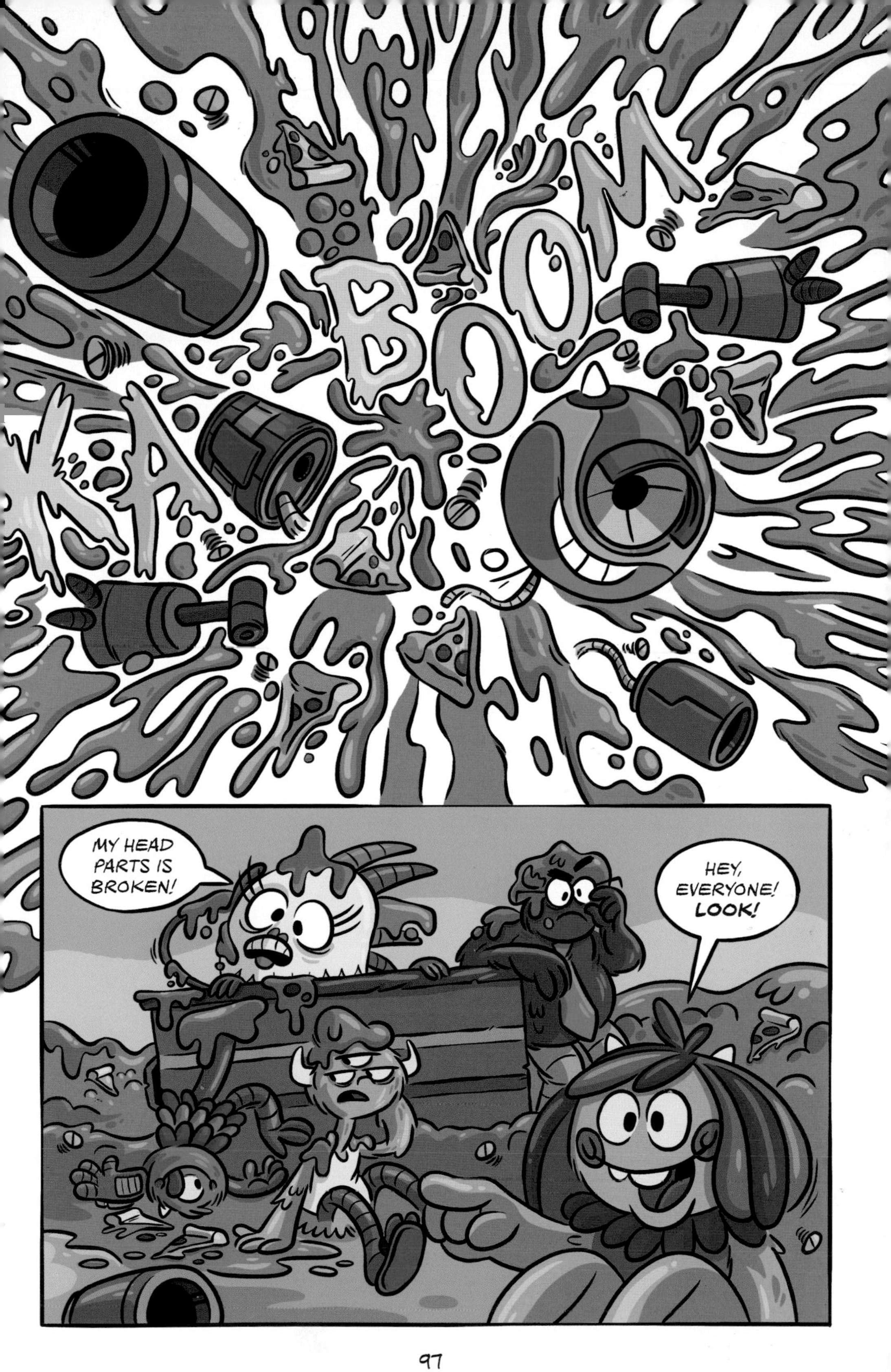
KA-BOOM
MY HEAD PARTS IS BROKEN!
HEY, EVERYONE! LOOK!

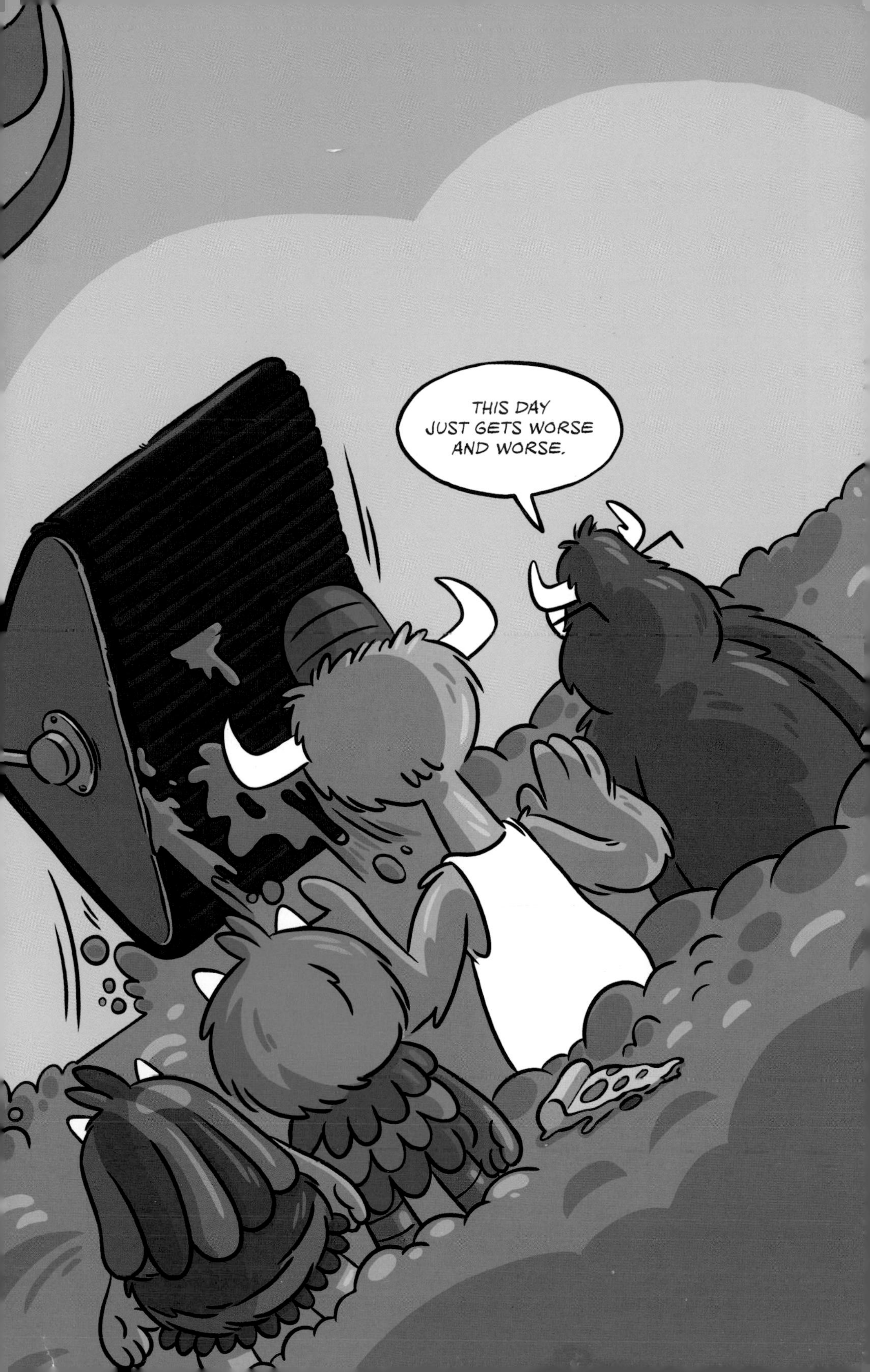
THIS DAY JUST GETS WORSE AND WORSE.

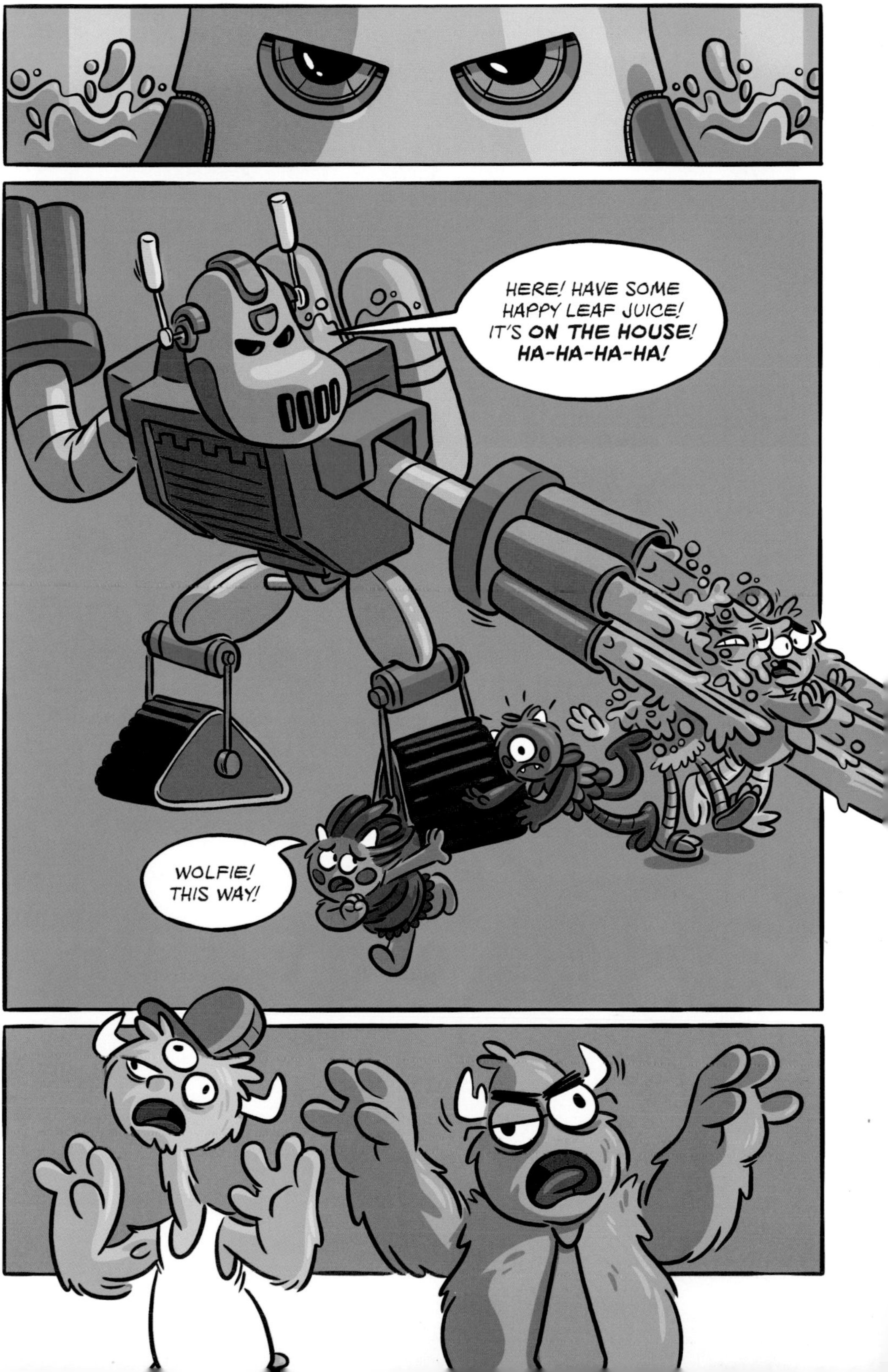
HERE! HAVE SOME HAPPY LEAF JUICE! IT'S **ON THE HOUSE! HA-HA-HA-HA!**
WOLFIE! THIS WAY!

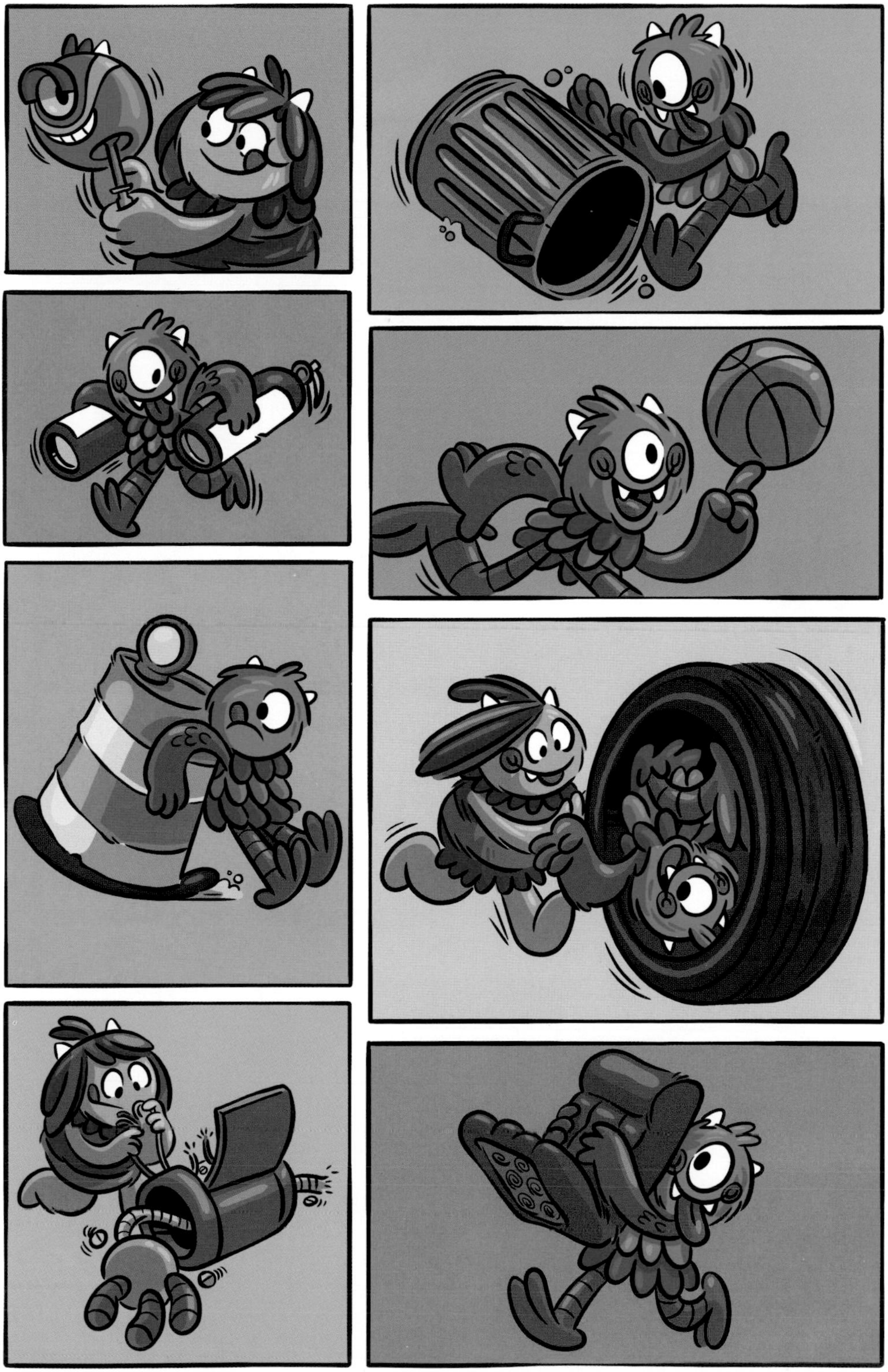

108

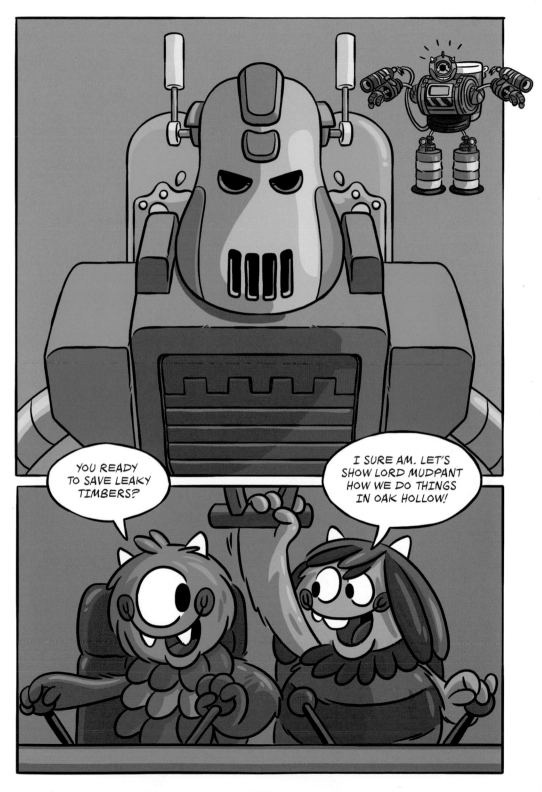

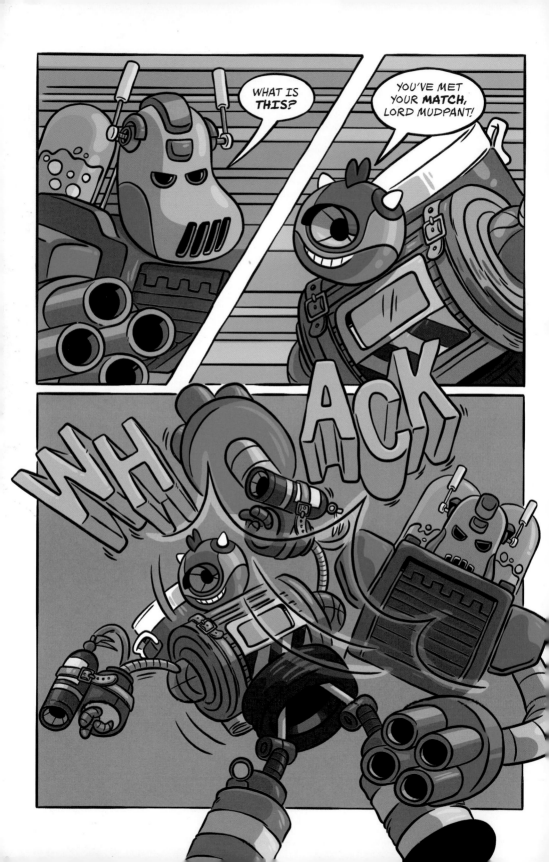

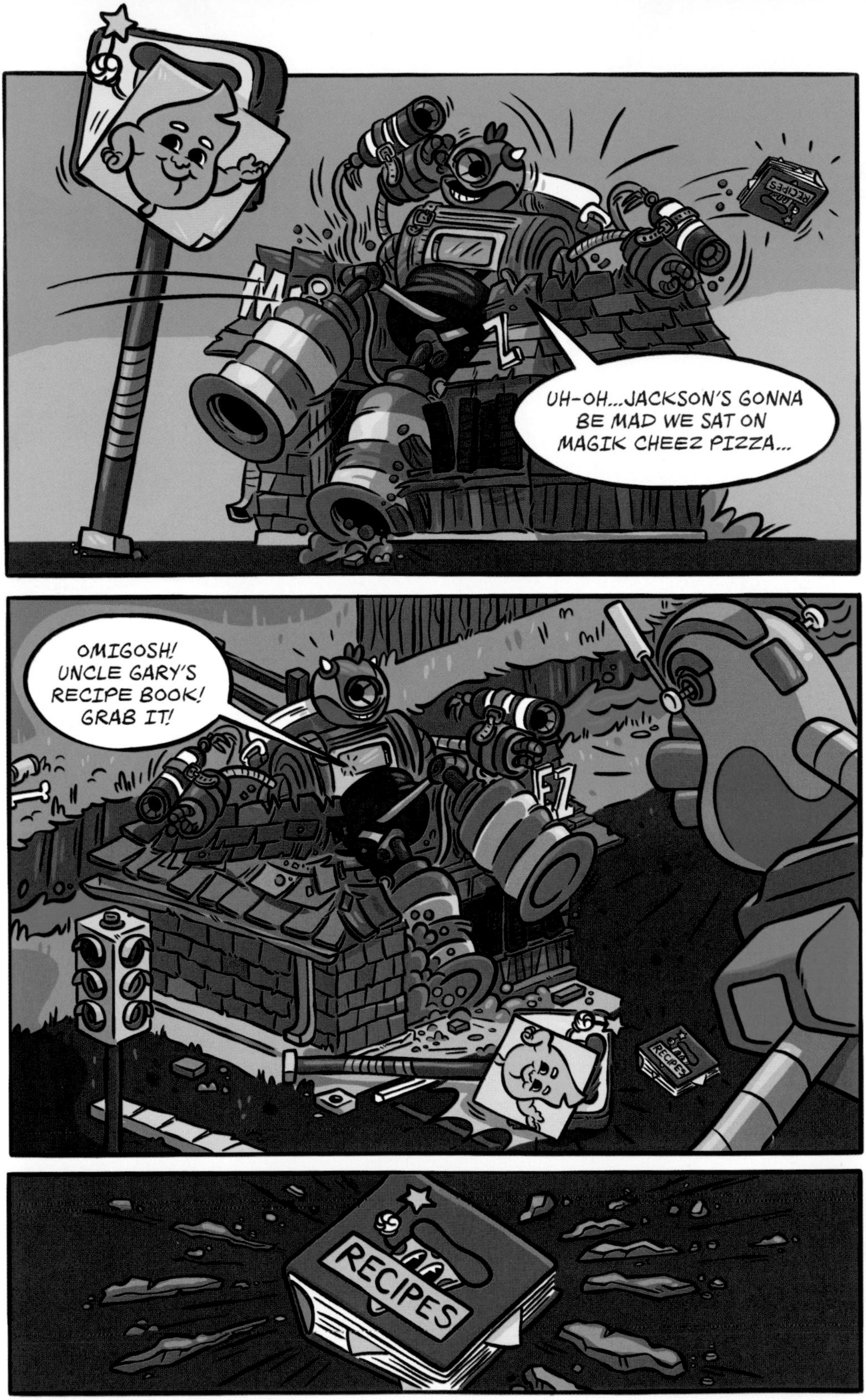
UH-OH...JACKSON'S GONNA BE MAD WE SAT ON MAGIK CHEEZ PIZZA...
RECIPES
OMIGOSH! UNCLE GARY'S RECIPE BOOK! GRAB IT!
RECIPES
RECIPES

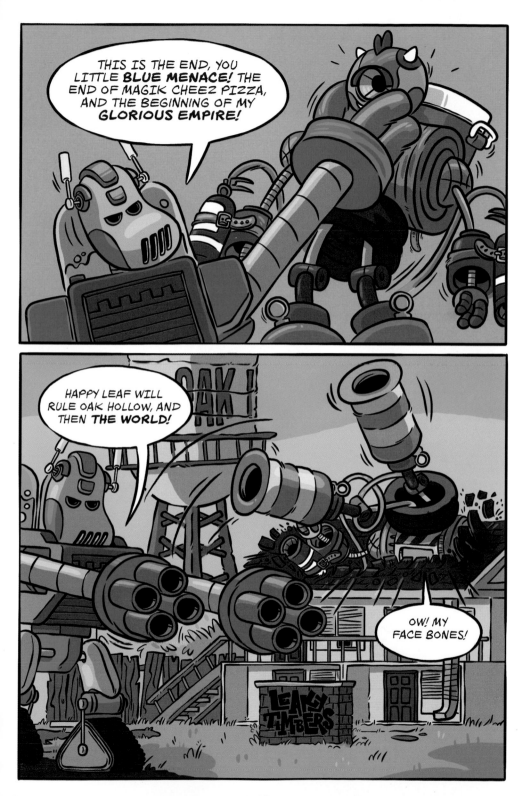

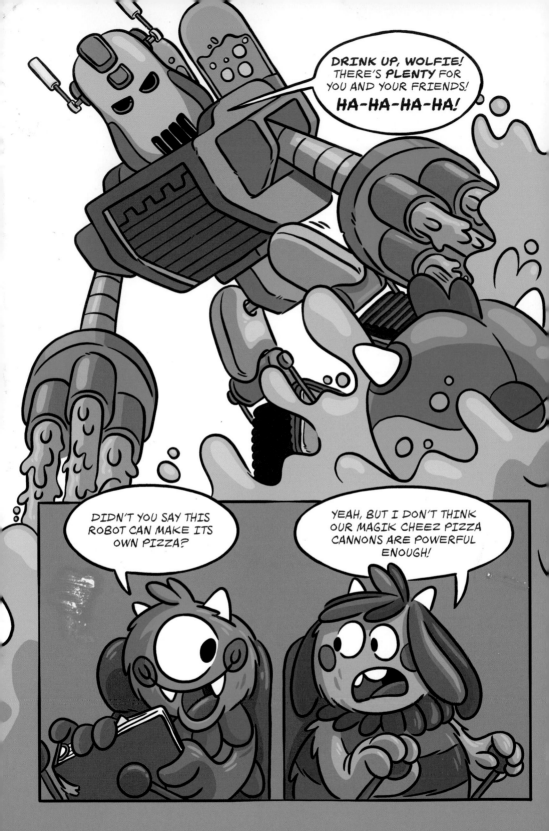

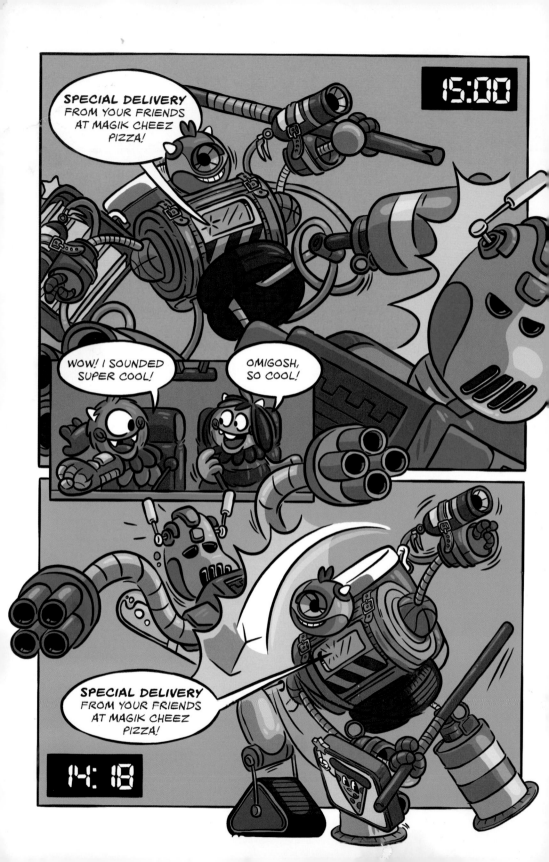

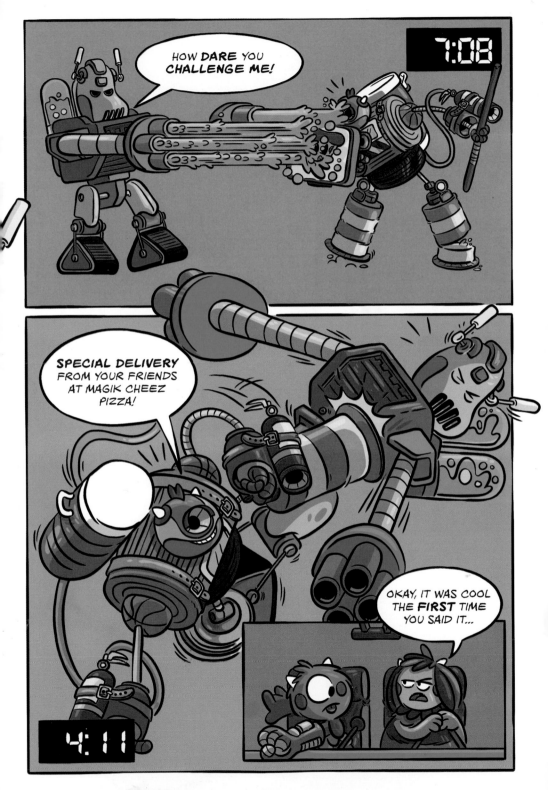

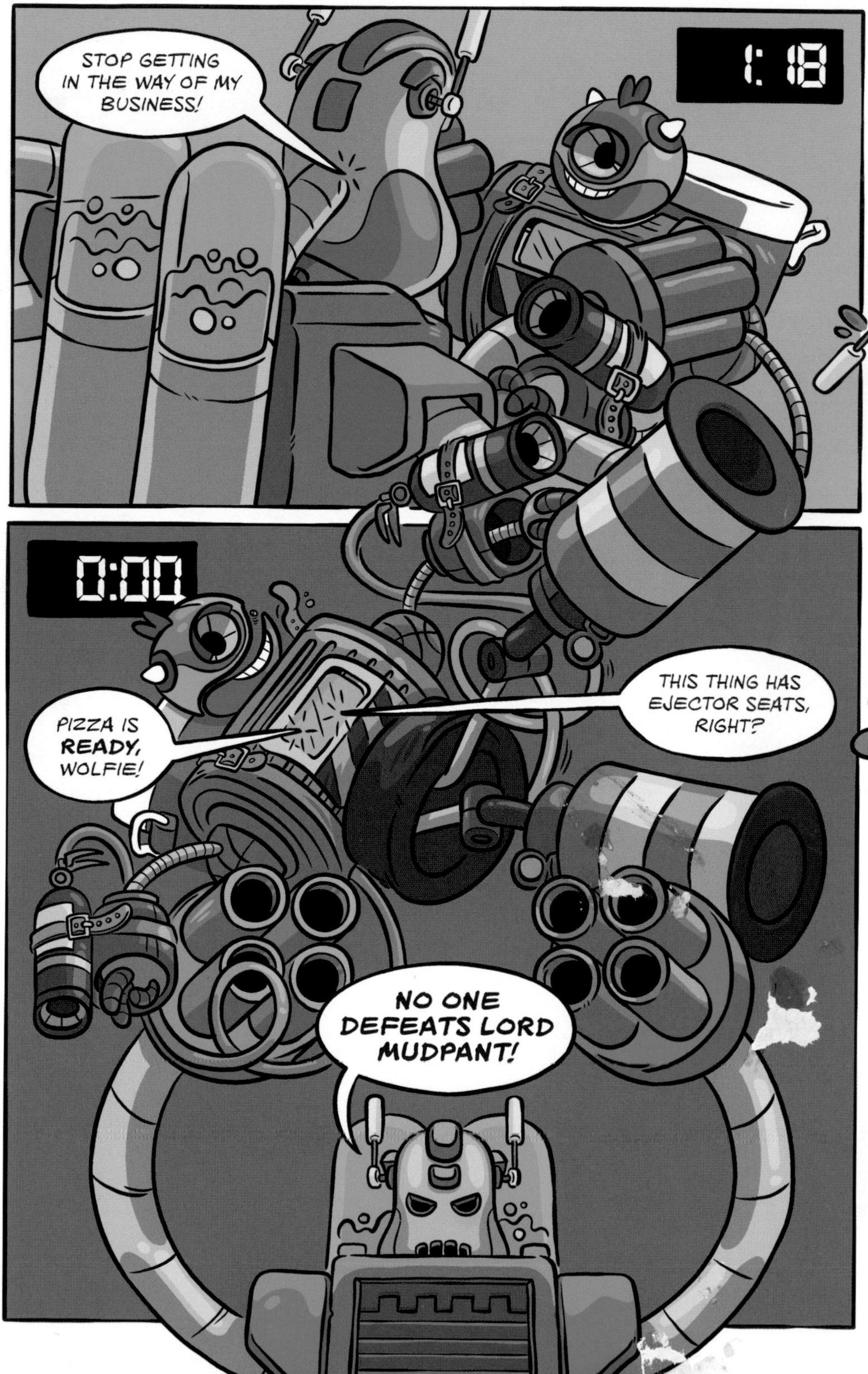
1:18
STOP GETTING IN THE WAY OF MY BUSINESS!
0:00
PIZZA IS **READY,** WOLFIE!
THIS THING HAS EJECTOR SEATS, RIGHT?
NO ONE DEFEATS LORD MUDPANT!

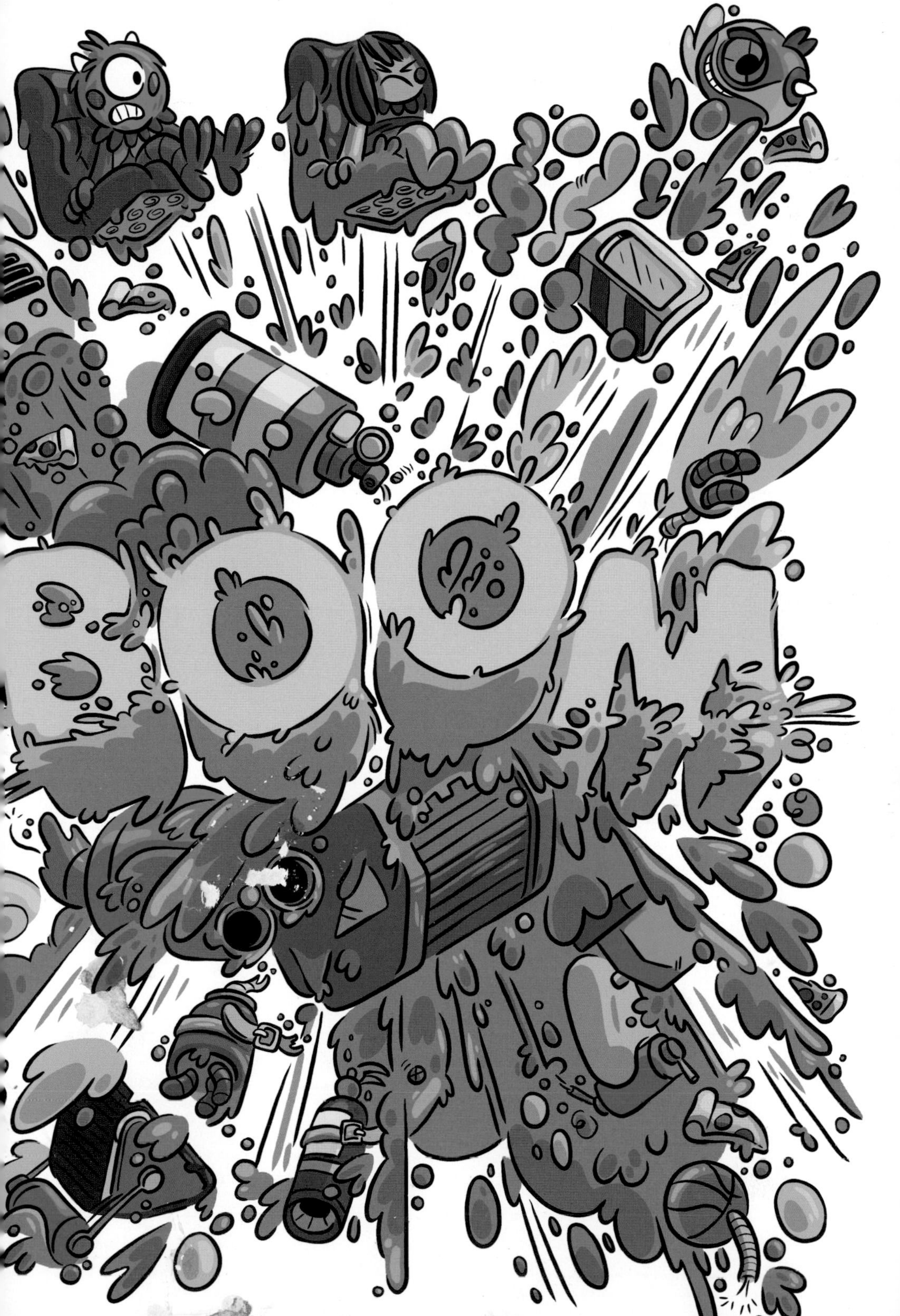
BOOM

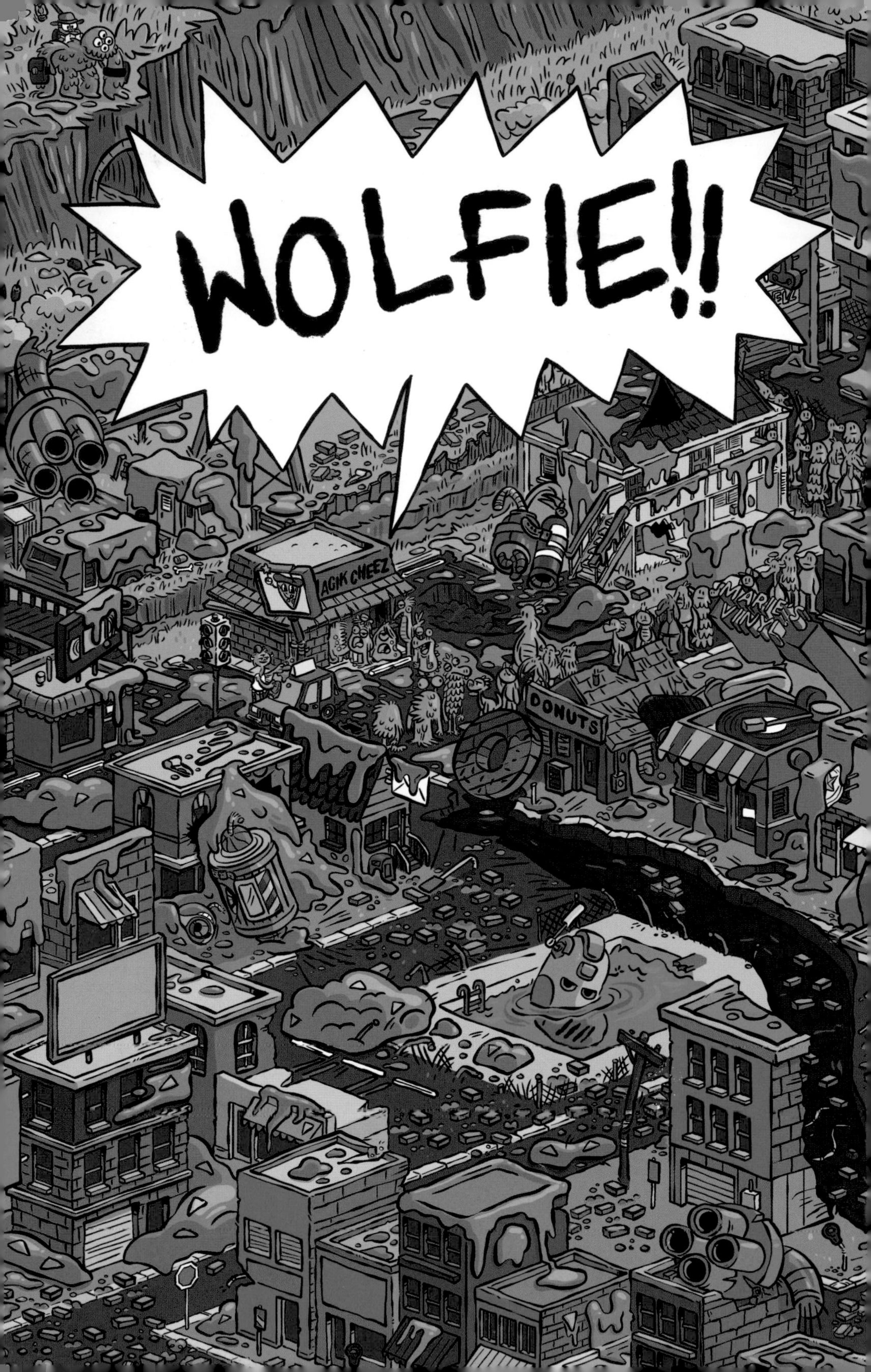
WOLFIE!!
AGIK CHEEZ
MARIE'S VINYL
DONUTS

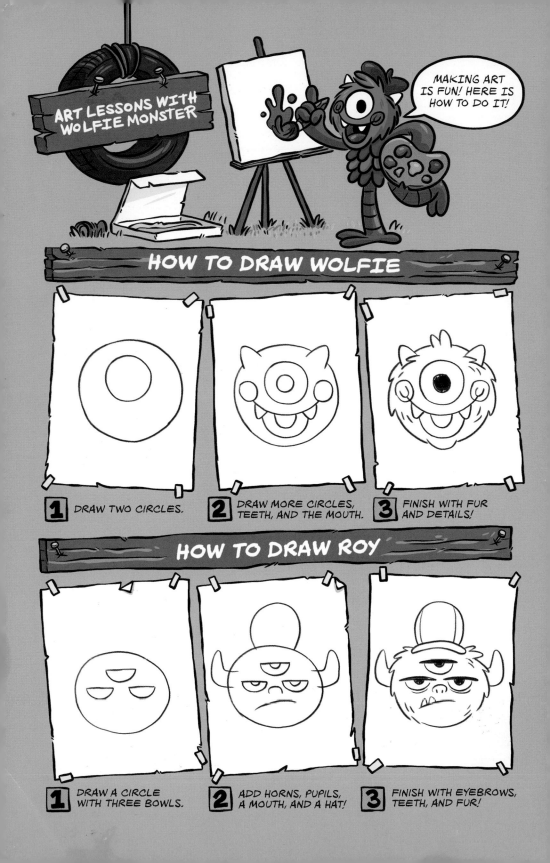

BORING
DESK PLANT

BOX OF SUPER
GATOR CRUNCH

BUSINESS
PHONE

THE ROYAL
PLUNGER

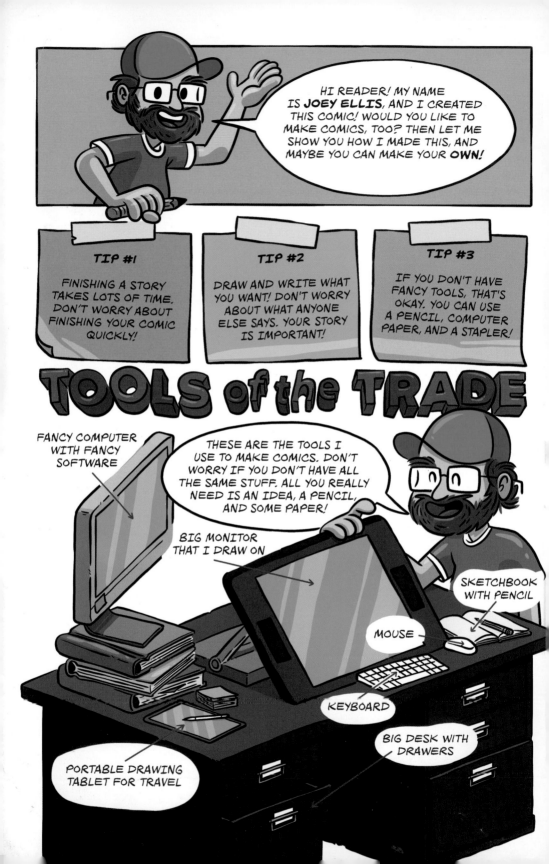

JOEY ELLIS has had his illustrations and character designs featured in *Highlights* magazine, *Boys' Life*, *Sports Illustrated*, ESPN.com, *Ranger Rick* magazine, The Walt Disney Company, and many others. Joey also performs puppetry and creates funny videos featuring his wacky characters. In his spare time, he collects toys and retro video games, and has fun with his family. Joey lives in Charlotte, North Carolina, with his wife, Erin, their two sons, James and Michael, and the family's sock-eating dog, Toby.

ACKNOWLEDGMENTS

Many thanks to Erin Ellis and Joey Weiser for their help with color flatting. Thank you also to Kyle Webster: This book wouldn't have happened without you. And Adam Rau, thank you for being my editor, you sweet and patient man.